Ego's Odyssey
By Robert Ensor

First Published as an e-book in the United Kingdom, 17 January 2023.

Paperback version first published 19 January.

For my father and my mother.

Acknowledgements

I'd like to acknowledge my mother for her constant support during the writing of this book.

Table of Contents

Chapter 1: In Media Res

I woke.

The first thing I saw was the snake. I felt it sliding slowly across my bare stomach with its hard, muscular body, coated in repulsive leathery scales. His dead cold eyes stared at me. They held less sympathy than the eyes of the worst killer in the world. The forked tongue poked from between the eerily motionless lips to tickle my clavicle in a devilish kiss. I squirmed in fright. The dull throbbing pain that suffused my entire body had sharpened to a knifepoint in my upper back. I groaned.

Then She appeared, emerging from the vague shadows at my bedside.

The nurse was clad all in white, except for the red cross on her tunic. Six feet tall and slim yet strongly built, with long dark blonde hair garlanded with red roses, small green eyes, a pert nose, well-defined jaw and full red lips. She was beautiful.

She lifted the serpent off my skin and set it down on the ground. It made a hiss of displeasure.

'How are you feeling?' she asked.

'Uh, terrible,' I said, groggy. I raised my head. 'I have a pain in my neck, shooting down the spine.'

She smiled and shook her head. The smile was absolutely radiant.

'No, how do you feel – in here,' she said, pointing at the stitched red cross over her heart.

'Terrible,' I said, grinning weakly at my humour, so pathetically inadequate before her beauty.

'Why?' she enquired. There was sympathy in her marvellous cat-green eyes. Those eyes seemed vaguely familiar, but I couldn't quite place them.

I groped for words, and, finding some, stumbled over them.

'I was joking. My wounds are physical, not mental. How bad are they?'

'To joke in such a condition would be a rare display of courage,' she said, with a note of scepticism.

'Your spine is broken in two places. And, in case you were wondering, you still have the plague,' said a nasal, sarcastic voice.

An old man hobbled into view. He was balding, with a large, bulbous, purple-tipped nose, and an abrasive demeanour. Addled as my brain was, I recognised him at once. He had been our ship's doctor. He wore loose, flowing white sheets and was supported by ingeniously carved wooden sticks that fit under his armpits. Such things were unknown in the land of my birth.

'Who are you?' she asked, turning to face the newcomer with a smile that concealed daggers of ice.

'Diodorus Placebo. *Doctor* Diodorus Placebo. And your patient will be dead within a week – no, three days, if you continue to treat him in this way. Step, aside, maiden, and let me conduct a proper examination.'

She stood firm, with two sturdy legs planted well apart on the marble floor. Of the two, she was clearly the stronger, especially in the old man's current enfeebled state.

He raised a sardonic eyebrow.

'I'm not sure what will kill him first: your snakes or your ineptitude. The men and I shall wager on it – could use a little sport around here.'

The lovely face hardened. There was granite behind those thick yet shapely brown brows.

'You are a patient here, not a doctor, and I shall use *our* methods to treat him. Now return to your bed!' she said, in a deep, strong voice, that was sufficiently controlled to avoid wide notice. The room darkened perceptibly, along with her face, which assumed an inhuman grey aspect. She towered over the weak old man, until she seemed seven feet tall.

At first, Placebo shrank from her magnificent wrath.

'Well, yes, my leg is hurting rather badly, come to think of it,' he said, shuffling off, as fast as he could safely manage.

After two steps, emboldened by the fresh distance between them, he turned and fixed her with a bitter sneer.

'I suppose it doesn't matter. Even if by some miracle he survives the ravages of the buboes, he'll be crippled for life. Your incompetence at least has the virtue of finishing off those wretches the gods have deemed unworthy of life.'

'He is worthy of life. More worthy than you: a small man who hides behind his profession, a man who has taken more lives than the worst criminal, who delights in the death of his patients as a relief of his workload and would rather die than be proven wrong. If it weren't for your stubbornness, you could recover, old man, but instead *you* will be dead within a week.'

The doctor stopped dead and shuddered. A sudden panic fear of demoralisation lit up his milky old eye, but only for an instant. The sneering mask was reassumed, though this time it was cracked a little, like antique pottery.

'If I wasn't suffering from a broken leg and dying of plague, I'd put you in your place, missy,' he muttered, then staggered off in exaggerated motions, so his crutches rapped obnoxiously against the marble floor.

Despite my pain, I couldn't help but smile upon witnessing that pompous hacklimb getting knocked down a peg or two.

'Someone should have said that to him years ago,' I said. She turned to face me.

I averted my eyes. The truth was, she terrified me, and the terror of her beauty was redoubled by her formidable strength. It seemed grossly unfair of the gods to endow one being with such splendour.

'Where am I?' I said, looking at the high coffered limestone ceiling.

She folded the white screen back, revealing a vast pillared hall of beds, filled with the groaning sick and injured, who were tended by innumerable women in white tunics, some of them maidenly, some older. The limestone pillars were carved with snakes curling around their circumference.

'In the Snake-Temple of Esklepios, on the Island of Tyria.'

'A temple?' I said, my mind racing at the impropriety of my naked torso. Our gods spoke often of modesty. 'But I'm not properly clothed —'

'The god does not care. The god asks only that you heal.'

I grimaced, surveying my ruined body, covered in taut, angry buboes, black as death, and blood-seeping bandages.

'I fear the god asks too much.'

'You will heal,' she said, with serene, perfect confidence. 'If you are truly willing to heal.'

I smiled, condescendingly. Clearly the girl was some naïve young nurse, in her first month at the work, who had not yet become jaded by years of drudgery and dead patients.

'There's only so much the will can do when confronted with a shattered body,' as I said the words, I felt first a lurch of dread at the yawning abyss of despair opening up before me, then a sharp pain in the spine.

'The will can work miracles, if you let it. For almost all health and all sickness are a matter of will. It is theoretically possible to live forever, for one in whom the will to life is unwavering.'

I couldn't help but laugh. Then I saw she was serious – quite deadly serious, in fact.

'Be careful of your cynicism, lest it become a self-fulfilling prophecy,' she said, making to leave.

'Wait! What's your name?'

She hesitated for a second. 'Anima,' she said, at last, with a beguiling half-smile.

'I'm Ego,' I said.

'I know.'

She knew. But how? The manifest had gone down with the ship. I assumed one of the crew must have told her, though it later transpired that nobody had.

Chapter 2: The Emperor of Maladies

That night, I had a strange dream.

I was in my sickbed, in the snake-temple. A woman approached my bedside. It was Anima, gloriously naked. A blood cross was carved in the smooth skin of her abdomen. She held a birch wand in her left hand, twined with serpents and tipped with a red stone. She touched the stone against my forehead, and I was flooded by torrents of rage and sorrow. Madness seized me. Tears streamed from my eyes. I rose from the bed, crying and screaming. My buboes popped in a painful black splash.

I woke again. It was day. A rectangle of sunlight lit up the bottom half of my bed.

I looked to my left.

Anima was sat on a stool, watching me with her cool green eyes. There was that ambiguous, condescending half-smile again. A huge white snake with black spots was sprawled across her broad shoulders and entwined around her right arm. It hissed at me.

'Is it deadly?'

She looked down at the snake's head, unconcerned.

'Yes. But we have plenty of anti-venom.'

'Where did you get that from?'

'It's made from the venom. The source of the sickness is the source of the cure.'

I pondered those words, which seemed allusive and strange. Then I winced.

'Do you have any opium?'

'You don't need it.'

'But my buboes – my back!' I cried, panicking. The pain seared my spine like a hot poker.

'Trust me,' she said, placing her hand on my forehead and caressing my skin gently, as if I were a child with a fever.

She seemed totally unconcerned about catching plague from me. If he wasn't already infected, Placebo wouldn't have come near me without his ibis-beaked plague doctor's mask, stuffed with garlic, cloves and other herbs said to ward off the malign spirits which caused the sickness. Her serene confidence was contagious. I calmed down.

'But —' I protested weakly.

'Shhh. Don't think about the pain,' she said, pressing a cup of scented water to my cracked, blue lips.

I sipped. The water was fragrant, laced with herbs. Only then did I realise how thirsty I was, how parched my throat. I gulped down some more. She pulled the brown earthenware cup away – too soon for my liking.

'Did you dream?'

'Yes.'

'Tell me your dream.'

'Why? It's nonsense and madness, like all dreams.'

'The world is as much nonsense as it is meaning, and there is a difference between madness and divine madness.'

'Well there was nothing divine about this dream, I assure you.'

'But we are in the Snake-Temple of Esklepios. The god sends his patients dreams that they might be cured.'

That made me think. Such a notion was unutterably alien to me, for our physicians relied on bloodletting and dismissed dreams as a kind of mental dungheap.

'Please. It is my duty as a sister here to interpret the dreams given you by the good god.'

Faintly embarrassed, I told her of my dream, though I substituted the goddess Melea for Anima.

She nodded, understanding perfectly.

'That is a good dream.'

'Good? It was frightening and painful and weird!'

'Those are the best dreams!'

'What does it mean?' I asked.

'It means your salvation lies in talking to me.'

Panic seized me, like a serpent crushing my ribs. I was in the care of a madwoman.

'I enjoy speaking with you, but doing so is hardly going to cure me. I really think I ought to be bled. Doctor Placebo says—'

'Tell me how you got here,' she said, ignoring my protestations.

'Well, surely you know? We were shipwrecked in a storm, in the Olearic sea.'

'No. From the beginning.'

'The beginning? Of the voyage?'

'If you like.'

'Well, I was persuaded to join the ship's crew. I was bored. At home, on the farm with mother.'

'Where was your father?'

'He died. Ten years ago.'

'How?'

'Apoplexy.'

'I am sorry to hear it,' she said, with due sympathy, but her eyes flashed with morbid interest.

'Yes, it was something of a relief when he finally died – for all of us,' I said, gravely.

She nodded. Her eyes glistened redly. Were those tears? It was impossible to tell, with me all bathed in golden light from the window behind my bed, and she in purple shadow. Her beautiful face certainly had a mournful aspect. She grabbed my hand and squeezed, gently. I felt myself overcome by a sudden surge of sorrow, but held it back.

'Anyway,' I said, carrying on hastily, 'since father died, we had to sell the fields and all of our livestock and could only keep the farmhouse. I was forced to work in the vineyards of our neighbour, picking grapes.'

'Hard work.'

'Bloody hard. And unpleasant. In the heat of summer.'

'Continue.'

'Well, I was slaving in the vineyards one day, when Nero, who worked with me – even then, the bastard always managed to steal some of my quota of grapes while my back was turned – Nero came up to me and tells me of an "opportunity."'

'Nero – he was one of the crew.'

'Yes, the tall, handsome one with the smug grin.'

'The one who looks like you?'

That gave me pause. I'd never thought of him like that.

'I suppose he does. He survived, then?'

'Oh yes. He's another one of my patients. He is badly injured.'

'Right. Well, if you hear what I have to say about him, maybe you'll think twice before emptying his bedpan.'

She giggled at that.

'Anyway, in those days, he was just as cocky, and he had a little dog, Rufus. Does he still have it, or did it die in the shipwreck?'

'Oh, you mean the little black thing?'

15

'Yes, the little yapping bastard.'

'He survived without so much as a scrape. I'm surprised you haven't heard him. He kept half the ward awake last night, so we moved him to the kennel.'

'I'm too exhausted, thank the gods; I slept like the dead last night. Anyway, Rufus was barking away at me as usual, when Nero offered me a job aboard ship.'

'Tell me exactly what each of you said, and describe the scene, to the best of your recollection.'

I thought this a strange request, but since there was nothing sensitive in our conversation, and she was beautiful, I decided to humour her.

'Very well. Ah, let's see. It was a bright sunny day in the vineyard. Afternoon. The earth was dry and dusty; we hadn't had a good rainfall in weeks. Many grapes were withering on the vine. I wore my old mud-stained tunic, and Nero, who was always better dressed than me, wore his fancy black toga.

"It pays five drachmae a month," he said, of the job aboard ship.

"And what do I have to do?"

"Loading and unloading cargo, maintaining the sails and ropes, cleaning the deck and scraping barnacles off the hull—"

"In other words, I'd be a deck hand."

"Hey, do you really want to stay here all your life, picking grapes and listening to your mother gripe about the harridans at the well?"

"No, but —"

"It may not be any more prestigious than picking grapes, but working on a ship gives you a chance to see the wider world. Have you ever travelled beyond the borders of Aeonia?"

"No," I admitted, grudgingly.

16

"Have you ever had a woman?" he said, a sleazy grin on his bronzed, handsome face.

I blushed. I had not.

"I knew it!" he cried, with some satisfaction. "Well look laddie, here's your big chance to wipe the mother's milk from your chops."

I demurred.

"You know, I woke up today and felt a terrible sense of impending doom," he said.

"What have you done this time?"

"Oh, nothing in particular. It's just, the idea of going to work again. The same old boring routine. Six days a week. Maybe a carouse and a tumble with Tabitha at the tavern on a feast day, if I'm lucky. Aren't you bored? I mean, really *bored to death*? Sick to the back teeth of it all, the smell, the backache, the ripe stench of the manure carts, the old neighbours and their complaints. I know I am."

"Well, yes, I am bored. But things could be worse."

"Things could be better! Riches are to be had on the high seas. Take my friend Alexius. He enlisted with a company of mercenaries, saved Princes Therosopore of Maleto – who apparently, was most grateful! – and my friend Papadopolous, who found buried treasure diving off the coast of Mesopoea! He now lives like a king, with a harem of Meso women hanging round his legs."

"That must be cumbersome."

He smiled at me.

"Look, these adventures all sound wonderful, but most men who take to the seas report bad food, squalid conditions, bilge rats, plague, fights among the crew, and getting lashed by their tyrant of a captain. It's not perfect here, but I have enough food and a roof over my head."

"Is that all you want from life? Because look at farmer Branso over there. Not a tooth left in his haggard old head. He was content with life here in the dung-fields of Aeonia. And he's still here. He's a greybeard, but he knows less of the world than a child. He is your future, if you stay here the rest of your life. Do you not want more out of life than that?"

"Of course I want more. But I have my mother to think about."

"Your mother will be fine without you. I think you need her more than she needs you."

"That's not true!"

"Alright, then prove me wrong. Be a man! Join the crew! Look," he said, "it's only for six months, then you can come back to mummy."

Seeing I was still on the fence, he went on:

"Besides, if you stick around here, there are no marriageable women except for your cousins, your mother will get old and sick and you'll have to take care of her. Wouldn't you rather be seducing beautiful nymphs on the salt isle of Thessalia? – which, by the way, is our first destination."

He had me at nymphs, the bastard.'

She smiled.

'Well, if you wanted nymphs, you have come to the right place. All of our nurses are nymphs: brood of the Goddess Aeola.'

My heart leapt. As a boy, nymphs had been the stuff of fairy-tale – and fantasy. Distant descendants of the gods, they were said to have magical powers of enchantment and, though they were mortal, to live longer than ordinary women.

'Are you a nymph?'

'No,' she shook her head, as if amused at my naïvete. 'Now please, go on.'

'Alright. Well, fool that I am, I was seduced by Nero's promises of riches and women, and I enlisted with him at the port. The captain, a gruff old salt named Piraeus, set me to work – and he was not shy about using the lash when I did a bad job, but that was to be expected. What I did not expect, was for Nero to turn on me like a viper the very instant we set sail. It was as if he was just waiting until it was too late for me to back out, before unleashing all of his malice upon me.'

'How do you mean?' She asked.

I frowned.

'It started out with mockery. He called me "piss-swill" because amongst my many onerous duties I had to empty the bucket we used for a lavatory. Then he and the men started pissing on deck so I would have to clean it before the captain surfaced in the morning – when I rose late, it was the lash for me. I was their sacrificial lamb. In this way he won a band of hangers on. My suffering was the rope that bound them,' I said, with bitterness.

'That must have felt terrible.'

'You think that's bad?' I shook my head. 'Soon they were saddling me and riding me about the deck like a donkey, and when I went to bathe, they mocked my manhood and snapped my naked body with towels, leaving me covered in red welts the size of rosebuds – and once, they emptied the shit bucket over me in my sleep!' I raved, indignant. 'Then Nero started stealing from our small cargo of apples. When the captain counted them, he started a witch-hunt. Nero denounced me as the thief; his thugs, who had also eaten of the fruit, backed him up. My punishment was to be tied to the mast and pelted with the apples. More and more joined in the fun, until the whole crew, Captain Piraeus included, were hurling apples at my head. They didn't mind that some apples flew overboard, and many were damaged, lowering the price they could fetch in the markets of Thessalia. "Tis to be expected with perishables," the captain said, with an insouciant shrug, when I pointed this out to him. He didn't care about the fruits, for the ones they threw were the crabbiest, and our main cargo was logs from the pine forests of Aeonia.

They called me scum, thief, goat-fucker, bastard, pervert – every name you can think of. The whole crew had nothing but contempt for me. In the face of such universal derision, I began to think there really was something to their claims. I came to see myself as scum, a bastard, a goat-fucker – even though I didn't steal the apples and have never so much as touched a goat. Being thought a thief made me into one; I found a stray apple by the gunwale and ate it. I was getting the blame for a crime I did not commit; why not reap the rewards?'

She shook her head, but was unable to supress the ghost of a smile. 'Did you not fight back?'

I grimaced and blushed with shame.

'Well, at first it wasn't so bad. It began as mere idle mockery and horseplay, and their attacks worsened slowly, so slowly that, like a frog in a pan of boiling water, I didn't notice how terrible my lot had become until he had turned the whole crew against me – and by then, it was too late to jump out! When I confronted Nero about his behaviour, he wrote it off as pranks between friends, and implied I was making too much of it. He was always more or less respectful to me in private. We even joked together, sometimes. It was only when he was with the others that something came over him and he became a tyrant as bad as any tyrant in the history books, and no less terrible for the modest scope of his dominion. I honestly believe he would have been

20

worse than Argo the Ripper, if Fate had but given him the opportunity to practise his depredations on the grand scale.'

'And later, when things got out of hand, you still refused to fight back?' she asked, unimpressed.

'By then, it was too late. Or so it seemed. For Nero had a friend – or rather, a crony, for such men are incapable of true friendship and know only slaves or rivals – a man named Doloma, who put the fear of god into us all.'

'Describe him to me. He may be among the patients here.'

'He will be. That man is like a cockroach; he is the kind of insect-scum that survives even the harshest conditions. Doloma is of middling height and balding, yet otherwise extremely hairy and ape-like, with long arms and short legs. He is wiry and prematurely aged, for he is ravaged by a terrible anxiety. You will know him by the lines of care on his high forehead and, if he is awake, his habit of direst pessimism.'

'Ah yes, I know the man of whom you speak. I had to muzzle him. He talked his bunkmates into killing themselves, after relating in great detail all the horrors of the plague, the awful painful death, the creeping buboes growing larger and more agonising every day, the bloody flux that awaited them all. I will repeat no more of what he said, for your sake. Merely to listen to him was a torment of lamentations worse than the fate he described – worse even than Nekriya, the darkest circle of the underworld, to any man possessed of an imagination.'

'Yes, that is he,' I said, grimly. 'He was always worrying about storms, aboard our ship, the *Olympias*. "Storms are bad on these seas!" he would say to me. "Just last week two ships were lost to storms! We will probably go the same way. I wrote my will before heading out. Did you?"

I said no.

"That was a gross oversight," he said. "A man should always be prepared to meet his end, because those who are not prepared are more likely to die.'"

'That is quite the crew you found yourself amongst,' she said, amazed at my misfortune.

I laughed, a short cynical bark.

'I have ere been a lucky man.'

'Carry on with the story, while I change your bandages,' she said, peeling one off the weeping bubo on my right forearm. The once pristine white bandage was black as the hand of a leper.

'Well, whenever I spoke of revenge, Doloma would chime in – he has an annoying and uncanny knack of being everywhere at once – and he warned me that if I tried anything of the sort, Nero's band of thugs would weigh in on his side and I would find myself outnumbered.

"They will beat you to a pulp and throw you to the sharks," he said, in his shrill, whining voice, the kind of voice that makes you want to cover your ears.'

'Sounds like idle talk. As you say, such men are incapable of inspiring true friendship. What loyalty could they possibly owe to Nero?'

'I do not know. He charmed them, as he charmed me into coming aboard the ship. Nero has a peculiar effect on people – he can be harsh and rude, but at other times he is personable and funny, his words are honeyed and well-chosen and there is a blind conviction to his every utterance, even his most blatant falsehoods, that is strangely compelling. The man once swayed a goatherd to give up his flock in exchange for a bag of rocks, by saying they were from the ruins of Thalamis' palace, and worth a fortune in the antique markets of Aeos.'

'I know the type,' she said, lowering her eyes and grimacing in sympathy. I might have asked her to elaborate, but I was too wrapped up in my own sorrows to spare a thought for hers.

'Anyway, I was glad I did not stand up to him. One man, the cook Mapiso, attacked him with the ladle, and it went as Doloma said; they beat him and cut him with knives – they dunked him headfirst in his bubbling cauldron and threw him overboard. He was never seen again.'

'What did they tell the captain?'

'That Mapiso was drunk last night – true enough – and must have fallen overboard in his stupor.'

'And he was believed?'

'Like I said, Nero is a good talker, and the very devil when it comes to slipping out of trouble or heaping the blame on some other fellow. If the captain harboured any suspicions, he kept them to himself. We were a crew of only fifty, and by then, Nero had sixteen followers – the sixteen toughest men aboard. I suppose Piraeus was scared, like the rest of us. A gang of murderous brutes had taken over his ship. And the most terrible of them all, the ringleader of this band of cutthroats, was my only friend; a man I had once regarded as a brother, for I have no natural brothers.'

'An awful betrayal,' she said, gravely. 'But tell me – is that all Nero did to you?'

'What do you mean?'

I had no idea what she was referring to.

She frowned. Her mouth squirmed with unease.

'The scars on your back?' she said, looking me straight in the eye.

My stomach lurched with dread. I became frantic, panicky, shrill.

'How do you—'

23

'When you washed up on the shore, you wore tattered rags. We stripped you and saw scars – healed, but recent.'

Then the memories came flooding back. Until then, I had honestly forgotten.

'I don't want to. I am ashamed. You will think less of me.' My voice was small and breaking, like a pubescent.

'My dear, I already know.'

'Then what use is there in me telling you what you already know?' I said, thinking she meant to humiliate me for her amusement.

'You cannot heal until you hear yourself say it,' she said, with considerable authority.

'How—'

'Just tell me.'

'They came upon me at night, in my hammock. The others muzzled me and tied me with their dirty loincloths and Nero...'

'Continue,' she said, with considerable urgency, as if my very life depended on my next utterance.

'Nero whipped me,' I blurted.

She grabbed my hand.

I began to sob. It was not the cruelty of Nero that finally moved me to tears, tears that had long been dammed up: it was her show of sympathy.

'The burns?' she prompted, gently.

'They poured scolding water from the kitchens on my back.'

'And what of the other men in the galley?'

'The others pretended to be asleep, but they heard. After that, Nero did not go down in their estimation; but I certainly did, for they had witnessed my weakness. I was every man's whipping boy, and what shreds of dignity remained to me, vanished,' I said,

24

in a wavering voice, fragile as glass. 'Ever since, I've felt dead inside.'

'You must be furious.'

'I want to kill him, I want to kill, kill, kill them all – I want to stab him in the gut and rip out his bowels! I want to slash his eyes, stab his throat and twist the knife and burn him alive!' I said, seething.

I seemed to lose myself in the blood-reverie, and she was so damn easy to speak to, such a good listener, and you could tell she understood everything I said – not only with the mind, but with the heart. Aside from anything, I was ashamed at my cowardice, especially before a woman of such beauty, and this, more than anything, fuelled my paroxysm of loathing.

'And how is your back?' she asked.

I blinked. I hadn't thought of my back in minutes, so engrossed was I in my story – in the burning intensity of my hatred for Nero.

'Better – it doesn't hurt so much.'

My spine, which had felt like a bag of broken glass, was now reduced to a dull ache.

She nodded, and smiled, smugly, as if this was all entirely foreseeable.

'You asked what my healing method was. This is it.'

'What? Talking? Ranting and raving?'

'Reliving traumatic memories and releasing buried emotions.'

'Nonsense! My ailments are of the body, not the mind! I came to you plaguey and crippled – not some lunatic who barks at the moon!' I said, with strange vehemence.

'Then how come your back is feeling better?'

I paused. She had me there.

'You took my mind off the pain, that's all. Distracted me from it.'

'Pain, illness, injury – these are the real distractions. They distract you from your worst emotions, your worst memories, from everything you have not done but wish that you had and everything you have experienced but do not want to think of – this we call the Unknown Mind, and it is the root of all earthly woes: the Emperor of Maladies. Such dark, unpleasant thoughts and feelings are thrown out of our minds like slops from the bucket, where they fester and nourish vermin – but they are the key to our salvation. How else could merely telling your story reduce the pain?'

'Well, even *if* your talking magic could alleviate my pain, my spine is still broken, and I'm riddled with plague!' I cried, in the grip of a curious hysteria.

She raised her thick right eyebrow.

'Take a look at your buboes.'

I leaned forward. The black blob on my stomach was no longer angry and taut; it had burst, and sagged, like a blister. I probed it with my fingers. Puss wept from the edges. It was a soft, squelchy, suppurating mass.

'But – that's impossible!' I could not believe my eyes. It was as if a goddess had come down from her throne and unveiled herself before me, in all her radiant splendour.

'You deny the evidence of your senses?'

I was speechless.

'But,' I stammered, thunderstruck, 'there must be some rational explanation – the potion you gave me must have healing properties – if it is not some such elixir, why do you give it to us?'

She threw back her golden head and laughed.

'The potion merely contains herbs to make you emotional and loosen your tongue. The same effect could be achieved with a bottle of wine, the only differences being that this sharpens your memory instead of dulling it, and there is no hangover afterwards.'

'I do not believe you!'

'And you do not believe!' she cried, much amused. 'The healing quickens, the more you believe. What care you how I work my miracles – you are delivered – is that not enough?'

'To believe is not enough for me. I wish to *know*.'

She regarded me with newfound respect, and a sly smile of secret knowledge, as if to say: 'We shall see.'

'To know you must first believe. For what becomes manifest in the world is conditioned by our beliefs. This is what the prophets meant by the "leap of faith."'

'Perhaps I would believe more if I knew more.'

She looked at me, appraising my worth, like a heifer at the market.

'You are the first man of the crew to make such a demand. Seekers of knowledge have ere been welcome on our isle.' She sighed. 'Ask what you will, and I shall answer what I can.'

I took a moment to formulate my question:

'How is this possible? I mean, how does merely talking of the past work a miracle like that?'

'There is inside every mind, a distinct personality, whose role it is to distract us from the Unknown and lead us into error. We call him The Deceiver. Pain, desire and fear are his weapons of choice, for nothing grabs our attention like suffering, sex and terror.'

'He sounds like Doloma.'

She nodded, serenely.

'As within, so without.'

I blinked. She remained silent, as if for dramatic effect, or to make a point.

'Care to explain your maxim?'

'Everything you see in the Material Realm, has a corresponding figure inside your mind: the source of the external manifestation.'

It was as if she had laid before me a banquet of the ripest fruits and choicest cuts in the land. I knew not where to begin. The truth was so profound I could not digest it all, before she had moved on:

'The purpose of The Deceiver is to keep us focused on the Material Realm, root of all pleasure, pain, desire and fear. Peer behind the veil, into the Unknown, that festering refuse heap of memory, grief, rage, trauma and guilt hidden in the darkest corners of every mind – and, like a confidence trickster caught in a lie, The Deceiver is forced to beat a retreat, or at least change tack, for to persist in a swindle before a disbelieving audience is a fruitless endeavour.'

'There is a certain logic to what you say. And it is hard to argue against such phenomenal results,' as I said these words, and my conviction grew, the burning pain in my spine began to seep away, as if doused by some secret water.

'This is nothing. I have seen men in worse condition than you recover from their ailments. I have healed scores of lepers. I have saved hundreds from the plague, the very old and the very young among them. I have banished malaria; conquered the pox; cleansed the blackest of lungs. I have mended broken necks and broken hearts; I have lifted the veil of darkness from the eyes of the blind; and I have shrunk cankers the size of hams,' she said, in a baritone of frightening solemnity.

'Incredible.' I was going to ask if she was serious, but nothing about the woman was facetious. 'Forgive me if I struggle to comprehend what you say, for it goes against everything I have ever been taught about medicine, philosophy – and life.'

'Of course, you will need time; time to reflect on all I have said, to test my truths against the experience of your life. You have heard enough for one day.' She turned to go.

'But—' I said, like an infant greedy for more milk.

She held up her hand.

'For now, all you need to know is that illness, all illness, all injury, all strife, is a distraction from that great storehouse of everything you think you are not – namely, the Unknown Mind; and that belief in this great truth, the secret law of all life, and a willingness to examine the darkest parts of yourself, is all that is required to heal – to make a full and complete recovery.'

'A full and complete recovery…' I murmured to myself.

Then I cried. Some knot inside me had been cut loose. I wept like a babe for I knew in my heart she spoke the truth. It was such a great relief from the miserable anxiety that had held me in its grip ever since I awoke to discover my back broken, and my body ravaged by plague.

She returned to my side, leaned down and embraced me; I wrapped my arms around her soft, fragrant neck and continued to weep shamelessly, my tears rolling down her bare shoulder. Strange, how joy made me cry more than despair ever could. When I had finished, she wished me a good night, rose and departed, her day's work complete.

Chapter 3: The Fraud

'Tell me more about Nero,' she said, sitting on the stool beside my bed the following morning.

'The worst part was, the attacks, they seemed to come out of nowhere. I couldn't understand it. I still can't,' I said, shaking my head.

She placed a tender hand on my wrist.

'Have you ever done anything to make him resent you?'

'No!' I almost shouted at her, eyes ablaze.

She remained impassive, unimpressed.

'Well,' I equivocated, sheepish now, 'there were some boyish pranks.'

'Such as?'

'I would call him names. When we were younger, you understand.'

'What names?'

'Coward. Bastard, son of a whore – it was well known throughout the village, his mother was promiscuous, and his parentage dubious. I was not the only one to make fun of this.'

She persisted in her withering glare. She knew I was holding back.

I sighed, reluctant and ashamed to divulge further misdeeds. Until now, I had been the wronged party. Now I was becoming the villain of the piece.

'And I suppose, I used to beat him when I caught him stealing milk from our goats, or when he lied to my mother and blamed me for drinking the wine that he and his friends had quaffed – and she believed him!'

'Is that all?'

'I called him goat-fucker. I do not know why. Maybe because he was always good with animals, whilst I feared them. Unjust, I know – but hardly proportionate to the horrors he would later inflict upon me!'

'And you feel no guilt for your misdeeds?'

'Of course not! If I'd known the monster he would become, I would have hit him ten times harder!'

'And what of the other village boys – did you never torment any of them?'

'There was one lad, Propius. I once threw a bucket of shit in his face and kicked him in the balls. Though he had stolen my book, he didn't exactly deserve it.'

'You feel guilty,' she said, her face hard as stone. It was not a question.

'I suppose so,' I said, mouth squirming in discomfort.

'Say it.'

'I feel guilty!' I said, hotly. 'There. Are you happy?'

'That depends,' she said, placing the back of her cool hand to my forehead. 'Your fever has broken. You are telling the truth.'

She was right. My limbs were no longer leaden, the throbbing in my head had ceased and I felt suffused with new life.

'You can tell whether I am lying or not from my physical symptoms?'

'The body does not lie. And it is not for nothing that the prophet said, "the truth shall set you free."'

I blinked. I had never considered this before. Like most of my countrymen, I no longer honoured the gods, and had written religion off as a crock of shit that was only good for the odd day off work. But her words added a new shade of meaning, of living colour, to the dry old catechism.

'Here, have more potion.'

I took a swig.

Instantly, my spirits lifted, my head cleared, my eyes brightened.

'Anyway, after the cook was killed, Nero took the man's place in the kitchen. Soon his cronies swapped jobs with the kitchen helpers, and next thing we knew, that gang of thieves had control of the food supply!'

She shook her head, sympathetically.

'You can guess what happened next. Nero and his gang grew fatter while the rest of us starved on half-rations. They kept the captain and first mate well fed, so they wouldn't complain. They were all too glad of an excuse not to confront Nero, the cowards. Then the water supply began to mysteriously dry up. We were reduced to two amphorae, which meant three swigs per day for every man. And the rats - the rats thrived, for Nero fed them the scraps from his bowl – he was ere an animal lover, that one! The damn vermin dined better than most of the men! If only he had shown me such compassion!

Well, the rats grew bigger and bolder and bit one of the men, an unlucky fellow named Scorpio. Whilst working in the kitchen one day, Scorpio fainted and took to his hammock. Then one day, as I was emptying his bedpan - for on Nero's ship I got all the best jobs! – I noticed there was a black blob under his armpit. I ran off, crying plague. This finally roused the ships doctor – your friend Placebo – to come take a look at the wretch.

"Mmm, that's not good," he says, after sticking his finger in the bubo and tasting the goo! You see, he thought it was a squashed prune or common boil!'

Anima burst out laughing – a harsh, violent cackle.

I stared at her askance.

'I suppose it is funny, but not to us! For half of the crew caught the disease off the very man they looked to for a cure! They came to him with jaundice, constipation, headache, the runs – the everyday niggling complaints most men suffer from on a poor ship's diet – and they left infected with plague!'

I shook my head.

'Hey, I'll hear no more against Doctor Diodorus Placebo, thank you very much!' came the jeering voice of my neighbour, a thickset rustic called Apos, who was also suffering from plague.

'And why not?' Anima asked, coolly.

'That man is a martyr! He's tending to the sick while 'is own body falls apart! Sure, he's not perfect, but the poor fella is trying 'is best fur us, so 'e is,' Apos said, stirred by anger to sit up in bed.

And just like that, the screen folded back and in stepped Placebo.

'What's this – have these charlatans been badmouthing me again?' the old man said, his choler rising.

Apos was right; the doctor was indeed falling apart. His eyelids drooped, and his face was riddled with buboes of all shapes and sizes; a cluster had spread from his jaw to the left side of his mouth and was beginning to slur his speech. They dangled off his sagging old arms like bunches of rotting grapes, and each time he took a step on his crutches, his festering armpits squelched. His feet were bulbous, trailing bloody unravelling bandages across the marble. He reeked as bad as he looked; like a rancid dead animal left by the wayside.

'Speak of the devil…' I muttered, under my breath.

'Keep yer damn quackery to yerself!' he rasped, eyes wild.

He raised a crutch to wave at Anima, threateningly, then lost his balance and clattered to the floor with a gruesome splash of exploding buboes.

Apos struggled out of bed, wincing with the pain. Placebo brushed aside his offers of help.

'Stop, fool, don't you know touching spreads the sickness!?'

'But doctor, you're already infected—'

'I said touching spreads the sickness, damn it!' he hissed.

Apos withdrew his hand, terrified.

Arms quivering, Placebo raised himself up on his crutches.

'You can have Ego here – there's no helping such simple-minded fools. But I'll not let you bewitch a good sensible lad like Apos, with your hocus pocus nonsense,' he croaked, between gasps.

'Ego here is recovering under my care. Ego, show him your buboes,' she commanded.

With a sadistic smile, I lifted the bandage on my stomach, and was shocked to find the bubo reduced to the size of a squashed plum.

Placebo's eyes flashed with annoyance, as if I had miraculously healed myself merely to show him up. The impudence!

'He never really had plague – it must have been some sort of benign tumour or rash.'

I laughed.

'What kind of tumour goes down that quickly? And all the other "tumours" are shrinking, too,' I said, showing off the ones on my arms and face.

'Well, it would take time to conduct a proper diagnosis – perhaps you have some strange foreign pox, unknown to our physicians.'

'How could I catch a foreign pox when we never visited any foreign lands on our voyage?'

'By frequenting the port brothels, which are packed to the rafters with foreign whores, all of them crawling with disease. In any case, one in ten men recover from the plague. Even if you *were* infected, your recovery is not due to this harlot and her witchcraft; you are simply blessed with a strong constitution.'

'Wish I was so lucky,' murmured Apos, resentfully.

'Me? A strong constitution? Do you not remember? I was always pestering you aboard ship with one complaint or another.'

'Oh, that? That was all in your head,' he said, waving my rebuttal aside.

'Maybe Ego is lucky. But if there is even the slightest chance my methods have healed him, why would you not try them for yourself? If, as Placebo says, you'll be dead within a week with his treatment, then you have nothing to lose by seeking alternatives,' Anima said.

The crude lines of Apos' homely peasant face scrunched in thought. He was not accustomed to pondering such subtle arguments – and doing so made him deeply uncomfortable.

'Do not listen to her. And do not envy Ego. Even if he is recovering from plague, the wretch is still a cripple for life, on account of the injuries to his spine! He'll never walk again! Better death than such a fate!'

My spirits sank at these cruel words, which Placebo took a strange relish in uttering.

Anima turned to look at me. She weighed me with her big green eyes.

'Ego, stand up,' she said.

'But—'

She placed her hand on my arm.

'Do not think. Stand up.' Her voice was calm but commanding.

Semi-hypnotised by those beautiful eyes, so full of compassion and understanding and implacable will, I absorbed some of her confidence, and before I knew it, I had swung my legs out of bed and sat up, all in one sudden movement.

'That's it. Now stand.'

Following her injunction to not think about what I was doing, but simply do it, I acted quickly and straightened my legs.

I stood. Quivering, uncertain – elated.

'Now walk!' she boomed, her voice extremely deep and loud.

Trembling, I took a step. Then a second. A third. The pain was there, but dull. I seemed to have caught it unawares. Then I began to falter, and she was there, by my side, taking me by the arm, murmuring, 'That's enough', and easing me back into a sitting position on my bed.

It was only now that I looked up to see the reaction of Placebo.

His mouth was open. So was Apos'. They were speechless.

Finally, Placebo regained his wits, such as they were. He cleared his throat.

'Well, it's obvious what has happened here,' he said, quite calmly and reasonably. '*You are a fraud*!' he screeched, levelling the trembling finger of accusation at me. 'Go on, admit it, you were never really ill, were you, you were just putting it on so you could win the sympathy of this ripe young whore! Liar, demon, *fornicator!*' he shrieked, hysterical with rage and stumbling toward me.

Anima punched him square in the face.

He flew backwards, like a leaf in the wind, and landed with a heavy thud that shook Apos' bedframe.

The entire ward, patients and nurses alike, had stopped to look. They were all speechless.

I couldn't help but laugh.

'Get out!' she said, calmly.

Placebo looked up. I'm sure the shock of the blow damn near killed him.

'Out! Back to your bed!'

Two nurses came to help him. Seeing his legs were quivering, they dragged him across the ward. He left a trail of black stinking ooze in his wake, like a giant slug.

'And you, Apos. What more proof do you need before you will believe?'

The big peasant whimpered like a kicked dog. He couldn't meet her eyes and folded himself back into bed. He lay staring, unblinking, at the ceiling. Events had surpassed his capacity to comprehend them.

'Suit yourself,' she said.

'That was incredible. How did you know I could walk?'

'After curing hundreds, one develops a certain feel for these things.'

'You could have warned me! I would have prepared myself!'

'If I had prepared you, I would also have prepared The Deceiver within you and given him time to plot his sabotage. When you plan, he plans. That is why it is best to ambush yourself – to catch The Deceiver off-guard.'

'You are right. By the gods, you are right. I must confess, at first I didn't believe this talk of a Deceiver – it all seemed rather abstract, and the thought even crossed my mind that he was some sort of bogeyman you had invented to keep me in line, as if I were a child.'

'You *were* a child. But today, you have taken the first steps towards adulthood.'

'Don't you think that's a little harsh?' I stammered, for I was no longer a youth.

'Grown-up children are the rule, not the exception. There are greybeards who know no more than babes at the teat. Placebo is such a one.'

I pondered what she said. As usual, a sentence from her could fill books written by others.

'Whatever doubts you have in future, remember this day; it will be valuable evidence to use against The Deceiver in the courtroom of your mind.'

Then she left.

Chapter 4: Ship of Fools

Two days passed.

I was walking around the ward. Since his outburst, I had avoided Placebo, but presently he was particularly animated, so I hobbled over on my cane to take a closer look at what all the fuss was about.

He was haranguing one of the patients, a man of our crew named Laertes, who had thus far escaped the plague. Laertes was a strapping young man who looked like a statue of a god, an athlete with thick black hair, full of life and gaiety – usually at my expense. Whereas I had been a regular at Placebo's cramped, dingy little cabin amidships, Laertes, with his naturally robust constitution, had never seen him once – until now.

Placebo was pointing to something on his groin. A black swelling. My heart sank, even though I hated Laertes as I did all the crew who had tormented me for weeks, it disheartened me to see such a proud specimen cut down in the flower of his youth.

'It's plague, I tell you!'

'But—'

'I swear by all the gods, young man, you'll be dead within a week!'

Laertes' face crumpled. All his hopes had been shattered at a single word from the doctor. He went pale.

Then something strange happened.

His eyes widened, his breathing became shallow, and he clutched his chest.

'Heart attack! He's having a heart attack!' I yelled, staggering forward, my dull pains forgotten in the imperative of the moment.

Placebo was too shocked to quibble with me. He unrolled his bag of knives on the bed, selected the longest, grabbed Laertes' arm and began to hack and slice away at his bicep like a man possessed.

'Stop! Stop, damn it, you'll kill him!' I yelled.

Anima emerged at my side. In all the excitement, I had not seen her approach, so her sudden appearance startled me.

Before she could stop him, Placebo pierced the black spot with his knife. Blood oozed out of it.

The young man gasped, leaning forward in bed and grabbing the doctor by his dirty, blood-spattered tunic.

'Help!' he croaked, between chapped lips.

Then he was seized by a sudden shudder, his eyes rolled into the top of his head and he slumped back onto the pillow. A long, deep sigh escaped his lips and peace stole across his handsome features.

Anima stepped in and checked his pulse.

'He's dead,' she said, in a quiet voice.

She turned, slowly, to face Placebo, who positively quailed before her. He turned and hobbled away, as fast as his crutches and his withered plague-ridden arms would take him.

She snatched up his bag of knives.

'You'll treat no more patients here!' she yelled after him.

I stared at the bleeding black spot on Laertes' exposed groin. It moved.

'What the…?'

Anima turned, leaned down and poked the black spot.

It wriggled a little. She pushed it off, revealing a small circle of blood.

'It's a leech.'

'The doctor was bleeding Laertes yesterday. He came back just now to remove the leeches. That's how he spotted the plague on him,' said Glaucus, the small, bearded man occupying the bed on the dead man's right. He too was riddled with plague.

'Probably that damn fool Placebo left it there yesterday and forgot all about it. His wits are addled from the fever. This man never had plague,' Anima said, decisively.

'But – he's dead!' Glaucus protested. 'Surely he must have had something wrong with him!'

'Dead of fright. I'd wager Placebo had just told him he'd be dead within a week.'

'He did,' I said, a shiver running down my spine.

She nodded, solemnly.

'His prognosis became a self-fulfilling prophecy. The patient died because he believed he would die. It is so for all the men who have died under the care of that pompous hacklimb. This case is just a little more obvious than the rest.'

'Now now, Placebo tries his best,' said Glaucus, in reasonable tones, as if Anima was allowing herself to be carried away by the emotion of the moment.

'How are you faring, Glaucus?' I asked.

He turned to face me and grimaced.

'Wonderful. Farting rainbows. I see you're up and about,' he said, without any particular relish.

'Getting better every day. Sometimes, every hour.'

'Aren't you the lucky one? I'm getting worse every day. Placebo said—'

'You'll be dead in a week?'

41

His mouth fell open.

'How did you know?'

'Oh, lucky guess,' I said, exchanging a sly smirk with Anima.

'It's alright for you. Placebo says you were never really sick. Just putting it on for the totty here, he reckons.'

'Ego is many things, but I doubt he'd want totty badly enough to lie for it,' said Leon, from the bed on Laertes' left, with the lopsided grin I had come to loathe.

'You saw me on the ship. Our hammocks were next to each other. I was plaguey back then, and there was no totty onboard, unless you count Marcus.'

'Oh yeah,' he said, stroking his chin.

'As for my spine, Placebo himself examined me and pronounced it broken. He said I would never walk again – and now look at me.'

'I know what's happened. It's a miracle,' said Leon, the grin wiped from his face.

'You could be right, friend. Fat chance either of us will get a miracle then. Everyone knows they crop up once in a blue moon,' said Glaucus.

'It is no miracle. Ego owes his recovery to my methods, from which anyone can benefit,' Anima said. 'Would you like to try?'

'Two miracles in the same hospital, in the same week – now I've 'eard it all! That'd be like lightning striking the same spot twice!' Leon said, chortling. He began to cough and splutter and had to stop.

Glaucus narrowed his eyes at the nurse.

'What does it involve? Strange herbs from The East? Animal sacrifice? *Black magic*?' he whispered, casting nervous glances to left and right, lest he be overheard.

'It is a kind of magic, but there is nothing black about it. Esklepios receives less sacrifices than the medicine of your friend Placebo. All I ask is that you be honest with yourself.'

'That doesn't sound too hard,' he said.

'You'd be surprised.'

'Honest – how?'

'You must tell me all your darkest secrets. Everything that ever angered you or made you sad.'

He quailed. Then he looked to me, unsure.

'It works,' I said, patting the scabs where the boils on my arm used to be. 'I'm living proof.'

'If you continue as you are, you're dead anyway. Talking could hardly make you any worse. What do you have to lose?' Anima said.

'Hmmm, I'll consider it. There must be something in what you say. After all, piss-swill here is well and truly on the mend.'

'I have to talk with Ego now. But I'll come and see you in an hour. Does that sound alright?'

'Yea, alright, why not? Like you say, it could hardly make me any worse.'

We walked back over to my bed. Only now was my back beginning to ache from the strain of movement.

'Well done. You've made good progress,' she said.

'I owe it all to you,' I said.

'Where were we, before Placebo interrupted?' she said, ignoring my starry eyes with a knowing smirk.

'You should keep him away from the other patients. The man is dangerous.'

43

'I've taken his knives. What would you have me do, put him in shackles?'

'Yes! Or at any rate, put him somewhere he can't speak to the others.'

'We have long since learned that one cannot persuade the truly ignorant, so we do not even try. We let them know there is another way, and we leave the decision to them. We believe that, just as health is a choice, so death is a choice, too. It is against our ethics to interfere with an individual's free will; still less, his Fate.'

'Placebo has no such qualms. He tells people their Fate all the time. I remember when I went to see him with a fever, he told me I had the plague and said I'd be dead within a week. I felt worse instantly. My buboes doubled in size over the next two days. Every time I saw him, he seemed to drain the life out of me and blacken my spirits. All he could do was bleed us and lance our boils, which naturally became infected. Everyone got worse after seeing him with the first signs. I assumed it was just the natural course of the illness to progressively worsen.'

'Is that what Placebo told you?'

'Yes – but, to be fair to the man, everyone knows that's how it is with plague and other such diseases. It's just common sense.'

'His common sense is killing him.'

'And the rest of the crew!'

'Do not concern yourself with him; he will be gone soon enough. He has pronounced his own death sentence.'

'I will not mourn him. The frustrating part is, most of the crew still listen to him, even though they can see me getting better. I suppose it's his training at the school of Hippolytus, they respect him for it, treat him as if he were some kind of demigod, even though all he did there was learn to cut open frogs.'

'It is frightening to think that the man with the power of life and death over you and your family has no idea what he's doing, so they place blind faith in authority.' She shrugged. 'If they want to die, that is their affair. Continue with your tale.'

'Well, there we were, starving, thirsty and plague-ridden aboard our ship of fools, when Nero tells us there's no more food. He blamed it on the rats. At this point, you'd expect the captain to say enough is enough and take back his vessel. But the captain was sick. Persona, the first mate, hated Nero, who always mocked his rather prudish morality, calling him an old maid, but even he daren't lift a finger to stop the tyrant who had taken the place of my friend. Soon we all developed scurvy and anaemia – all except Nero and his cronies. Seeing the cowardice of the men, I resolved to act. I got together with Persona and began plotting a coup.

"Nero is hoarding the food and water."

"But, he said the rats—"

"Nonsense. We had ample provisions for a two-month voyage when we embarked. It's only been four weeks since we set sail. The rats would have to be bigger than the crew to finish the supplies in this time."

Persona's noble brow furrowed. He's not the quickest of chaps, you know, though he is very good looking.

"Even if what you say is true, what can we do about it? The kitchen is always guarded by at least five of his thugs."

"A majority of the men are not being fed. Even though we are weaker, we outnumber Nero's gang three to one. A fight will see many of us dead or wounded, but it's our best and only chance of survival."

"The others won't believe you. They hate you, and they've got their heads buried in the sand where Nero is concerned."

"What if we showed them proof?"

"How could you prove he's stealing our food?"

"I know they all get together in the kitchen at night and eat. I can hear them from my hammock. We could show the captain. The others would take *him* at his word."

Persona persuaded the captain that thieves had stolen our food. By this point, it was obvious; the rats couldn't possibly eat so much. Later that night, I led them down to the hold, where I had heard the gang eating the night before. Nobody was there. To this day, I do not know why. Perhaps we were overheard plotting by one of Nero's men; it is hard to keep secrets on a ship.

But the captain, now *he* was starving, persisted in his investigation. The next morning, he was inspecting our hammocks, when in comes Doloma, screaming his head off: "The ship, sir – she's sprung a leak! Water's up to our knees down in the hold cap'n! We're doomed we're doomed we're all FUCKIN' DOOMED!"

Seeing they were bound to be caught sooner or later, I assume Nero and his men made holes in the hull to buy themselves time and distract the captain from his inquiries. Anyway, if that was their game, it worked. The captain had us all down in the hold, bucketing out the water and fashioning the logs into planks, that we might plug the holes. While I was tipping the water to the next man in the chain, I saw Nero and Doloma slip away from their stations. Suspicious, I followed them up onto the deck.

The sky ahead was black, there was a soft under-breeze, and the waters were curiously still. I passed the mast and saw Nero and Doloma giggling by the gunwale. Doloma was holding an amphora by the neck.

Nero's eyes met mine. At first they were startled, then he tried to hold me with his basilisk stare.

My heart leapt into my throat. I knew this was my chance for revenge. Failure would mean certain death at the hands of Nero and his posse.

"Thieves! I have found the thieves!" I bellowed, at the top of my lungs.

Five men were within earshot, Persona among them; all came running. Nero drew his knife, but we had them outnumbered and he knew it.

Nero muttered something to Doloma and the bald man nodded. Suddenly, he jerked his arm out over the gunwale and said, "Come one step closer and I drop the amphora into the sea!"

This gave us pause. In our condition, that amphora could have made the difference between life and death, for despite dying of thirst, we were only five days sail from the isle of Telos, where we could resupply. We approached the two thieves cautiously.

"Lower us a rowboat and we shall leave you the water," Nero said, with his usual bluster. But I could tell he was nervous; the man is a coward at heart.

"Alright, just don't drop the damn amphora!" cried Persona, frantic with worry.

He ran over to the gunwale and began to lower their boat.

"Wait – how do we know he'll keep his word?" I said. Knowing Nero as I did, I imagined him rowing off with the boat *and* the amphora of water.

"You don't. But I'll drop the water *right now* if you don't do as I say!" Doloma barked.

The ship rocked from side to side; the waves were growing choppier.

"If he does, he'll die of thirst: he's bluffing!" one of the five men cried, though he sounded unsure of himself.

"If I hand myself over to you, I'll hang from the gallows at Telos or Thessalia! I might as well die of thirst."

"Besides, we just had a good long drink; that should keep us alive longer than the rest of you, should the water go into the sea," added Nero, with his sleazy grin and dead eyes.

Then came a deafening thunderclap that made us all shudder; the deck lit up brighter than a summer's day, for though the heavens were dry, they were black, and out of the deepest blackness a jagged fork of lightning struck the mast. Splinters flew; the mast cracked, creaked and fell sideways, tilting the ship dangerously to port.

I heard a clatter. Doloma had dropped the amphora. No water was spilled.

It was empty.

The captain came rushing out on deck. Then the heavens opened, the waves grew larger, and a sudden gust of wind blew us further to port. We were buffeted by a wave and the deck slanted till the ship was near-vertical; she almost capsized. I wrapped my arms around the base of the mast. The captain lost his footing and grabbed onto the gunwale. But, already weakened by starvation, thirst and plague, he had not the strength to hold on. The sea claimed him.

The upper part of the mast fell off into the sea. Then the ship righted herself.

I ran to the quarterdeck and almost slipped, for it was slick with seawater. Although we were down to one mast and one sail, we still had a working rudder and with the captain gone, someone had to take charge. Having witnessed the appalling conduct of the crew over the past month, I knew that someone must be me.

"Man the oars!" I bellowed, and the men did as I commanded.

I looked ahead and saw a narrow fjord between two cliffs. By the cliff on our right, a giant swirling hole had opened up in the sea, roiling the surrounding waters to a hideous froth. I had never seen anything like it before. Then I saw two massive tentacles the colour of human skin, sprawled over the rocks on our left. More pink suckered arms appeared, and a huge bulbous mantle, grotesquely phallic, poked out of the frothing sea. The black eye, large as a dinner plate, stared at me with wanton malice and the tentacles flailed hideously in mid-air, waiting for us to enter their range.

We were headed right for those jagged rocks and that horror of the deep. A tentacle grasped the prow, entwining itself around our maidenhead.

Seized by animal terror, I spun the wheel to starboard, for I would rather chance the whirlpool than be pulled under by the kraken, and I knew the creature would not dare approach the roiling waters.

A second appendage slammed onto the deck, with the suddenness of a whiplash. The pink arm wrapped itself around Marcus' waist and lifted him away, writhing and screaming. The beast dropped him into its gaping maw where his legs were gnashed and chewed by the hideous black beak.

We entered the radius of the whirlpool. The ship was sucked into the vortex by an irresistible force, and we circled the hole before finally plunging into that horrible roaring blackness.

I remember drowning and being tossed about like a doll by the frightful maelstrom. Then there was a sharp pain in my back, and I passed out; I must have hit a rock.

I came to, coughing saltwater, and caught a glimpse of a beach and a fair maiden clad in a blue peplos. She ran across the sand toward me. I passed out again. Next thing I knew, I was lying here with a broken back.'

Anima was quiet for a moment, absorbing all I had told her. I knew that I had found a most discerning listener and that no detail of what was said, or unsaid, would be lost on her.

'That was an interesting story. I must see to Glaucus now; his need is more urgent.'

Then she got up and left.

Chapter 5: The Plateau

Our next meeting was in the gardens of the temple. Snakes slithered through the manicured lawns. Hummingbirds and sparrows fluttered from the cypresses that lined the narrow, gravelled path. The flowerbeds were many-coloured, fragrant and humming with bees. Deer frolicked in the sun-dappled bowers of the pine forest bordering the gardens, and the sky was a fierce blue.

The path led past a small ornamental pond wriggling with red fish to a domed pavilion whose marble columns were dazzling white in the sunlight. Inside the pavilion was a small stone bench. It was for this bench that I was headed, praying my back would not give out.

Sweat rolled down my forehead as I hobbled along on my cane. My breathing became laboured. Then, out of nowhere, my hip spasmed; there was a frightening loose feeling deep in the joint, as though my leg might give way at any moment and render me a crumpled heap on the ground. I groaned, involuntarily, for the pain was beyond my ability to supress it. Anima pretended not to notice.

At last, we made it. I sat down with an audible groan, glad to take the weight off my burning hips.

From the bench we had a clear view of the Temple of Esklepios, a rectangular, columned building with a triangular, red-tiled roof, flanked by rows of cypresses. The blue pediment was adorned with two intertwined golden serpents of healing.

We had been talking about my life in Aeonia, until I had gotten out of breath.

'Threw my hip out, on that last bit. Now it burns like the fires of Nekriya!' I seethed. 'And I thought I was making progress! What went wrong?'

'The pain has changed location. This is good.'

'How is it good?'

'You've got The Deceiver on the run. He knows back pain does not distract you anymore, so he's changing tactics, like a general losing a battle.'

'Doesn't feel like he's losing. My hip is hurting as bad as my back ever did.'

'I assure you the hip is fine. The sisters examined you when you arrived. There is no damage to the bone or the muscle whatsoever.'

'Then why does it hurt so bad?'

'Sometimes, symptoms can intensify when you are close to a breakthrough – in a last-ditch attempt to forestall the coming insight.'

'What breakthrough? I haven't made any progress in days.'

'Tell me about your father,' she said.

'He was a tall man, with thinning red hair, large yellow eyes and a ready smile,' I said, somewhat peeved at her unconcerned attitude, which I took for a lack of sympathy. 'He was a simple man, a good-natured farmer, content with his family and five acres, his tavern-friends and modest flock – not at all like me. He was conscripted to fight in the Miletian war, but he never spoke of it, though he was honoured for exemplary valour. All in all, I have little cause for complaint: he was a good father, he never struck me and we seldom had serious disagreements.'

Anima arched her thick eyebrows. I was holding back, and she knew it.

'Though I am grateful for all he did for me and my mother, our contrary temperaments prevented us from ever becoming truly close,' I muttered, sheepishly.

'Now you appreciate the healing power of honesty, I thought you might have something to say about his illness.'

I squirmed on the hard, stone bench. I suspected she would ask such a question. My hip burned, right in the hinge of the joint. I braced myself.

'Well, truth be told, I could not stand to see the man I admired most reduced to a wreck, unable to walk, feed himself, wash himself or even take a piss without help. So I left home; I abandoned my mother to care for him alone, stole some of my father's money and wandered the roads. I squandered the coin on wine and was robbed of my clothes; I know not by whom, for I was dead drunk at the time. I barely made it back alive. When I returned to the farm, I was dishevelled, hungover and reeked like a vagabond. And my father was dead.'

'How did that make you feel?'

'Truth be told, I felt nothing but relief that the suffering was over – for all of us.'

'You must feel grief: he was your father.'

'No, for I had mourned his passing in advance, when the local hacklimb pronounced the case hopeless; I cried for two months after that,' I said, curiously calm. 'Now I wonder if that was really so; if your methods could have saved him – but we knew nothing of such things at the time, and hindsight is a wonderful thing.'

'Ego, do you trust me?'

'If it weren't for you, I'd be dead,' I said, somewhat guardedly, for after Nero I had solemnly vowed never to trust another human being again.

'Do you respect my understanding, then?' she said, sensing my equivocation.

'Of course! You seem to know my mind better than I do.'

'Then repeat after me: "I mourn my dead father. I miss him."'

'But I—'

'We have heard enough from the I. If your recovery is to go any further, it is the not-I that must speak. Say it!'

'I mourn my dead father. I miss him,' I said, somewhat churlishly, like a boy forced to repeat a catechism.

'Louder!'

'I mourn my dead father. I miss him!'

'Again!'

'I mourn my dead father. I miss him!' I screamed, breaking the arcadian tranquillity of the garden scene. The deer in the forest turned their heads and sprang away.

Perhaps it was the effect of Anima's potion, but I saw him, in my mind's eye; not the drooling wreck of the final years, but my father as he was in his prime: a strong, happy, caring man who liked to wrestle with his son and fish in the local river. He did not deserve his fate. Of that there could be no doubt. Then the emotion hit me like a wave; I had to hold onto the pillar to keep my balance. I began to cry. The tears rolled freely, uninhibitedly down my cheeks and my large frame, hollowed by malnutrition, was racked by sobs. This time I did not even try to hold back.

Anima placed a gentle hand on my shoulder and waited, silently, for me to stop. An hour passed before the tears finally abated, but she never left my side.

'And how is your hip?'

'Better.' I had noticed the pain diminish; that is why I had prolonged my tears. Only when I was sure no more relief could be wrung from my sorrow, did I stop. I had become canny in my suffering.

'Now you see how we turn shit into gold,' she said, smirking.

I wanted to kiss her. Was there ever such a perfect woman?

Then a thought struck me, and I blushed.

'What is it?'

'During our acquaintance, I have only talked of myself and never asked about you.'

She was taken aback for a second. Then a radiant smile burst forth, like the sun emerging from behind the clouds. The eyes though, seemed curiously void of warmth.

'Well, before our appointment, I saw Glaucus.'

'How is he?'

'Bad. When I appeared at his bedside, he dismissed me, saying Placebo was taking care of him. When I reminded him of our appointment, his face was blank. It was as if he had completely forgotten our earlier conversation. Then, in an effort to persuade, I told him what wonderful progress you were making under my care. He said, "Ego was never really sick. It was all in his head. *My* wounds and buboes are real! Look at them!" as if the very rancidness of his body were somehow proof of his character. Seeing he was obstinate, I simply gave up,' she said, with that vaguely melancholy air I had observed before, as if she were a genius whose fate was to be eternally misunderstood by the greater portion of mankind.

'What a fool,' I said, shaking my head. 'If only the others could recognise your wisdom as I do.'

She cast a glance at me and smiled, wryly.

'You flatter me.'

'And why not? You are beautiful and wise as Sophia herself.'

'I am not so wonderful as you think. And if I have earned wisdom, it was at too great a price.'

Again, I sensed a vague allusion to a tragic past.

'Why are you so melancholy?' I said, shuffling closer to her on the bench.

She looked at me and hesitated. Her reticence created a stifling mystique; I resolved to penetrate it, to find the warm girl buried alive within this immovable statue.

'Sometimes I cry. For days at a time.'

'When I am sad, I write poetry,' I said, trying to be helpful. 'It's like your healing magic; better out than in.'

Her mouth fell open; she was at a loss. Something strange was happening, something beyond our comprehension.

'I am a poet too,' she admitted, with strange gravity.

I was thunderstruck. What were the chances?

'Historical poems?' I ventured, for this was my forte.

She nodded. Her arms folded, and she shuffled across the bench, away from me. She seemed intimidated by our similarities, the uncanniness of the encounter.

'I wrote a poem about the Miletian War. It describes the siege of Miletus, the great deeds of the hero Kleon and the rout of the Miletian Army by the wily general Andromachus.'

'I would like to read it – if it was not lost in the storm?'

I grimaced.

'It wasn't lost. I didn't bring it with me. But I have it up here,' I said, tapping my forehead.

'You memorised it?'

'I had to. In my village, few can read, and the work must be performed orally if anyone is to understand it.'

'Let's hear it.'

'Alright, but I warn you; I am a poet, not a singer.'

She smiled.

I prepared myself and stared across the garden.

Then the muses spoke, and the words came:

'Beneath a rosy-fingered dawn,
The blood tide was coming in,
Shield, sword, spear and horn,
Wine left in the skin,

Corpses far as sight can reach,
Sacrifices to the god of war,
After ten days' battle on the beach,
The brave Miletians fought no more,'

Here I stopped, for the whole poem ran for 5,000 lines.

She smiled at me, as if I were a precocious child.

'That was good. And good poets are hard to come by, these days.'

'Thank you. What is your poem about?' I said, trying to draw her out.

'The truth.'

'Dangerous theme.'

'Yes, but poetic fancy is a fine guise for dangerous truths, don't you think?'

I paused. I had nurtured such thoughts myself, but never dared speak them aloud. A shiver ran down my spine. Such encounters reeked of Fate, and the mischief of the Gods.

Then a thought occurred to me.

'You spoke earlier of having known men like Nero. Did some fool of a lover once betray you?' I hazarded.

Her eyes flashed with alarm. She rose from her seat.

'I am needed in the temple. I'm already late. Please excuse me.'

Then she left.

****

That night, I woke to the hooting of the owl. Every night since I had arrived in the snake-temple, I had heard the owl, though when I mentioned it to the others, they knew not what I was talking about.

A noise. The rap of wood on stone. Getting closer.

Placebo.

I broke out in a sweat. He was headed my way. What business did he have with me, at this hour?

I tensed my muscles, but kept my eyes shut and pretended to sleep.

I heard a rustling at the foot of my bed. Then a faint clatter as he dropped something metallic. Muttered curses. Sighs.

Then I felt his hot breath on my face, breath that reeked of decay. The sheets were whipped off, revealing my body, naked except for a loincloth.

A pause. Then the cursing started.

'Where are the damn buboes!' he hissed, amazed at the smoothness of my skin. He began pawing at me with his wrinkled claws.

'This can't be possible! The swine *must* have been lying all along!'

Then I felt the cold bronze of the knife on the soft skin of my neck. My eyes opened and I saw his hideous swollen face, wrinkled and sagging with buboes, the eyes glinting mad with animal hatred of the opposite.

I grabbed his narrow, dotard's wrist and gave it a sharp twist. He punched me in the face left-handed, stunning me with the desperate strength of the damned, and I lost my hold on him.

'I'll punish you, bastard, for making a fool of me!' he hissed, drawing back his knife-hand for a killing blow.

And then he was seized by a violent fit of coughing. He vomited all over my naked chest; in the moonlight it looked black, and it had the coppery smell of blood. I jerked violently out of bed and stood on the far side, ready for another attack. His stomach gurgled audibly, and he bent double, clutching his gut. He voided his bowels all over the marble floor beside my bed; a never-ending torrent of hot, liquid shit – for I could see it steaming, and it hit the floor with such force I had to shield my eyes from the splashing.

When the geyser of violent dysentery finally abated, he gave a long, drawn-out groan and keeled over. By now, the braziers had flickered to life, and the nurses were rushing over. One of them leaned down to check his pulse.

'He's dead,' she said, without the faintest trace of sorrow.

I later counted back the days from when Placebo diagnosed himself. It was exactly a week before.

Chapter 6: The Telling Omission

'I heard about Placebo. I will not mourn him.'

'Nor will I,' I said, troubled. 'Why do you think he tried to kill me?'

'Because you were the living refutation of his medical theories, which he had come to identify with, and elevated to the status of a religious creed.'

'And he was too scared to attack *you*,' I said.

Anima smiled, her eyes flashed with demonic sadism and my heart skipped a beat in terror. Then the moment passed, and her normal, placid expression returned.

We were walking through the garden again, but this time, the sky was overcast.

'There is one thing that still bothers me about him.'

'The mess he made of your bed? Don't worry, I had the nurses provide fresh sheets.'

'No, not that.'

'Well, what is it?'

Apparently, she couldn't read my mind all the time.

'Well, it's just – I came to Placebo once, with stomach pains. He bled me and the pain went away. Bleeding worked for the others, as well – up to a point. I mean, for simple things like rashes, clap and jaundice. Why is that?'

'Because you all believed in him and by extension, you believed in his treatment. Also, I suspect the pain of bleeding is distracting enough to substitute entirely for the pain of various minor maladies. Even with grave illnesses, it can have a relieving effect, by absorbing a modicum of the attention that would otherwise be given wholly to suffering, worry and despair.'

'Interesting.'

A gust of weird wind caught the underside of the leaves.

'Your shipmates told me of a man named Xanthus,' she said, suddenly. 'They said you were close. Why have you never mentioned him?'

My bowels lurched with dread. I had been trying not to think of Xanthus.

'Perhaps I would be more forthcoming with you, if you told me even a little about yourself. I've placed a lot of trust in you, told you more secrets than I've ever divulged to anyone else, even Nero, and what have you confided in me? Nothing. Absolutely nothing,' I said, with a bitterness that surprised even me.

'What would you like to know?' she said, warily.

'For starters, I want to hear about this fool who spurned you.'

At that moment, the heavens opened. She dashed over to the pavilion. Unthinking, I ran after her. Then I realised – I was running! Praise be to the gods!

A bolt of pain shot down my back, into my left buttock and all the way down my hamstring. I staggered and lost my balance, falling into a bed of roses. As I tried to push myself up, I felt my arms snag on the thorns.

After watching me struggle for what I thought an indecent interval, Anima came over to help me to the bench, where I lay down. My muscles were still twitching; another spasm threatened to come at any moment. And I was soaked.

'There is only one way to end your torment,' she said, placing a hand on the pillar, the easy motions of her youthful body taunting me in my moment of infirmity.

I knew she was referring to Xanthus.

'No,' I said, stubbornly. 'I won't tell you about Xanthus, unless you tell me about your lover.'

She sighed.

'Very well. My lover came to me when I was but a maiden. He seduced me with the promise of forbidden wisdom – truths known only to the gods, truths that could take away the pains that ailed me. Knowledge of life's mysteries, of the beginning and the end of all things and the frightful power that comes with that knowledge.'

'Let me guess. He lied.'

'Oh no, he was as good as his word – and therein lay his betrayal. For I did not realise that knowledge is a prison from which there is no escape,' she said, a faraway look in her melancholy eyes.

The downpour intensified.

'He was unfaithful, of course, for "trust no one" was the first lesson. He used his knowledge to control me without my realising, talked me into doing things, disgusting things that were against my nature—' she stopped herself and looked up at me, her eyes red-rimmed. 'And now I shall hold you to your promise,' she said.

My bottom vertebrae exploded in fireworks of agony. I gasped; the pain took my breath away.

'Alright. Well, Xanthus was my friend. He had a mop of unruly blond hair and was kinder than the rest. Out of a crew of 50, he was the only one who defended me from the bullies. It happened, one day, when they were pelting me with apples. He stepped in and punched Nero in the mouth. Broke a few of his teeth. Then Nero's thugs set about him with oars. One blow caught him on the top of the head. Xanthus was a big man, and he dropped like a felled oak. When he finally recovered consciousness, he wasn't the same. His brain was damaged, and it soon transpired he was unable to speak, see or walk more than a few steps unaided. What's more, Placebo said he was unlikely to ever regain his faculties. The only decent man aboard, and how was his decency rewarded? The bastards made him a vegetable.' I shook my head, bitterly.

'Well, since he was my friend, and nobody else would do it, least of all Placebo, whose prescription was to throw the poor man to the sharks, I was given the job of looking after him. It was not a role I was suited to, not least because I was half-starved to death myself. For therein lay the difficulty: around this time, Nero's gang, through their thieving, had reduced us all to half-rations. Nero, in his misanthropy, refused to feed Xanthus. He called him "dead weight" and advised me to put the poor sod out of his misery. Naturally, I blanched at such callousness and at first, I gave my ward almost half my share of food and water; then the rumblings of the stomach tormented me, and I could bear no more. I reduced Xanthus to a quarter of my ration. As my condition worsened, I was faced with a dilemma. If I didn't start consuming my full ration, I would surely die of thirst, as Placebo said, and for once he was right,' my voice wavered, and my eyes watered. 'It was him or me! I had no choice!' I said, pleading with Anima to understand. She remained impassive and kept her peace. I went on: 'I finally took Placebo's advice and stopped feeding and watering Xanthus altogether. Soon his mewling and moaning were driving us all crazy. I tried gagging him but that didn't work; he still made enough noise at night to keep us all awake. On the second night of this racket, Nero could take no more. He came up to Xanthus's hammock, which was next to mine, and slit the wretch's throat. As I watched him bleed to death, I swear I saw his eyes glare at me in reproach; in some way, he knew I was his killer! And afterward, they ate him. The bastards *ate* him!' I wailed, before breaking down into sobs.

'Are you finished?' Anima asked, her voice hard. 'Or is there anything else you would like to add?'

I was alarmed at the harshness of her tone. My heart jumped into my throat.

'No. What do you mean?'

'That's the first lie you've told me. I do not like being lied to.'

Her face was grim and stony. Without knowing exactly why, I was terrified.

'I told you no lies! Have I not bared enough of my soul to you! What more do you want from me?'

'Honesty! Honesty or death!'

'You want honesty? Fine, I'll give you honesty; more than you can damn well handle. I think you're a prying bitch who needs to learn to mind her own business. Just because your boyfriend lied to you once upon a time doesn't mean you have to take it out on me!'

'On this island, the penalty for murder is death. If you do not tell me the whole truth right now, I will inform the magistrate and see you hanged.'

My viscera plummeted. I stared, aghast, at her dread livid countenance. She meant it; she meant every word of it.

'Since you already seem to know, what does it matter if you hear me say the words?' I protested, weakly.

'It does not matter to me. It matters to you; for your recovery,' she said. And just like that the demonic fire went out of her eyes, to be replaced by a look of profound human sympathy.

'I killed him! I slit his throat and – not Nero. It was me,' I said, in a small voice. 'I ate him, too. I didn't want to at first, but I was so damn hungry. I picked at the scraps, when the others had eaten their fill. He was my only friend and I killed him.'

Upon hearing those words that I had scarcely dared to think, I felt faintly nauseated; I was disgusted with myself. But with the nausea came a complete and total cessation of all bodily pains – and I became conscious of a voracious hunger.

The sun blasted through the cloud and a rainbow appeared over the forest, shockingly clear and transparent; I felt I could almost touch it.

She placed her hand on my shoulder. Her eyes were brimming with tears, tears of true sympathy and true understanding.

I kissed her.

Her lips felt warm and soft. My head began to swim.

After a tantalising few moments, she pulled away.

Then she left.

Chapter 7: Silence

One by one, those who recovered left the hospital. They never returned to visit those of us who remained. I was the only one of our crew who made use of Anima's talking magic; the other convalescents were fortunate enough to have avoided the plague and serious injury during the shipwreck. When I asked what had become of them, I was told by a sister they were living comfortably in the palace and waiting for us to join them.

Because of my progress, I was the fourth such to leave. When the time came, I was glad to depart the temple, for I had not seen Anima since our last conversation, and she was said to live in the palace. She had left me in a torment of anxiety; had my crimes revolted her? I reckoned this unlikely, since she seemed to have known all about them before our fateful interview. I remained largely ignorant of the customs here, the relations between men and women. Perhaps I had gone too far by kissing her, crossed some invisible line? She had certainly reciprocated. But then she darted off, without so much as a word in parting. Why?

With this question burning in my mind, I was led by a sister through the hall of the snake-temple and across a rolling meadow, brimming with yellow wildflowers. It was a golden morning and the sky was blue.

A well-trodden path cut across the meadow. Rabbits and deer frolicked on the grass, unconcerned by our presence. In the distance lay a rural idyll of breath-taking beauty: miles of rolling gold-tinged canopies ringed by mountains with pine-clad slopes and rocky peaks.

The meadow gave way to a manicured lawn. The path here was gravelled and lined with cypresses. Then we crested a gentle hill, and I saw the palace for the first time, gleaming like a pearl in the distance; a white façade with a long colonnade leading to the entrance.

Entering the welcome shade of the colonnade, I stared awestruck at the towering marble pillars. Everything was on the grand scale here; so grand it could scarcely have been built by human hands. For a fleeting moment, I wondered if I had died on the ship and this was the afterlife.

Other than the bronze lions flanking the double doors of the entrance, there were no guards. The doors were not even closed. I could scarcely believe such fabulous wealth lay unguarded! These maids were lucky *we* had washed up on their shores, and not a band of rapacious pirates! A slight, brown-haired nymph, clad in diaphanous blue robes, slipped out of the crack between doors and stood, waiting for me.

She introduced herself as Helen, and explained that before I could enter the palace, I must receive a tattoo; a mark of my status as an honoured guest.

I thought this a curious thing to do with one's guests, for in my homeland only criminals and slaves were tattooed. But who was I to question the customs of my generous hosts? Overwhelmed by my august surrounds and grateful for all the sisters had done for me, I agreed.

She led me into the high-vaulted entrance hall. The floor was marble; the ceiling, coffered and frescoed with lions and figures of nymphs carrying water. A broad stairway in the centre of the hall led to a balustraded mezzanine.

My footsteps echoed as Helen showed me to a small wooden chair. Helen sat down on the chair next to mine and set to work on my hand with her needles.

The tattoo was small and the nymph skilled at her art, so it was over quickly and with a minimum of pain. It depicted a thorny red rose intertwined with a snake. Perhaps it was a sign of healing, for I knew the serpents were associated with the God of Medicine, Esklepios.

Then I was led through into the Hall of the Moon.

It was a vast square room. The high domed ceiling had an oculus in the centre, enabling a shaft of sunlight to blaze through the gloom and illuminate my side of the hall. Before me was a semi-circular dais of white marble; pillars supported the roof on either side of the four steps, which began in the centre of the hall.

My heart jerked when I saw the animals lounging at the foot of the dais: a tiger with bright orange fur, a male lion, and a wolf. The predators regarded me with lethargic disinterest; the lion raised his head as if he might trouble himself to roar, then thought better of it and settled back down into a regal slumber.

Seeing my fright, the nymph tittered.

'Oh, you needn't worry about the animals. They won't hurt you, unless you attempt to mount the dais.'

'Why would I want to "mount the dais"?'

As if in answer to my query, through the shadowy purple veil at the back of the dais, stepped Anima. Her hair was loose, garlanded with red roses and crowned by a silver tiara. A serpent hung around her neck. She wore a translucent white peplos through which I got a tantalising glimpse of her pert breasts and pink nipples. She had a snake and rose tattoo like mine on her left wrist. In her right hand, she carried a short wooden rod. She looked otherworldly and mysterious in the relative darkness of the dais.

But something was wrong. She did not greet me, nor did she even so much as look at me, but instead sat down on a throne of ivory, which rested upon a small dot of white marble, encircled by a snake of blackest quartz. The backrest of the throne was a square mirror, in which I could see my bearded mouth agape, above her right shoulder. Anima stroked the wolf which had ambled over to lick her hand. Then she began to play the harp, positioned beside the throne for this very purpose.

Mystified and irritated by her rudeness, I asked the nymph, 'Why is it forbidden to climb the dais?'

'That is a sacred place. The sanctuary of the goddess. No mortal man may enter.'

'Which goddess? Melea?' I said, for I had seen frescoes of Melea and her serpents in the snake-temple.

She shook her head, surprised I did not know.

'Anima.'

'Wait – Anima's a goddess?' I asked, stunned.

'Of course. I thought she would have told you by now, since you were in her care.'

'She was rather reticent on the subject of herself,' I muttered, bitterly.

In hindsight, I should have seen it coming: the magic, the mystery, the snakes.

The nymph tittered. She and Anima exchanged an amused glance.

'Since you did not know, I'm sure your lapse will be forgiven.'

'What lapse?'

'When the goddess enters the Hall of the Moon, you must kneel before her.'

'Kneel?' I cried, indignant.

She nodded patiently, as if I were merely slow. Then she lowered herself onto one knee.

'Like this. See?'

Reluctantly, I followed her example. Anima refused to acknowledge my obeisance.

'Where are the three men who preceded me?'

'On the dais.'

I looked again. I saw no men. Only Anima, and the animals.

Then a horrific thought struck me: there were three animals.

I turned to the nymph, aghast. 'You can't mean?'

She nodded, grinning. All this was marvellous sport to her.

'Yes. Anima turned them into beasts.'

'How the devil did she do that?'

'With her wand,' Helen said, blandly.

'Her wand?'

'Yes, you can see it right there, resting against her throne,' she said, helpfully.

I studied the rod more closely. On the tip was a small red stone; a ruby, or some kind of crystal.

'Why did she turn them into beasts?' I asked, bewildered and frightened.

'Because Anima loves pets; and mortal men are not allowed on the dais.'

Frustrated by this non-answer, I began to pace the quartz floor, eyeing the exit cagily. I had a sudden impulse to run for my life and never look back.

'Fear not; Anima has no desire to turn *you* into a beast,' Helen said, reading my mind.

'*Why not?*' I half screamed.

Still Anima did not deign to notice me. She kept playing her harp, the soft music wafting across the airy hall like incense. Against my will, I felt the melancholy strains relaxing me. The tension seeped out of my muscles.

'You are to be her court poet and immortalise her splendour for posterity.'

I was taken aback. So she *had* liked my poem. I felt privileged and punished, simultaneously. It was all so damn confusing.

'If she wants me to write her poems, she can ask me herself!' I yelled, insolently.

Anima did not so much as look up from her harp. Her beautiful face remained maddeningly indifferent.

'Really, there is no need for such histrionics. You will be well fed and taken care of here. There is a chamber set aside for you, upstairs. But if you wish to spurn her patronage, you are free to go. That may prove difficult though, since your ship is destroyed and Tyria is an island,' Helen said, with a sadistic smirk.

'You don't possess your own ships?'

'No. Why would we?'

'In case you want to leave!'

'Why would we want to leave?'

Then some men wearing orange togas shuffled in. They made their ritual obeisance before the goddess, who ignored them as she had me, lay their red cushions down on the floor and sat on them.

'Who are they?' I asked.

'These are the goddess' priests.'

Their faces held strange enraptured expressions. Their eyes were filled with teary devotion. They were all bald, and their bodies and faces, though not fat, were strangely soft.

'Priests? They don't seem to be doing much preaching.'

'Oh, I forgot your ways are different from ours. Here, the title is purely honorific.'

Bemused, I decided to grab a cushion and sit down. For the first time, I noticed the pattern on the floor, the counterpart to the one on the dais: a black spot in the centre of a white marble uroboros, within a black quartz semicircle. Looking closely at the floor, I saw it was slightly convex, with carefully concealed drainage holes. The triangular spaces between semicircle and wall were paved with white marble. Entranced by the music and the patterns, I sat on the black spot. A pleasant weariness came over me, as if I had been soaking for hours in a hot bath, though the day had just begun.

'Dinner is at sunset,' Helen said, and made to go. Then she stopped herself.

'I almost forgot. There are but three rules on this island. You must not touch any of the nymphs. As well as the dais, you are forbidden from entering the sacred grove, by which I mean the olive trees to the rear of the palace.'

I thought these directions curiously precise; perhaps, since I was a newcomer, she wanted me to be clear on where exactly it was that I must avoid.

'What happens if I do?' I asked, dreamily.

'*Men* are not permitted to enter the grove,' Helen repeated, firmly and somewhat allusively.

I felt a sudden lurch of dread, without quite knowing why.

Then she glided across the hall and through a door to Anima's left.

Chapter 8: The Beast-Master

Days passed. All who were going to recover, had recovered, and all who were going to die, had died. Glaucus, Apos and Leon were among the latter group, passing according to the schedule Placebo had given them. Unfortunately, Nero survived. Worse still, he was one of only four crew members who were not turned into beasts, the others being Persona, Doloma and myself. Truth be told, I always knew Fate would preserve him, if only to spite me.

I asked Helen, why us four?

'Since you are to be the court poet, you can hardly be expected to write with cloven hooves. Doloma is a skilled mimic and actor; he entertained us in the temple. Persona has kept his form because he is pleasing to look upon,' she said, with an admiring glance at his bronzed, godlike physique.

'And Nero?'

'He is good with animals.'

And so a newcomer was appointed beast-master, a position of considerable trust, since he now had thirteen beasts in his keeping, some of which were dangerous. As well as the lion, wolf and tiger, the men had become oxen, sheep, pigs and a snake. I couldn't help but think their new forms befitted their characters; aboard ship the majority had behaved like herd animals, terrified of the predatory few and their master, Nero. In that sense, little had changed. The snake joined the other predators on the steps of the dais, while the herd animals grazed on the lawn outside and sometimes wandered into the palace.

Nero's good fortune mystified me, especially since I had told Anima of his true nature. But the scoundrel had ingratiated himself with his hosts. During the shipwreck, he received a wound to his abdomen that became infected. He claimed the god Esklepios came to him in a dream and told him to place a sprig of myrtle in his bandages. The nurses, being holy women, eagerly followed his instructions, and after that the wound soon began to heal. I was of the mind that the wound would have healed regardless of the myrtle, but our hosts made a great fuss of him and said he was chosen by the good god of healing.

Nero saw little point in mocking me anymore; now most of the crew were incapable of appreciating his insults, the nymphs were curiously aloof, and Persona hated him, Doloma was his only remaining audience. For my part, I was less intimidated than before, though the sight of Nero wandering the grounds with the wolf that was Megaron, filled me with dread. As two of only four crew members in the palace, an uneasy truce emerged between us.

We settled into a routine. Each day we took our two meals in the dining hall, a grand affair with red marble walls, adorned with frescoes of Anima healing the sick, feeding the island's native deer and playing her harp, all bordered by gold meander. The knives and spoons were silver. The pots, bowls, amphorae and goblets were of clay, but even these were finely adorned with black and red images of Anima. The fare was ample and good, if simple: barley porridge, bread lathered with gobs of fresh butter from the palace's dairy, shiny red apples, roasted chickens, venison steaks, grapes, figs and olives, washed down with milk, wine and fresh water from the spring. Doloma had started a rumour the liquids were laced with poison that would either kill us or turn us into animals. After the second day, sheer thirst overcame our fears. We were relieved to find ourselves free of tails upon waking the following morn.

As for the goddess, she was present, but remained oddly silent. She looked lonely up on her vast dais, which filled half the hall's floor-space, playing her harp and weaving her loom, with only beasts for company. Gradually I got used to her aloofness and she became almost like an actor on the stage, albeit one cast in a curiously boring play.

Nonetheless, I was well and truly bewitched, as worshippers are by their silent idols. I spent most of each day at the desk in my room, composing poems on the papyri I was given; mostly love poems, dedicated to her, since that was my remit. I placed them as ritual offerings on the altar before the dais and handed them to Helen, who passed them on to Anima, but still she remained maddeningly indifferent. When I asked Helen what the goddess thought of my work, she shrugged her shoulders and said, she can't think too badly of it, or you would be oinking and rolling around in your own shit by now.

Her enigmatic silence only deepened my obsession. The more she ignored me, the more desperately I wanted her. Thoughts of her chased themselves around my head; did she love me, or hate me? Had I done something wrong? What could I do to get her to notice me? When Doloma, dressed as a satyr, juggled balls or put on one of his farces with Nero, I was too distracted to laugh along with the others. Her image burned itself into my mind's eye until there was scarcely room for any other thoughts.

Doloma didn't help. He began whispering that she had turned most of us into animals and ignored the remainder because of something I had said to her of our voyage. The others took this with a pinch of salt, but the seed was sown; occasionally, I caught Nero staring at me balefully from across the dinner table. Doloma also described her wondrous body to me and regaled me with his detailed sexual fantasies even when she was absent, or we were in a different room, so that I couldn't free myself of her enchanting image.

The nymphs were no more accessible than their mistress. Though they fed us, watered us, cleaned up after us and washed our clothes, they never showed the faintest flicker of human interest in us – with the sole exception of Persona, but even he, they regarded with the detachment of aesthetes admiring a sculpture. We debated breaking the rule against seducing the nymphs, but I was put off by Doloma's idea that the penalty for lawbreakers would be death, and the large snakes each of the nymphs wore around their shoulders in imitation of their goddess, which hissed whenever one drew near.

Nero was not so easily deterred. Surrounded by so much beauty within touching distance, he could not restrain himself. For a man such as he, taboos and prohibitions only added to the excitement. Yet even he dared not approach Anima, for he shared our awe of the goddess. So, ever the pragmatist, he set his sights a little lower and directed his amorous attentions towards the nymphs; an extremely dangerous business, though he seemed unfazed by their snakes, threats and cold rebuffs. I saw him one day, walking in the woods with a nymph named Lucilla; a voluptuous little minx with blonde hair and a mischievous smile. Her snake was muzzled with a loincloth and their clothes were dishevelled. He gave me a suggestive wink.

I no longer needed my cane and began taking progressively longer walks through the forest, in a vain attempt to free myself of Anima's image by removing myself from her person. But how could I, when my very ability to walk was thanks to her? Each step I took was a reminder of my sublime benefactress.

I roved the secret ways of the forests, admiring the gnarled roots of the oaks, the sighing maroon canopies of the copper beeches, the spongy tread of pine needles underfoot and the startling beauty of sunlight filtering through the green leaves of the birches. I saw a little owl, not much larger than a sparrow, on the branch of a pine, and it stared back at me for a long while before fluttering away. I watched the deer leaping across the undergrowth and the eagles soaring high above the mountain peaks, all the while racking my mind for some way to impress her, or to escape her influence. Though sound of body, I was perturbed of mind.

It was on one of these walks that I caught glimpse of a man in a dirty, weather-beaten brown cloak, tramping through the woods. His hood was up, but I could tell he was old from his long, drooping grey beard, which descended to his waist. Though he carried a walking staff, he was still hale; I struggled to keep pace with him. Then the strangest thing happened. He put his fingers to his mouth and made a shrill whistle. The little owl came fluttering in like a jay and landed on his shoulder. In the end I had to leave off following him, as he was climbing higher and higher up the mountain slope, and my food was getting cold.

At the dinner table, I was burning with curiosity about the old man. He was a bright spot of colour in my comfortable but frustrating existence. The priests were as reticent as the nymphs about the affairs of the island, but since Phidias was something of a leader and spokesman among them, I asked him first.

'Ah, you mean Mentor. You needn't concern yourself with him. He is little more than a vagabond,' the priest said, his soft, venerable features contorting into a contemptuous sneer.

'He is not a priest, then?'

Phidias barked with scornful laughter.

'Nay, he was once a petty sorcerer, specialising in herb-craft, but is now nought but a broken-down old fool.'

'You speak of Mentor the Madman? He's not filling your head with his inane ramblings, is he?' chimed another, his venerable monkish eyes blazing with malice.

'No, I have yet to speak with him. But I am curious about him. How did he come to be on this island?'

'He was a pilgrim. A holy fool, from the east, he came to pay his respects to the goddess. Once she learned what little she could from him about herblore, she lost interest, but by then the poor sod was besotted!'

Cackles of laughter erupted among the priests.

'He lingers here in the hope of a kind word or even so much as a glance from her.'

'I have seen the way you look at her,' said Phidias, somewhat gravely. 'I assure you any efforts in that direction are forlorn and counsel you to give them up, lest you go the same way as Mentor the Madman.'

'Why?' I said, stubbornly. 'She made me her court poet. Why is it so hopeless? And why does she ignore us all?'

The priests grinned at me for a naïve young fool, but Phidias cast a nervous glance around the dining room. He waited until the nymph Gothia had disappeared into the kitchen with dirty bowls before answering.

'Anima is a goddess, and as such, she will only wed a god.'

'Bachelor gods being somewhat thin on the ground in these latter days, she remains alone and devotes herself to healing the sick and looking after her pets,' explained Phidias' friend, in a low, amused whisper, as if the very idea of her making an exception for a mere mortal like me was stupid beyond ridicule.

'And how did *you* come to be here?' I asked, seeking to take advantage of the priests' newfound loquaciousness. Nero had asked this question before, but they had given him nought but frightened looks and evasive replies.

Silence.

The priests glanced at each other, furtively. Phidias was about to say something, when Helen emerged from behind and gathered up his empty bowl and knife to be washed, startling us all. I did not know why, but that nymph positively frightened me; and I began to understand the nameless terror of the priests. We spoke no more and returned to our meals.

The next day, I walked in the pine forest again, hoping to catch another glimpse of Mentor. I ranged the forests all day, bringing with me a packed lunch of cold venison, buttered bread and a skin of wine, but I had no luck. The old man was elusive as a deer. Finally, as the sun was westering and the sky turned violet, I returned to the palace.

My bedchamber was large. The bed itself was extremely soft and comfortable, the sheets were of silk, the pillows feathery soft and scented with sprigs of lavender. Since my arrival in the palace I had experienced the most vivid dreams.

In one of them, I was back in my homeland, in the grounds of the palace of Laertius. A horned owl landed on my arm and flew off, killed a rabbit with its talons and landed to peck its guts out. Then I went over to the rabbit, sat down on the grass and ate its ripe red innards like a ravenous wolf. The owl stared at me reproachfully. It was angry at me for stealing its quarry. I punched the owl in the face, and it flew off. I wanted the rabbit to myself.

When I woke, it was late morning. Since there was little to do, I had taken to rising late, and other slovenly habits. I staggered over to the bathroom and splashed water from the basin on my face and looked at myself in the square mirror hanging from the wall. Though still skinny, I no longer appeared emaciated and my walks had given me a healthy bronze skin. But as I grew stronger in body, I became weaker in mind.

When I arrived at the breakfast table, everyone was unusually quiet. Then I noticed Persona was absent. I asked Nero what was going on.

'It's Persona,' he said, 'last night, he was caught *in flagrante* with the nymph Helen.'

'Really? I thought her interest in him was purely aesthetic?'

Nero raised a bushy eyebrow.

'If you really believed that, you're even more of a fool than I supposed.'

'What happened to him?' I said, ignoring the barb. I had grown accustomed to insults.

'The nymphs ordered him to come with them.'

'And he just obeyed?'

Nero nodded.

'You know how that fool is. He has faith in the justice of the law, though that didn't stop him from breaking it.'

'They took him through the door, on the right of the dais. We haven't seen him since,' Doloma added, a worried look on his lined face.

'What is to become of him?'

'The nymphs are sure to kill him,' Doloma said, gravely.

Nero shrugged.

'That is speculation. In truth, we do not know. But I mean to find out.'

'Lucilla.'

He nodded.

'I will ask her.'

80

'It will be a thorough questioning, I do not doubt,' said Doloma, grinning. 'Be careful, or you shall go the way of Persona.'

I returned to my room and worked on my poem. I could not concentrate. Doloma's words of doom rolled around in my head. Though I did not care much for Persona, since Anima had stopped talking to me, he was the closest thing I had to a friend.

Nero appeared in the shadows of the threshold. I started; I had not heard him approach.

He grinned.

'Fear not, old friend, it is I.'

'Have you news of Persona?'

He nodded.

Then he glanced down the marble corridor, closed the door gently behind him and sat down on my bed.

'I had a word with Lucilla. She says that Persona is God for a Day. That means he gets to fuck all the nymphs all day, with the sole exception of Anima. He can do whatever he likes with them and gorge himself on the island's finest foods and wines.'

'Some punishment,' I said, incredulous.

'That's what I thought. But being a god isn't all orgies and feasts. There's a ritual tonight, in the sacred grove. The black wedding, Lucilla calls it. She was vague on the details but hinted that it would not go well for Persona. Perhaps they mean to sacrifice him, as Doloma says. We should watch the ritual, from the trees.'

'No. If we were caught, we could be killed too.'

'Lucilla has agreed to show us to a place where we will not be seen.'

'It's too risky. And how do you know you can trust her?'

'She and I are close. Besides, I for one will not sit idly by and let them harm my friend.'

'But you hate Persona!'

'That is irrelevant. We have to stick together. There are only four of us from the ship still in human form. We are outnumbered, stranded in a strange land. We owe it to Persona to at least try and save him; I do not doubt he would do the same for us.'

I felt a pang of guilt. If even a bastard like Nero was willing to risk his life for Persona, what did it say about me if I refused?

'What is your plan?' I asked, tentatively.

'If Persona is in danger, and something can be done, I shall return to the kennel and fetch my beasts. I'll use them to create a chaos in which he might be freed.'

'And leave me alone?'

'Lucilla will be there with us. And Doloma.'

This did not exactly fill me with confidence.

Seeing my doubt, Nero went on, 'If no opportunity presents itself, of course we will refrain from making the attempt, and return quietly to our bedchambers.'

I equivocated; hesitated.

Finally, Nero could take no more.

'Look, the risk is small. Are you coming? Or are you a coward?' he said, his dark eyes boring into my soul.

Damn him. For all my hatred of Nero, and all the scorn he had poured on me, part of me still coveted his good opinion.

'Alright. I'll come.' Even as I said the words, I felt the dread.

Nero smiled and clapped me on the back.

Chapter 9: The Sacred Grove

It was night. The moon was full and red. A blood moon, Doloma said. An ill omen if ever there was one. Still, the others were all for pressing on, and I had to show courage; or rather, I had not the courage to disappoint them.

As we made our way through the olive grove, the moonglow filtering redly through the canopies, I heard the hoot of an owl. I froze dead and scanned the weird silhouettes of the gnarled old trees, but saw nothing untoward.

'Relax, Ego,' said Lucilla, giggling. 'You must understand, there are two kinds of rules on the island: those you can break, and those you cannot. The prohibition on men entering the sacred grove belongs to the latter category.' The serpent she carried with her at all times was wound around her shoulders but muzzled with a loincloth. Evidently it was hers, for I could see her otherwise naked bottom jiggle through the diaphanous white dress as she walked ahead of me. I envied Nero.

'Where I come from, there is only one kind of law, and it cannot be broken,' I replied, churlishly.

'Nonsense. It is an antiquated law, a relic from bygone times. Nobody pays it much heed anymore, since it is bound to be broken. Indeed, we *expect* you to violate the sacred grove. You would not be a man, if you were not tempted.'

'Shh, quiet,' Nero said, for we were approaching the clearing.

I saw a fire in the distance. We crept through the moon-dappled bowers, keeping low. Fallen leaves crunched beneath our feet. There was a ripe crack behind me. I swivelled; it was Doloma, looking worried and sheepish. He must have stood on a twig.

We came to the edge of the treeline and peered through the undergrowth.

There was a large circular glade. In the centre of the clearing was a tree stump. Nymphs stood naked around the stump, a ring of fire at their backs. They wore terrible wood-carved masks of scowling horned demons. Each woman held a long wooden phallus in her right hand, like a club. Persona sat naked on the tree stump, his godlike physique on full display. The nymphs advanced on him.

The eye, confronted with so much ripe young flesh, knew not where to look. But far from being aroused, I was terrified. And disgusted. Recalling what Nero had said about the God for a Day, I assumed he had knowingly lured me to a sex rite.

'If you wish to play the voyeur, go ahead, but I shall not be drawn into your perversions,' I whispered in his ear, and turned to go.

A scream. Hideous, shrill. Seized by morbid curiosity, I looked back.

The women had made a ring around Persona. My view of him was blocked by their naked bodies. But I saw a hand thrust skyward, clutching something fleshy and bleeding. Then, horror-struck, I realised. It was Persona's manhood.

The organ was tossed carelessly from the circle and landed on the grass beyond the flames. It shrivelled rapidly, now it was cut off from the blood supply.

Another scream. Then the phalluses descended; the women smashed and battered Persona with the wooden sticks. Their cries pierced the stillness of the night.

Horrified, I ran.

I ran as fast as I could through the undergrowth, my breathing ragged, scratching my legs on brambles and briar patches. I heard rustling and cursing behind me, but dare not turn to see who it was.

Finally, once I was well clear of the grove, I stopped to catch my breath and wait for the others.

They were not far behind.

'What are you doing, coward? You could have got us all killed!' Doloma hissed.

'I'm sorry, I just—'

'Save it,' said Nero. Even he appeared troubled by what we had witnessed. Lucilla was the only one of our company who remained unperturbed. 'We will return to our quarters. Never speak of this again.'

We did as he said.

The following day, Nero cornered me in the corridor, on our way to breakfast.

'You'll kindly come to my bedchamber at sundown.'

My heart leapt into my chest. I recalled the horrors of the ship.

'Why should I?' I said, defiant, but I had a creeping sense of dread at what he might say next.

'If you don't, I'll have Lucilla report you for profaning the mysteries of the sacred grove.'

'But you did it too!' I protested, indignant.

Nero grabbed me by the skin of the neck and pushed me against the wall.

'She won't tell on me; the wench loves me. But she owes no loyalty to you and as a nymph, there is no taboo on her witnessing the ceremony,' he hissed, eyes burning with bloodlust.

'Is Lucilla not enough diversion for you?'

He stepped closer, till our lips almost touched and I could feel his hot breath on my face.

'Have you learnt nothing from my acquaintance? What we do is about power, not sex. Anyway, I can't do it to her; she would not let me, and the nymphs see each other naked when they bathe, so questions would be raised.'

Then he thrust his knee into my groin. I bent double, wheezing, and slid down the wall as he marched off for breakfast.

So this is how it must be, I thought, sinking into a morbid depression. Since his cronies could no longer hold me down, he had used guile to make me his whipping boy. I felt nauseated.

At the breakfast table, Doloma was filling our heads with dread once again.

'I was speaking with the nymphs. Turns out your predecessor as court poet, Iambus, mounted the dais,' he said, addressing me.

I looked up from my half-eaten bread, my eyes glazed over with despair. I was not hungry.

'Oh yes. He fashioned a spear from a fallen branch, stole a knife from the kitchen and hacked away at the beasts. Back then, there were only two wolves, and he got past them and up onto the dais where, such was the lunacy of the poor besotted fool, he even kissed Anima!' Doloma laughed. 'Anima soon restrained him with her wand and his boldness was rewarded with castration, followed by ritual sacrifice. They slaughtered him in the grove. He did not even receive the consolation of being God for a Day!'

Cheered by these dire threats, I spent the greater part of the day holed up in my room, trying to compose the final stanzas of my latest poem. Since all my previous efforts had been rejected, I was resolved to write Anima the greatest love poem of all time.

That, she could not possibly ignore! I knew I had it in me; or at least, I thought I did.

But I was too distracted by the prospects of the evening ahead to get much work done. I did however concoct a plan to spare myself; I would threaten to tell Lucilla of Nero's cruel demand. If he lost her affections, he had nought to hold over me, though she might well prove as sadistic as her lover, or see us both made eunuchs out of spite.

That evening, when I crept into his room, I was shocked to see Lucilla there, lying on the bed next to Nero. They were both naked. So much for my plan. My stomach plummeted, but my heart raced.

Lucilla patted the bed next to her and, hoping I might at least get a turn, I decided to play along.

I did not get a turn.

The next morning, I woke in agony. My back screamed with pain from a dozen cuts and bruises. Mercifully, Nero had avoided my face, arms and legs and the nurse Lucilla had bandaged my wounds afterwards, lest they attract notice. I tried to use Anima's talking magic, but the pain burned and burned so much I could not concentrate. Worse than the pain was the knowledge of the malice Nero bore me, and the soul-crushing humiliation. I felt worthless, for I was enslaved to the cruellest of masters and treated worse than a beast. I sank deeper into the dark waters of despair.

At the breakfast table, Nero told me that I was to muck out the kennel and stables. Helpless and morose, I agreed. My spirit was already broken; what was one more indignity? Knowing my fear of animals, he ensured the predators remained while I worked. He kept the wolf on a lead but allowed it to bite me in the leg. I smashed it in the nose with the shovel, but that just made Nero laugh. All our years of friendship were being used against me. I swore I would never trust anyone again.

After three days of drudgery and three nights of torment, I racked my brain for a way out. I had it! I would finish my grand love poem to Anima, she would be so grateful she would talk to me once more and give me the chance to woo her. As her consort, I would be in a position to revenge myself upon Nero and his cruel mistress.

But I knew she wouldn't have me, for I wasn't a god. I may nonetheless be granted an audience, where I could tell her of my predicament and throw myself on her mercy. I convinced myself Anima must be unaware of the black wedding, for the sweet, empathetic girl of the snake-temple could never countenance such barbarities. My reasoning was weak, but I was desperate.

At last, the work was finished.

I regaled the others around the breakfast table, singing the lyrics. Everyone clapped. Phidias said it was the greatest poem he had ever heard; some of the priests wept; even Nero was forced to grudgingly admit it 'wasn't a bad piece of poesy.'

Brimming with confidence, I presented it to Helen, who said Anima would read it that morning.

After mucking out the animals, I sat in the Hall of the Moon for hours, waiting for my deliverer to appear. When the goddess finally emerged on the dais, she sat on her throne and began to play her harp. She did not so much as glance in my direction, let alone make comment on my work.

She was totally indifferent.

I had just presented her the greatest love poem ever composed by mortal hand and she hadn't so much as farted in my direction. I felt absurdly undervalued. I began to question my talent, which had hitherto been the one certainty in my life.

Frantic, I saw Helen passing through the hall to the kitchen, to oversee the preparations for dinner. I ran over and would have grabbed her by the arm, if it wasn't for the snake that rose hissing from her shoulders. I stepped back and asked her if the goddess had a word of praise for my poem.

'No,' she said, as if it was strange that I should even ask.

That was the final straw.

Furious, I stormed over to the bottom step of the dais. The beasts stirred themselves from their languor and began to growl at me. The lion's ear-ripping roar was amplified by the acoustics of the hall. I did not care.

'I just wrote you the best damn poem of all time!' I yelled.

Anima's face remained impassive. This only served to further enrage me.

'If you want me to continue to be your poet, you must praise me, clap me, acknowledge me – criticise me! Anything is better than this infernal silence!' I thundered.

The priests were gobsmacked. Even Nero was surprised.

'To Nekriya with you, witch! I am no longer your poet! I am leaving this godforsaken island!' I stormed out of the Hall of the Moon, passing Nero, who smirked at me, as if he knew full well that I would return to the comforts of the palace before sundown.

His condescending demeanour only intensified my resolve to leave. I ran upstairs, grabbed my cloak, and then gathered some giblets and leftover bread from the kitchen.

Doloma ran after me as I marched across the lawn.

'Where do you think you're going? There's no way off the damn island!'

'I'll build a fucking raft.'

'You'll drown!'

I rounded on him.

'Look at me,' I said, staring at him with the wild eyes of a spooked horse. 'I don't fucking care!'

Then I stormed off. He did not chase me. Nobody did.

After three hours' morose trudging, I reached the beach. There, I found the few bits of driftwood that had washed ashore from the shipwreck. I needed some rope or twine to bind them together into a raft. It was already nearing sunset; not a propitious time to set sail, and I was a long way off having a seaworthy vessel.

Finding no rope amongst the wreckage, I set about searching for brambles in the nearby copse of scrubby pines. Having scratched my fingers yanking some loose, I returned to the beach and started trying to lash the boards together with the brambles. I cut my hand, for the fifth time, and cursed.

'Seek not your freedom in the world,' said a booming voice of incredible gravitas.

I turned.

Stood before me on the beach was a tall man in a brown weather-beaten cloak with a long, grey beard and an owl on his shoulder. The hood shrouded his face in darkness, but I knew who it was.

Mentor the Madman.

Chapter 10: A Hermit in the Woods

'Oh really? And where else *should* I seek my freedom, if not in the world?' I asked, with peevish sarcasm.

'Seek it within thyself,' he said, stepping forward and removing his hood to reveal a thick head of straggly grey hair and a forehead as deeply lined as the bark of an oak. He had a large, ruddy nose and his blue eyes sparkled like the sun on the face of the waters.

I was too tired and demoralised to bandy words with this halfwit, so I returned to my brambles and planks.

'And they call *me* a madman,' he said, chuckling at my pathetic efforts.

'Piss off, vagabond! Get back to your hovel!'

'You'll not leave the island that way.'

'And why not?'

'It would require the sturdiest of vessels to withstand these storm-tossed seas, and if your efforts are ought to judge by, you're no shipwright,' he said, with considerable amusement.

'What do you suggest?'

'There is another way to leave.'

'What way is that?'

A long pause. The surf crashed against the beach and drew back in a long, sighing ebb.

'It's getting dark. You must be thirsty. Come to my hut, it's not far from here.'

I regarded my pitiable efforts to string a couple of rotten planks together. Then I looked up.

Mentor's large, bagged eyes twinkled with kindliness.

'Why not? This day could hardly get much worse.'

We walked a few miles through the scrubby hills and sparse stone pines. Then the path rose into the highlands. The underfoot shifted from sand to mud and we found ourselves surrounded by gloomy mountain pines.

At last, we arrived at a modest single-storey hutment, somewhat dilapidated and so small that at first, I assumed it was merely used for storing wood. Then I saw blue smoke rising from the chimney. Behind the shack stood a mighty oak with a broad trunk, twisting branches and gnarled roots. The bower was littered with molehills.

'Welcome to my home.' The old man chuckled.

We both had to stoop to enter.

Inside, the hut was more spacious than I first thought. There was a rustic table with two chairs, an old chest, a hay mattress in the corner and a large pile of logs. The only light came from a fire. A cauldron was suspended above it, bubbling with broth. The old man dolloped the brew into greasy chipped bowls and plonked them down on the small table. Everything here was worn, uneven and spoke of shoddy workmanship.

'Please.'

I sat down opposite him. Then he removed a flask from the folds of his cloak and filled a wineskin for me, while the owl pecked at his broth.

'Eat. Drink.'

Too tired to protest, I did as he bid me.

The wine was cool and rich, and the broth tasted meaty and warmed my stomach.

'So, what have you heard about me?'

'That you're a vagabond, a hermit, a madman.'

'Well, I am a hermit, but as you can see, I have a home, modest though it may be. As for whither or no I am mad, I shall leave that for you to decide.'

'As far as I can tell, you have not made yourself unwelcome in the palace. Why do you choose to live alone?'

The old man barked with laughter.

'You have lived in that den of temptation, and you wonder why I choose the life of a hermit?' he asked, incredulous. 'The nymphs drove me to distraction with their transparent shawls. And I wearied of those bald-headed mincers they call priests. I needed somewhere I could be alone! Somewhere I could think!'

I could see his point.

'And you? What drove you from the walls of the palace?'

'Anima ignored my poem.'

The old man laughed.

'It was a great poem!' I protested, hotly.

'Even if it was, that makes no difference to the stone-hearted maiden they call a goddess. Even The Poet himself would leave her unmoved.'

'The priests told me she stopped talking to you.'

The old man sighed.

'Yes, that is true enough. She learned what she could from me, and when she had no further use for me, I was discarded, like yesterday's scraps,' he said, glowering into his bowl.

'It's so confusing. In the snake-temple, when I was convalescent, she seemed so friendly and understanding. We had so much in common. She's a poet too! We even kissed! And then she makes me court poet but acts as if I don't exist. I don't understand!'

I took an angry swig of the wine.

'That's deities for you, my boy. Fickle as the winds!'

I took another swig.

'I understand why you shunned the palace, but why do you remain here on the island?'

The old man slurped his broth. His table manners were atrocious.

'You are not like me. If you built this hut, you could build a boat, if you set your mind to it,' I said.

'Aye, mayhaps I could build a boat, but I could never leave.'

'Why's that?'

'I am a prisoner on this island.'

'How so? I see no guards.'

'Anima put a curse on me. I'm bewitched; I cannot leave because I do not want to leave.'

'If she has no further use for you, why not lift the spell?'

'The same reason she turns most castaways into beasts.'

'And that is?'

'Power. The snake-witch is jealous of worshippers. Isolated here on her island, she is envious of the greater gods of the mainland and she means to make up for it, any chance she gets.'

'But she is a healer! She saved my life!'

'Aye, that she might win a devoted follower for her cult.'

'I don't believe you.' I swigged the wine. A warm glow permeated my body, from my stomach to my head.

'Believe what you like, it'll do you no good. She'll only marry a god; everyone knows that.'

'Then what do you suggest?'

I sensed this old man was no madman at all; that his crude habits and stained cloak concealed a monstrous shrewdness borne of erudition and vast experience. Besides, in my despair, I would have sought advice from anyone willing to give it, even a holy fool.

'It is as I said to you on the beach. Look *within.*'

'Does that really mean anything, or is it just a vague mantra to make you sound wise?' My dealings with the human race thus far had made me cynical.

The old man smiled at me, cracking his chapped lips. The owl fluttered its wings restlessly and left a dropping on the table.

'Had any dreams lately?' he asked, ignoring my question.

I rolled my eyes.

'What is it with you people and dreams?'

'Dreams are the gateway to the soul.'

'Yes. A dream I had in the snake-temple helped me to heal. But I have recovered; my quarrel now is with the world.'

'The soul is a tree whose roots lie deep in the earth.'

I sighed. I was at my wits end, and willing to try anything.

'Alright. There was a dream I had a few times. I was stood on a small boat in the middle of a lake. It was a bright summer's day. I looked at my reflection in the waters and saw Nero staring back at me. He raised a spear, as if to throw it at me. I dived in, trying to strangle him, but the waters were heart-stopping cold. I drowned and woke up.'

The old man fished a pipe out of the folds of his cloak and lit it with a twig from the fire. He sat down again, leaned back in his rocking chair, and puffed away contentedly.

'Who is Nero?' he asked, at last.

'He was among the crew of our vessel. We were shipwrecked here in a storm.' Though I did not trust this wily old fart, I was past caring whether he betrayed my confidence or no.

'The whirlpool and the kraken?' he said, exhaling slowly.

I nodded.

He puffed again, wrapping his chapped lips around the smooth ebony of the pipe.

'Is he the other reason you left the palace?' he said; the old bugger was far too shrewd to suppose I had forsaken such creature comforts merely on account of a broken heart.

I grimaced and nodded.

'Giving you a hard time, is he?'

'Yes, you could say that. Can you tell me what it means or not?' I asked, impatient and reluctant to divulge more to a stranger.

'Each man contains a world in miniature. All the fish of the sea and the birds of the air dwell inside of us. If it was not so, how could the world exist?'

'The world was created by the gods,' I said, repeating the mantra I was taught at school.

'That is what they want you to believe, that they might cling to power. In truth, you create your world from the Unknown Mind, and nothing can happen to you in the World Without, that has not first occurred Within. Why else would omens appear to us in the guts of chickens, and the flight of birds? And how else can seers predict the future from their dreams and visions?'

'What does that *mean*?' I demanded, infuriated by his vagueness.

'Everyone in the World Without represents a part of ourselves we are not aware of.'

I pondered his words, which I felt to be unnecessarily cryptic. My head throbbed with confusion and anger.

'So you're saying I'm like Nero?' I scoffed. 'There's no way I'm as bad as that bastard. He's a murderer, a sadist, a bully and a thief.'

'Do you hate him?'

'Yes! I want to kill him!' I blurted, then instantly regretted my indiscretion.

The old man nodded sagely, and exhaled a thin plume of blue smoke, which gathered about the cobwebbed rafters.

'Then yes, you are akin. Not identical, but akin.'

'How?' I asked, bewildered.

'All hatred is self-loathing in disguise.'

'We couldn't be more different!'

'We hate men who express those aspects of our character we conceal, even from ourselves. Do not be fooled; contraries are sisters under the skin.'

Though I couldn't fully comprehend his words, I had an inkling there was more to them than mere sophistry.

'What should I do? In practical terms.'

'I know of certain herbs, that can induce a wakeless slumber. Have you the stomach for murder?'

I was taken aback.

'No!'

'Just a question,' he said, raising his bushy eyebrows, as if I had overreacted. Then he picked the crumbs out of his beard and fed them to the owl.

'Well?!' I demanded.

He looked up and frowned at me, as if he'd forgotten I was there.

'You must first admit you share many characteristics with this blackguard, that you may not be as bad as him, but that you *could* be even worse, if you had a mind – and take it from me, *you* could tyrannise on a scale that would make this rogue seem a gutter rat by comparison.'

His words resonated with something deep inside of me; something half-suppressed, half-hidden; something that had been on the tip of my tongue all my life, that I had never dared express.

'Alright, assuming I do as you say. Then what?'

'Then you must make a pact with the devil. But you must never, *never* forget: it is one thing to barter with the devil and quite another to be possessed,' he said, with the utmost gravity.

'What does that *mean*?' I asked, unable to keep the desperate curiosity from my voice.

'Accept the Devil Within; the part of yourself that shames and disgusts you. And then your fear of this boy will diminish. When your mind is no longer distracted by terror, a strategy will occur to you, and you will see through Nero's mummery; for a knave is a hard man to cheat. Remember: as a mere projection of the World Within, an extension of yourself, it is within your power to influence Nero: to defeat him. He grows larger, the more you hide your dark side from yourself. Find your hidden darkness, scour the record of your life for it, and then embrace it. Embrace it like a long-lost brother and this Nero will shrink to the size of a gnat,' he said, contemptuously.

I sat silent, letting his words of wisdom sink into my soul.

'What kind of sorcerer are you?' I asked, since his every word reeked of black magic.

'The kind that could kill with a look,' he said, his gnarled features twisting into a glare of pure malice. The shadows seemed to lengthen. The little owl fluttered out of the open door. The wood walls of the shack creaked as they would in a gale.

Then the storm cloud passed from his face, as if there were never the least threat of rain. He burst into reams of rich, belly-shaking laughter.

'I jest. I am a mere herbalist. Though, during the course of my travels, I dabbled in philosophy and eastern fire-magic.'

 'You have been to the east?'

'Oh yes, so far east it was nearly the west!'

I laughed.

'What did you see on your travels?'

'Wonders without number, every species of depravity and much that was banal.'

'Tell me of the wonders?'

'I saw a man raised from the dead.'

'Necromancy? I thought such things were mere legends.'

'All legends have their roots in fact.'

I was intrigued; I could have listened to him talk all night.

'Truly, Mentor, at first I thought you were crazy, like the others. But now I see there is far more to you than meets the eye.'

'I could say the same about you, my boy.'

The old man's eye twinkled. When it caught the light, it was fiercely bright, like a diamond. Far from being a madman, I already got the sense Mentor was the wisest man I had ever known.

'It's getting late. An old man like me needs his rest. You may sleep on the floor,' he said, laying his tattered cloak down on the splintery boards. 'That will have to do.'

Chapter 11: The Devil's Pact

I could not sleep. The planks of the floor were uneven, and Mentor's cloak made for a lumpy mattress; the pockets were filled with trinkets, flasks and bones.

I used the time to ponder what he said about the World Within. Though the old man's ideas were strange to me, Anima's words had prepared me for it, and I was unable to refute it on logical grounds. After all, our philosophers could not account for my miraculous recovery. But the old man's wisdom certainly could, and a good deal else besides.

Scouring the record of my life, I recalled that as a boy, I had attacked and bullied other lads in the village. That I had beaten Nero. That I had played the wastrel while my parents needed me at home. I had killed Xanthus, my only friend, and eaten him. Was my betrayal of Xanthus not as terrible as Nero's betrayal of me? I was forced to admit that it was worse. And would I not like to do to Nero, all the things he had done to me? The nausea hit me. The revulsion at the deed. But the old man had said I must accept my darkness. I might be able to admit I was a murdering cannibal, and that had healed me, but there was a world of difference between acknowledging a deed and accepting it – let alone taking ghastly pride in one's most monstrous acts. How could I love the ravenous beast inside of me?

I was desperate and willing to stop at nothing to free myself of Nero and revenge myself upon him. I had tried to be good, and it had led me to misery and defeat and the life of a slave. Goodness alone had failed me. I was quite willing to treat with the devil and sacrifice my goodness on his altar if it meant an end to my torment.

'I accept you,' I said, to the dark side of my soul.

Movement, in the corner of my eye. I saw a shadow on the wall. Following the shadow back to its source, I rolled over.

And then I saw him.

A livid red-faced demon with curving ibex horns and a repulsive grin, wearing the brown cassock of a monk. He stepped toward me, his cloven hooves clattering on the planks of the shack. He made so much noise, I wondered that the old man did not wake.

'Who are you?' I asked, startled. I sat up.

'Is it not obvious?' he said.

On closer inspection, his face was that of Nero's. My heart hammered in my chest.

'Are you Nero?' I asked, casting about for a weapon; the old man's staff leaned against the door.

He laughed.

'I am not he. I am you; as much a part of you as your hair and nails. Fear not, for I cannot harm you physically.' He muttered that last word with a sly grin.

'Why have you remained invisible until now?'

'You turned your back on me.'

I swallowed a lump in my throat. A lump of guilt. I felt guilty for shutting out the devil. Had he not a right to be heard?

'That is true. I wish to speak with you. To make a deal.'

'This parlay is long overdue. State your terms, and I shall state mine.'

'I want revenge.'

The devil laughed.

'Of course you do. All men seek revenge. But few of them are worthy of my aid. What marks you out from the unthinking mass?'

'I am willing to accept you as my brother. All I ask is that you give me revenge.'

'And what constitutes revenge? For it is the aggrieved party who defines the word.'

'Victory over Nero.'

The devil considered my terms.

'I will do as you ask. But I require one thing more for our pact to be sealed: your soul.'

'What does that mean? Exactly?'

'You must listen only to me. You must do as I bid you, forever.'

I recalled the old man's warning, not to let myself become possessed, and I was seized with the panic terror of the fires of Nekriya. Even to bandy words with such a one as he was to imperil the soul.

'No. I will listen to everything you have to say. But I will not be your puppet.'

'You are strong. Many have thought themselves stronger than I; many have proven themselves fools,' he said, in a voice velvety smooth and rich in contempt.

'Those are my terms.'

'You bluff. You cannot go on living as you are. For you it is a matter of life or death. You need me more than I need you.'

'If I die, you die with me, since you are a part of me.'

The devil considered my riddle.

'Death is not so very terrible for one such as me. I have a mortal part that dies with my host, and an immortal part that lives on in others, and will prevail as long as there are men to walk the earth and be tempted.'

'Very well. I shall revise my terms. What if I were to make a more modest demand of you? Would you renounce the claim on my soul and be content with a seat at the council table of my mind?'

'I am listening.' The devil said, stroking his red chin sceptically.

'All I *need* is freedom. You desire it for me too.'

'Of what concern is it to me whither you are free or no?'

'There are limits to what the devil can do with a mere slave; a free man has greater scope for good and evil.'

'What of victory. What of revenge??'

'Revenge is a luxury – and one I cannot afford, at the price of my soul.'

'Have it your way,' the devil said, somewhat peeved, like a merchant selling his goods at a meagre margin. 'Fear has clouded your mind and made you forgetful. There is something you have missed: in the snake-temple, Anima knew when you were lying. She knew all about you; this knowledge guided her questioning. Perhaps she asked around beforehand; then again, she is a goddess. Chances are, she can read men's minds as if they were open books. Even if she lacks this power, she is a wise woman and will not be deceived by a petty knave like Nero.'

'So what if she cannot be deceived? How would it help me?'

'Ask the nymph Helen about jurisprudence on the island. As the ruler of such a small community, Anima may well be the judge, and if Nero were to accuse you, a word from you would see him thrown in the dock beside you.'

'But Nero can rely on Lucilla's testimony. As a votary of the goddess and a native of Tyria, she will be believed more readily than I, and I have no evidence to produce against them.'

'A judge that cannot be deceived has no need of proof. The very words from their mouths would condemn him.'

'I see. So you're saying Nero is bluffing?'

'I am the Father of Lies; I know a fraud when I see one.'

'If you are the Father of Lies, how can I believe you?'

'You know I speak the truth. Remember the empty amphora.'

'The empty amphora,' I murmured. We could have killed him on the deck, if we hadn't believed his threats, and I would not have suffered further torments. Anger rose in me, like magma bubbling deep in the bowels of a volcano. 'He dare not denounce me, else we would both be for the chop,' I said, smirking in the darkness.

'That is the long and short of it.'

'I had no idea freedom would be so easily won.'

'Any man who wills it can be free. But Nero is violent and will not take kindly to being outwitted. For that reason, it would be wise to take certain precautions.'

'What precautions?'

'The one you call Mentor is a herbalist. Ask him for two sprigs of the belladonna Sagittarius. A *nonlethal* poison, it is weaker than ordinary belladonna because it sprouted during the sign of Sagittarius. The old man would agree to such a request; he has few scruples; he suggested murder. Nero is usually in his cups by sundown; put it in his wine.'

'How?'

'Under the pretence of helping the nymphs of the kitchen at their chores.'

'Then what?' I asked, fervently. My heart was racing.

'Then, steal a knife from the kitchen.'

'Won't they notice?'

'These are busy wenches; they will not miss one knife.'

'You speak of murder.'

'As you well know, in some situations, murder is the only road to freedom.' Xanthus's gashed throat flashed through my mind. 'But not this one.'

'Why the knife, then?'

'For your protection. You must go to his bedchamber at sundown and confront him. Call his bluff. If he tries to attack you, the belladonna will have weakened him; and you will be armed. It is sometimes necessary to frighten such men.'

I grinned.

'I like the way you think.'

'I am relieved you are wise enough to heed my counsel. So many scorn my words out of superstition.'

I basked in the warm glow of the devil's praise. Then a thought occurred to me – a worry.

'What if Anima is not the judge?' I mused, staring at the ceiling.

'Then you must resort to the way of poison and knife,' he whispered.

'What if we fight, and he dies?' I cried, desperate for guidance and racked by all the terrors of the night. 'Would you demand my soul as the price of vengeance?' I turned to face the devil.

But he was gone.

The next morning, I woke early. The fire was reduced to smouldering embers, but sunlight streamed in through the cracks between planks. I had only snatched a few hours' sleep, but I nonetheless felt revitalised and strangely wholesome. I rolled over and looked at the old man. He was still snoring.

I rose and looked about the hovel by the light of dawn.

There were all sorts of trinkets and beakers and vessels in the farthest corner. Were they for cooking? There was some pipe weed and an amphora of wine: uninteresting. Then there was the strongbox, in the corner.

Curious, I walked over, careful to avoid the creaking floorboards. I cast a nervous glance at Mentor; he slumbered yet.

I lifted the lid. The chest was not locked.

A giddy thrill rising in my chest, I looked inside.

A handful of gold coins. A bronze idol of a goddess – Anima? A few old stones. And a book.

The book was heavy, with a black leather cover. There was gold lettering on the front, in ancient script, but I could not make it out.

I reached down and blew the cobwebs off the book's front cover. It read: The Book of Forbidden Wisdom. A shiver went down my spine.

'Put that down!'

I nearly leapt out of my skin. Before I knew it, the book was out of my hands and the lid of the chest slammed shut, almost catching my fingertips.

'What's the fuss? It's just a book.'

'Just a book?' the old man cried, incredulous. 'That book contains – never mind.'

'What does it contain?'

'You are not ready for such a book.'

'Why not?' I asked, indignant.

'In all of human history, only a handful of men have been able to read it and understand its contents without killing themselves or going mad.'

I was intrigued; the old man could not have sold it to me better if he had tried.

'You exaggerate!'

'I most certainly do not. I pride myself on speaking the truth.'

'I saw it was called the Book of Forbidden Wisdom.'

'You saw too much. I have said too much!' he cried, despairing.

'What's it about, that it drives men mad?'

'I told you, you are not ready! Perhaps one day – but not now!' he thundered. The room darkened. Outside, the birds flew, cawing, from the trees.

It took all my will not to flinch from his gaze in terror.

'Very well. It's your book,' I said, placatingly. I had other matters in mind, anyway. 'I am grateful for your succour and even more so for your counsel, but tell me, would I be presuming too much of your hospitality to ask you one more favour?'

'Speak,' the old man said, wearily rubbing the sleep from his eye.

'You said you were a herbalist. Do you have two sprigs of the belladonna Saggitarius?'

The old man smirked.

'I see you have changed your mind about murder.'

'No! I said nothing of murder.'

'But two sprigs would surely kill the boy!' the old man said, peering at me with his canny grey eye.

A worm of unease wriggled in my belly. Had the devil knowingly given me false counsel?

'You have me wrong. I wish only to render my quarry docile – docile, but awake, for I have a mind to speak harsh words with him.'

He weighed me carefully.

'I have that which you seek. But I ask a price.'

'I have no money to my name.'

'Gold is not my price.'

'Then name it.'

'I wish to know if Anima still thinks of me. Ask the nymphs if she has mentioned my name, would you?'

'Of course,' I said, relieved that the price was so small.

'Oh, and while you're in the kitchen, place a dash of belladonna in Phidias' cup.'

I grinned and nodded.

The old man sighed, with some relief. Then he rooted around in his pockets and produced a sprig of the herb. 'Grind it to powder. It dissolves in wine.' I took it.

'I'm afraid I have no more food to offer; but since you are resolved on returning to the palace, you can breakfast there,' he said, brusquely, and showed me out of the door. He offered me his hand. It was gnarled, bronzed and huge. I shook it. His grip was hearty and bone-crushing. 'You are always welcome here, should you be in need of further counsel, or if you just want to hear more drivel from the chapped lips of an old fool.'

'Thank you.' I turned to go.

'And one more thing; do not mistake your shadow for yourself,' he said, gravely. Then he tramped off into the woods, and the owl descended from the old oak to land on his shoulder.

Chapter 12: The Temptation of Ego

I returned to the palace a more confident man. Nobody stopped me. Despite my tirade against the goddess, it appeared I was not banished from the palace. Doloma jeered as I made my way to the kitchen. I passed Nero in the Hall of the Moon. 'Back so soon?' he asked, grinning. I grinned back. Mildly discomfited, he stared after me.

The kitchen was vast, with baskets of grain and bread, tripods, *klebanos*, braziers, and long wood tables where nymphs were preparing the fish and vegetables for tonight's dinner. I scoured the nymphs' faces for Lucilla but could not see her.

Good.

I knew that on holy days she worked in the snake-temple. This was vital to my plan, for she was usually too tired to romp with Nero after tending to the sick and she could not be present when I confronted him.

Helen saw me and stopped dead.

'I would like to atone for insulting the goddess,' I said, hanging my head in solemn contrition, 'by working in the kitchens.'

Helen marched over, looked me up and down. Her countenance was hard for such a slight young woman.

'Very well. Since the goddess has not seen fit to banish you, it is not for me to stop you from making yourself useful around here. You can start by chopping those pomegranates.'

I did as she asked, and slyly ground the belladonna when she was looking the other way, all the while scouring the kitchen for the wine. I saw a nymph, Clotilda, emerging from the cellar with an amphora. When she returned to make the next trip, I offered to get it for her. She shrugged her shoulders.

I went down into the cellar. I was alone down there. It was cool and quiet. Casks of wine were lined up in rows on either side of the aisle. There was enough here to intoxicate the gods.

I grabbed an amphora and brought it up to the kitchen. I did not want to mix the poison until I could be sure Nero would drink from it.

'Mistress, I would like to serve our guests at table. Especially the wine; I know who is liable to get drunk and am prepared to dilute the wine accordingly.'

Helen understood my oblique reference to the hedonistic Nero, who all the kitchen nymphs went in terror of, especially when he was in his cups.

'Well, what's brought about the sudden change of attitude?'

'I remembered all you have done for me. If it wasn't for Anima, I'd be dead or crippled. I owe the goddess my life; the least I can give her is my service.'

'Hmmph. We shall see.'

I took that for assent and made to return to my chores.

'And Ego?'

I stopped, dead. Had she seen me grind the herb?

'Yes, mistress?'

'Keep it up.' There was the ghost of a smile, and then she returned to gutting the fish.

When dinner came, I served the men their fish, vegetables and bread, to howls of laughter and derision. 'Look here, if it isn't Vestia, goddess of hearth and home!' Doloma brayed. When I walked off towards the kitchen, Nero slapped me on the bottom as if I were a tavern wench.

I blushed with shame and bit my tongue; I was going to savour my revenge.

The wine was next. I checked nobody was looking, then grabbed the ground herb from my pocket and sprinkled it into the amphora.

'Hurry up! The boys will be expecting their wine!' cried Helen, from directly behind me.

I almost jumped.

'Yes, right away, mistress!' I said, grabbing the handle and marching over to the table.

In my haste to be revenged, I made straight for Nero's cup. Then Doloma shouted, 'Hey! Don't I get any?'

I murmured my apologies, backtracked and poured him a cup. Then I went over to Nero, who was staring at me thoughtfully. As I was about to pour, he grabbed my wrist.

'Why the sudden bout of matronliness?'

My heart pounded. I had erred by going to him first. I was acting out of character. He suspected something!

'I thought they wouldn't have me back if I didn't make a show of contrition,' I said, with a cracked voice.

I tried to hold his flinty gaze. The urge to look away was unbearable; within those black eyes lay all the horrors of the underworld.

He released me and nodded, but remained watchful.

I poured the wine. My hand was trembling; this was not lost on Nero. I had no doubt he would kill me if he knew what I intended. I could see where this was headed and made a silent plea to the devil within; I thought of Xanthus.

My hand steadied. I even mustered the spirit to glare sullenly at Nero. His insolent smirk returned. This was the resentful slave he knew and loathed.

As the evening wore on, I heard Nero and Doloma singing. Nero in particular grew increasingly obnoxious with the nymphs. He made a grab for my crotch as I refilled his wine, but he was so drunk I was able to dodge his wandering hands.

Back in the kitchen, work was winding down. Most of the girls had quit for the day and gone to their rooms. Only Helen and I were left.

I had yet to ask her about Tyria's judiciary. Now was my chance.

'Mistress, may I trouble you with a question about the laws here?'

This was curious enough to get her attention. Her smooth brow wrinkled.

'The laws? They are simple enough. Why should you want to know about them?'

'You said Anima has not banished me. Am I right to assume that Anima judges all cases of suspected lawbreaking on the island?'

'That is correct.'

'I should think she is a most sagacious judge.'

'Indeed she is.'

'And difficult to deceive.'

Helen scoffed.

'Difficult? It is impossible to deceive her, for she is a goddess, and can read men's minds as if they were open books.'

'I thought as much,' I said, concealing my inner relief.

'Why do you ask? Planning to commit a crime?'

'Not anymore!' I said, with an insouciant wink. I didn't know what came over me, but there it was, done.

Helen's stern matronly façade cracked a little and she giggled.

'I am pleased with your work today. I know you have been frustrated by the goddess. She is hard to please. But not all of us are so picky,' she said, running her finger down my bronzed arm.

You can have her, whispered the voice in my head, the voice of my devil. My heart pounded. Persona had her – and look what happened to him. Perhaps she always meant for them to be caught *in flagrante* and wanted him to be castrated, out of sadism or a twisted sense of piety. Perhaps my manhood was to be the next sacrifice for the goddess.

'It must be difficult, with the prohibition on contact with men.'

'Oh, we're not banned from touching men. You're just banned from touching *us*,' she said, slipping her hand down my tunic. The snake hissed; lust and terror comingled in me.

She's begging for it. Do it. Why not?

'I see. That's quite the ah, loophole. But what about the snakes?'

'Oh, these? They may bite, but we removed their venom years ago. They are an empty threat,' she said, setting hers down on the table. 'And they are not the only snakes we are interested in.' She stepped forward and pressed her body against mine. My fears dissolved in the flames of lust.

I heard a noise. Footsteps, coming our way. We pulled away. I grabbed a mushroom and started chopping, just to look busy, though dinner was already served.

It was Agnes, a busty nymph with red hair.

'What is it?' Helen asked.

'I forgot,' Agnes said, after staring at us silently for a while. 'I must go to the snake-temple tomorrow. My husband needs my care. Can you find someone to cover my shift?'

Husband? I remembered the black wedding and wondered.

113

'Yes, of course, Hermione will do it.'

'Thanks,' she said, and left.

Helen and I stared at each other, our eyes burning with wanton lust.

'Not here.'

'Where?'

'I'll think of something. I trust you'll be helping us tomorrow as well?'

I nodded. 'I'll finish up here. You go to bed.'

'Goodnight, Ego.'

'Goodnight, Helen.'

When she was out of sight, I grabbed a knife and slipped it inside the folds of my tunic. Then I took a swig of non-poisoned wine to fortify myself and raced up the stairs. I paused outside Nero's bedchamber. I heard no giggles, sighs or moans. Just some drunken stumbling. It didn't sound as if Lucilla was there. Bracing myself, I stepped inside.

Nero lay flat on his bed.

At first, I thought he was asleep, and prepared to slap him awake. Then he stirred and gave me his sleazy grin.

'I was wondering where you'd gotten to – and Lucilla. Don't think I've forgotten about our arrangement. I'm pretty drunk, but not so drunk I can't give you a good thrashing!' he jeered, beckoning me.

His obnoxious manner grated. My choler rose. This was going to be easier than I thought.

'Silence, drunken fool! I shall be your slave no more!' I said, firmly.

The grin disappeared from his handsome face. He sat up; he knew something had changed in me.

'What makes you think I will tolerate such insolence?'

114

'I spoke to Helen. If you denounced me, I would accuse you and Anima would know I spoke the truth. You would make eunuchs of us both; and we both know you could not bear to lose your manhood.'

'So that's why you were lurking in the kitchen. And here I was thinking you meant to poison me!' he said, lurching to his feet.

'You were right. I put ground belladonna in your wine.'

'Gads! That's what it is. I thought I'd lost my head for drink.' He swayed, drunkenly, but his eyes were black as coals and his fists clenched.

'You never had a head for drink.'

Then something strange happened. I saw, faintly at first, a red, horned devil in the shadows on Nero's left. The devil looked like mine, only this one had my face, not his. 'He's a coward. Force will keep him in line,' the devil hissed into Nero's ear.

'Your words are bold, but empty. I do not need blackmail to make you my whipping boy – you're like a cur, a good beating is all it will take to bring you to heel!' he said, staggering toward me.

I drew the knife.

'Stay back! Or I will kill you!'

This gave him pause. But the wine had emboldened him.

'You couldn't kill me! I may be half-poisoned, but I'm no invalid!' he cackled and threw a right hook.

I darted aside, dodging his blow easily. He lost his balance and fell to his hands and knees. The magma rose inside of me. *'This is your chance. Kill him you fool – or he'll kill you!'* hissed the devil in my ear. I felt something on my chest – someone was touching me. I looked down and my devil's red vascular hand was tweaking my nipple. *'Stab him, castrate him – slit his throat!'*

Nero was stumbling to his feet.

I screamed and punched him in the face and stabbed him in the gut. I felt the blade pierce him; it felt good. I twisted and pulled it out and stabbed again and again and again, the blade making a wet sucking noise as it flew in and out of the flesh. He doubled over in agony. I felt a dark thrill ripple through my chest. I had him, I finally had the bastard, after all these years of beating and humiliation, at last I would make him feel my wrath!

Then I shoved him; he slumped to the floor. I grabbed the mirror off the wall and smashed it over his head. He groaned. Then I leapt on him, rolled him over and broke his nose and cheekbone with the knife's wooden handle. His face was a bloody ruin and he was dazed, beyond fighting back. I put the cold bronze blade to his throat. My eyes shone with bloodlust.

'*Do it! Kill him!*' hissed the devil, making obscene gestures at Nero's semi-comatose form.

I looked up at the devil – saw his eyes shining with sadistic glee – and then down at Nero, moaning and struggling to open his swollen-shut eyes. There was terror in those tiny bloodshot slits; the same terror I had felt at his hands. Then the old man's words came to me: 'Do not confuse your shadow with yourself.' I saw my devil had tricked me, I half-suspected it ever since the old man said two sprigs was enough to kill, but I had played along because in my heart, I wanted Nero dead. I wrestled with myself for a moment, growling in the agony of indecision, my soul in the balance. These prevarications were not enough to stay my blade, for the bloodlust was upon me. Maybe I would be damned, but I would have my revenge. I began to make my cut.

'Don't! I'm your brother!' he croaked, the blood already pouring from his neck.

I stopped, but I kept the knife at his throat. I hadn't the time to absorb the meaning of his words.

'You lie!' I yelled.

'No! It's the truth.'

'Prove it!' I said, my hand quivering with rage.

'Our lives are the proof! Look at us,' he said, grabbing the smashed mirror off the floor. I saw my reflection; my eyes were soulless, life-sucking pits – Nero's eyes. 'We are the same!'

I slashed his wrist, lest he use the mirror shard to attack me.

He cursed, grabbed his bleeding wrist and stared at me with fear and loathing as I jabbed the knife point to his carotid. There was much of myself in that baleful look: too much.

'We share the same father!' he pleaded.

I pressed the knifepoint deeper into the soft skin of his neck.

'You call my mother a whore?'

'Is there any answer I can give that would not enrage you?' he moaned, plaintively. 'Tell me what to say and I'll say it,' he said, and broke down into sobs. 'Just don't kill me.'

'You are a coward. I knew it.'

'Of course I'm a damn coward!' he said, angrily. 'Do you really think a brave man would pick on the friendless and the weak?'

'If I am so weak, why do you hate me?' I hissed.

'Because I am jealous!'

'Jealous??' This had never occurred to me before as a possibility. What was so good about my wretched life to inspire envy? 'What are you jealous of?'

'You are smarter and stronger than me. You have that rare stuff that makes a great man. All I have is a quick tongue and rat cunning.'

'Why did you whip me, beat me, mock me?'

'My step-father did worse to me,' he said, in a fragile voice, brittle as glass. 'Hurting you made me feel better about the indignities I had suffered at his hands; if I played the wolf, I could forget I had ever been the sheep.'

'Why me and why not some other fellow?' I was determined to get to the bottom of this; to have it out of him.

'I told you, I am jealous.'

'Is it because I reminded you of yourself?'

'Yes,' he croaked, weakly. 'It is true. *I hate* myself. How could I not? There is nothing to like here. There are times where I almost killed myself.'

'Instead you tormented me and made my life unbearable so I would want to kill *myself*?' I shook my head, for I knew it to be true. 'And you did all this, knowing I was your brother?'

'It didn't stop my step-father from doing the same to me,' he said, shrugging.

I stood up, disgusted with him, as if he were leprous carrion. I spat in his face. He winced and wiped it off.

'Lucilla keeps the bandages in the bathroom. Cover your wounds and say the beasts attacked when you went to feed them. Make sure Lucilla is the only one to see your wounds in the snake-temple.'

I made to leave. Then I stopped. A thought had occurred to me.

'If you try to kill me, I have left a letter with a friend of mine,' I said. 'It contains a full account of our trip to the sacred grove. He has instructions to hand it in to the palace nymphs if I am murdered, grievously wounded or die under mysterious circumstances. We are finished.'

And then I left.

Chapter 13: The Book of Forbidden Wisdom

With Nero no longer troubling me, my restless mind gave all its attention to Anima, and the temptress Helen. When I was working next day in the kitchens, the latter gave my buttocks a surreptitious squeeze and placed a note in my hand.

'Meet me in the wine cellar after hours,' it read.

I carried on with my tasks, chopping mushrooms, moving grain and preparing fish for lunch and supper. As I was removing the fish heads, she leaned in and murmured 'good work' in my ear. After lunch was served and the dishes washed, I asked Helen if I might be excused.

'Of course, you've done a full day's work. Just make sure you're back here for dinner.'

I swallowed the lump in my throat and promised her I would be.

I walked into the Hall of the Moon and saw Anima sat on her Mirror-Throne, remote as a distant star, and my reflection, filled with mortal longing. Nero shuffled past, regarding me warily, and mumbled a vague greeting. His face was bandaged. I was unable to stop the smile from creeping over my lips. I had not exactly revenged myself, when all of Nero's depredations against me were stacked up, but at least he respected me now.

My situation was still wretched; I had thrown off the shackles of one master, only to be faced with another who would prove far more difficult to shake. For Anima was a thousand times lovelier than Nero; and that made her a thousand times more dangerous.

I took to the forest to clear my head, for my mind was a buzzing beehive of lust, whirling with images of Helen's small breasts and piquant nipples, her fragrant auburn hair, plump red lips and bold blue eyes. And then there was Anima; her creamy skin and divine form but above all, the memory of her sympathy, the only sympathy I had received from anyone except for my parents. And now this absurd indifference. I needed to speak with Mentor. If anyone could solve this maddening riddle, it was he.

I remembered the way to his hut. It was another glorious day for a tramp through the woods. I reached Mentor's abode within an hour and knocked on the door.

'Who is it?' came a gruff voice.

'Ego.'

'Ah, come in my boy, come in,' the old man said, and the door swung open.

When I stepped inside, he was stood across the far side of the shack; he couldn't possibly have opened the door and returned to his jars and alembics in such time.

My eye leapt to the jar on top of the chest. It contained a two-headed foetus. My stomach sank at the sight of it. My instincts had been right; the old man was a black magician. The hut was filled with an atmosphere of stifling, almost unbearable tension. I felt, rather than saw, the presence of a third party: a formless darkness of crushing willpower.

'I'll just be a moment,' he said, pouring a vial of purple liquid into the jar.

'What on earth are you doing?' I asked, repelled and fascinated.

'Proving the physicians wrong. Trying to, anyway,' he muttered, distractedly.

When the substance dissolved in the yellowish waters of the jar, the foetus' leg kicked.

'The sleeper wakes!' the old man cried out in triumph.

'It's alive?!' I cried, horrified.

'Shhh,' the old man said, pressing his finger to his lips. 'You'll startle him.'

Then he grabbed a twig from the table and poked the creature in its bulbous head.

The leg kicked again. The black eye opened.

'Hello there, little master! I am your father!' Mentor said, jubilant. He came over all gooey-eyed and started making baby noises. 'You're daddy's little abomination. Yes you are, yes you are!' Then he tipped a pail of milk into the jar and the creature began to lap it up like a goldfish. Only the larger of the two heads seemed conscious; the other remained limp and mole-like. When the mouth opened, I saw it was full of sharp little teeth.

Mentor beamed with the pride of a mother cradling her new-born.

A wave of nausea hit me. I felt a sudden impulse to turn and run; nought good could come of the unnatural.

'How is this possible?'

'Anything is possible, if you know the secrets of life,' Mentor said. 'Come, sit!'

I took the proffered chair, careful to avoid the rusty nail protruding from the edge of the seat. I had come to him with my own problems but found myself morbidly fascinated by his work.

'Where did you procure an infant like that?'

'The nymphs sometimes get pregnant *out of season* and have stillborn children,' he said, suggestively. 'I rid them of their burden and give the poor babe a second chance at life.'

'Has it ever worked?'

121

Mentor's haggard face clouded.

'Nay,' he muttered, irritably. 'Most of them die before the week is out. I fear little Clitus the Foetus will fare no better than his brothers and sisters, but I live in hope.'

My mind's eye leapt to the little mounds at the back of the shack. I had assumed they were molehills. Now I realised they were probably the graves of other 'abominations.'

I stared at the creature.

'Why does he have two heads?'

'Two heads are better than one!' the old man said, cackling madly. 'If only because the odds are better that one will survive.'

'I see.' I stared transfixed at the pink wriggling horror reborn in the jar, felt a wave of nausea rising and stifled a retch.

'Anyway, enough of my work. How did you fare with your tormentor?'

'I am free of him. Your counsel worked. I made a pact with my devil and he showed me the way.'

'He did not trick you?'

'He tried; the fiend almost made a murderer of me, but I resisted the temptation.'

'You did the right thing. For as the scriptures have it: "he who kills his brother, kills himself" – or rather, the part of himself embodied by his brother.'

I wondered at his use of the word brother but let it pass; the holy texts he quoted referred to all men as brothers and the old man already knew too much of my business.

'So, you are free of your tormentor. Yet you are troubled. Why else would you come to visit a mad hermit?'

'I am tempted and frustrated.'

'Still besotted with Anima, eh? I can't blame you. I'm half-bewitched myself.'

The old man leaned forward conspiratorially and whispered, 'The conflict between good and evil is but a trifle compared to the problem posed by the riddle of the sexes. It is this that kills most folk.'

'You refer to murder?'

'Not murder, so much, though it is more common for spouses to kill one another than for criminals to kill the innocent and for men to die in battle.'

'What then? How do people kill one another, if not by murder?'

'The cup of love is sweet at first but leaves a bitter aftertaste. Heartbreak, frustrated longing, regret, the guilt and rage of infidelity, and the simmering hatred of domesticity; thousands more have died of such causes than have perished by scheming poison and jealous knife, though the world says the life was stolen by heart attack, cancer, plague, pox, cough or fever. To choose a husband or wife is to choose the way you want to live – and the way you want to die.'

'You make marriage sound so dangerous! Is it not also a source of happiness?'

'Do you know the customs of this island?' He said, eyebrow raised.

I took this as an oblique reference to the black wedding.

'I know a little, yes,' I said, cagily.

I had just escaped one blackmailer; I would not put myself at the mercy of another. Then again, he already knew about my poisoning of Nero, so it seemed senseless to be overly reticent, and the prohibition was on witnessing the sacred grove mysteries, not knowing of them at second hand.

'Then you see why I am a hermit!' he chuckled. 'Though for most natures, loneliness proves more deadly still than marriage.'

'Having been initiated into the mysteries of Esklepios by Anima, I can well understand how Unknown emotions can kill; and woman is the source of much feeling in man – partly acknowledged, but mostly hidden.'

The wizard nodded. 'The principle is the same.'

'Your magic is akin to hers,' I observed.

'Where do you think she learned it from?'

'You taught her how to heal?' Though I had come to respect his intelligence and had just witnessed him resurrect a stillborn infant, somehow I had never thought this muddy vagabond to be so grand a figure.

'Of course. You think I merely taught her herb-craft?' the old man chuckled.

'That is what you said,' I replied churlishly.

'That was before we knew each other. But we are friends now, are we not?' he said, offering me his wineskin. I took a pull.

'A friend would get to the point!' I said, feeling the warm burn in the pit of my stomach.

'Your impatience will cause you much grief. But luckily for you, Clitus the Foetus has put me in a forgiving mood. In a word, self-knowledge would help you to forget Anima.'

'I do not wish to forget her. I wish to marry her!' I said, startled by my own boldness. But there it was.

The old man did not laugh, as I expected him to. He stared at me appraisingly, as one would a cow at the market.

'Though I know it is hopeless as I am not a god,' I added, hastily, ashamed at my presumptuousness.

The old man grabbed his pipe from the table and puffed, his brow furrowed.

'Hot words may be rash, but they are spoken from the heart, and that is not without value.'

'What value can there be in hopeless fantasies?'

The old man grinned.

'Far more than one would suspect. And your hope may not be so forlorn as you think.'

I looked up, sceptical. I daren't let myself hope.

'What do you mean?'

'Perhaps you are ready,' he murmured, half to himself, chewing on the ebony pipe.

'Ready for what?' I demanded, urgency filling my voice.

'You accepted the teaching of Esklepios in order to heal; you listened to my counsel about the knave in the palace. You didn't recoil at Clitus, as most would; you have a stomach for dangerous truths.'

Had I stumbled upon Mentor at the very moment he brought his abomination to life, by pure coincidence? Or had he known I was coming and timed it so, as a test?

'I will stop at nothing to win her.'

The old man stared at me with his milky eye for a good long time. I felt the weight of a crushing will bearing down on me. It took an immense effort to hold his hard gaze.

'There is a way for mortals to become gods,' he said, quietly.

The shack stopped creaking; the wind had ceased blowing outside. The birds fell silent.

'The Book of Forbidden Wisdom?' I hazarded.

He nodded, deadly grave.

'Before we go any further though, I should warn you—'

'Most men who read it go mad or kill themselves, I know.'

'Very well. Have it your way. But know that whatever happens next, *you* willed it so.'

'If it will help me win Anima, I accept the consequences.'

The old man settled down in his chair, making himself comfortable.

'You should not *want* Anima. If you do, you will not have her. What you should aim for is to rid yourself of *all* desire; this is what you need to be free of her dominating influence. Just as knowledge of your likeness to Nero eased your fears, understanding your likeness to Anima would lessen the burden of your obsession.'

'You say I am like a woman!' I exploded. In my homeland such things were always meant as insults and typically preceded a beating.

'Calm yourself. All men are alike to women. It is nothing to be ashamed of; indeed, shame at your feminine traits is the root of your trouble. For every individual has an Unknown Mind that is contrary to their Known Mind; the two are opposites. The precise character of the Unknown Mind depends on the individual, but since *you* regard yourself as masculine, you would call your Unknown Mind feminine – an Inner Woman. Like many such men, you reject your Inner Woman from your Known Mind, and she is forced to manifest as a woman in the outside world; the more hotly you deny and suppress the Woman Within, the more strongly you come under the spell of the Woman Without. She seems to be of an opposite character to you, but this is trickery, for she is identical (or near as damn it) with those aspects of your Unknown Mind you would see as feminine – *if* you could see them. The consequence is love.'

'I do not love Anima!'

126

'Call it obsession, desire or hate, then, if that is more in keeping with your sensibility; in the end, there is not much difference,' the old man said, unfazed by my rage.

'You speak in riddles, dotard. I am disappointed; I thought your dangerous truths would be grander, more profound.' I had no idea why his words angered me so; I had shocked myself by my reaction. 'Even if what you say is true, it does not help me at all!'

'Bear with me and listen closely,' the old man said, more amused than offended by my truculence, as if he had seen such childishness before. 'Obsession, desire – and for that matter, love – can only occur if there is an unseen commonality between you and the object of your obsession. You wish to be free of your obsession? Find and embrace the commonality, and your thoughts of her will diminish. When your mind is not distracted by obsession, that heady brew of love-hate and lust, you will think clearly and know how to free yourself.'

I pondered his words.

'Well, you were certainly right about Nero. My obsession with him was due to an unknown kinship; in that case, a literal one. He is my brother – or he claims to be, anyway.'

The old man was taken aback. I had not meant to reveal this; but I had to tell *somebody*, and before I knew it the words were out. I made a mental note to drink less of his wine in future. The damn stuff loosened my tongue abominably.

'You believe him?'

'I do. As you said, we are similar at heart; that is why we hate each other. And what two men are more similar than brothers? We even look alike.'

'What are the odds?'

'Not bad, actually. We were born in the same village. He was the one who got me the job aboard ship.

'I see.'

'But where Anima is concerned, I see no commonality. We are as different as the sun and the moon.'

'Are you sure? Search your heart.'

Then I remembered our conversation in the pavilion of Esklepios.

'Well, I suppose we are both poets and share the solitary, melancholy temperament of poets,' I said, grudgingly.

'You most certainly do!'

I ignored the old man's barb.

'She said she had been betrayed as I had been betrayed by Nero. Our thoughts seemed to follow the same patterns.'

'And you both have a quenchless thirst for knowledge – or you wouldn't be caught dead riddling with a madman such as myself!' The old wizard chuckled.

'Yes. And we were both compelled by illness to accept the wisdom of Esklepios into our hearts. That is the most striking commonality of all, since it is a rare path to tread.'

I fell silent and frowned.

'A good deal of these shared traits are not what is commonly thought of as masculine, are they?' Mentor said, a canny glint in his eye.

The old man was right, damn him. I grunted a surly 'no.'

'You may be embarrassed by these revelations but like I said, such things are so common as to be ubiquitous. What is not common is to acknowledge them.'

At that, the old man rose from his chair and opened the chest. He removed the Book of Forbidden Wisdom and blew dust from the jacket.

'It has been a long time since my last initiate.'

'Initiate? Do you belong to some sort of cult?'

He laughed.

'You know me; I am not a joiner. No, this book is the central text of the secret, nameless religion that exists behind all public religions. Its devotees are but a handful of wise men who discover the mysteries for themselves, without the aid of priests or temples.'

'Is it secret because of all the suicide and madness?'

The old man laughed.

'That was a harmless ruse on my part, to dissuade those who are not serious, and tickle your fancy. No, in the majority of cases, the real danger lies in forgetting the wisdom or dismissing it as nonsense.'

I blushed; I felt angry at the old man's deception.

'If you lie about such things, how can I believe a word that you say?'

'The great test of any truth is how it makes you *feel*: distracted, or content. How *do* you feel?' he asked, solicitously.

'Embarrassed, as you said,' I admitted.

'But not quite so smitten as before, I'll wager?'

This gave me pause.

He was right. That tumultuous dazed-bewitched feeling had certainly dissipated and, by focusing on myself, I had given less of my thought to Anima's beguiling loveliness.

'No. I'm not,' I said, curiously relieved.

'As the prophet said: the stone the builders rejected, this I shall make my cornerstone. We all have a stone we rejected whilst building our characters because it was ugly or did not fit with the other bricks. For those of us who think more than they feel, our stone is feeling: love, emotion, ethics. For those who withdraw from company, who prefer to live in their heads, their relations with other people and the physical world – the undiscovered practical side of their nature – constitutes the Rejected Stone. The reverse is also true.'

I suspected the old man, under the guise of generalities, was actually talking about me. I quailed at the prospect of becoming more sociable, more worldly; more loving.

'You are asking me to become someone I'm not; to betray myself,' I said, recoiling in disgust from Mentor's perverse ideal.

'Not at all. I am asking you to become who you *really* are.'

I scoffed.

'You think me practical? Physical? Ethical? There is little evidence for such suppositions in the record of my life,' I said, haughty with sarcasm.

'There was little evidence for the emotions that almost killed you in the snake-temple. And yet they were there all the same, working their secret poison.'

'True,' I admitted, reluctantly.

'While our Rejected Stones are unknown, they are weaknesses, blemishes, and others who manifest our unknown traits seem poisonous to us. But if we make the rejected stone our cornerstone, then our flaws become less ugly, and those who manifest such traits become less dangerous to us.'

'This is a formidable undertaking. I am not sure I can do what you ask.'

'You have already begun to do so. Look at yourself and Nero; since you embraced what he represented inside of you, he has been less of a hindrance, has he not?'

There was truth in the old man's words; more than I would like to admit. Nero was outgoing, popular, glib and physical; an athlete and a rakehell. He was everything I was not, everything I hated. And yet there had been an underlying commonality, hadn't there?

'I can certainly see why the wisdom is forbidden, or rather, unpopular.'

The old man chuckled.

'There is good reason the nameless religion has few adherents, aside from common prejudice against magic. The gods themselves have suppressed the knowledge contained herein, for such knowledge is the hidden root of their power; the source of their divinity. In these latter days they have succeeded in perverting the outlook of mankind so far that even if one was bold enough to speak the truth openly, he need not be struck down by divine vengeance; he would simply be ignored – or mocked and derided as a madman.'

'Mentor the Madman.'

He nodded, gravely.

'I am trying my best. You have been right about many other things; probably you're right about this, too, and I am just too dull-witted to see it. But, please explain – why should I have an Unknown Mind? How did things come to be this way?'

'What I say will seem strange to you and go against everything you have been taught. I ask only that you suspend judgement and listen with an open mind.'

I nodded. My hand trembled; I was seized by a strange excitement, though I half-suspected the whole thing was either madness or a confidence trick, like all obscure and unorthodox cults.

'In the beginning, man and woman were one: a sexless, androgynous spirit who roamed the heavens in divine bliss, though one can very well imagine such a state to be boring. Enter The Deceiver. He tempted us into the Material Realm with the promise of sex and power. This we call the Fall. Thus was evil born; for there can be no evil without matter.'

I was seized by a sudden urge to interrupt.

'Why is that so? Matter is not inherently evil. Surely, like a sword, it depends on the use to which it is put?'

'Think about what you say. When there was no matter, there was no suffering and no temptation because there was nothing to want and nothing to fight over.'

'But matter is also the source of all pleasure; everything that makes life worth living!'

'That may be so, but pleasure stimulates desire for *more* pleasure.' The old man smiled at his cleverness. 'Make no mistake, desire is the sister of pain and every bit as distracting, since they both lead us away from the truths concealed within our Unknown Mind.'

'That makes sense.'

'So you see, reality is an illusion; and we are trapped in this vale of tears because we were deceived at the dawn of time, and continue to be deceived.'

'Why did God allow The Deceiver to trick us so?' I asked, suspending my disbelief for the sake of argument.

'Good question. This is where it gets complicated. The Deceiver is not really the antagonist of God.' Mentor shook his head. 'He is God. Part of God. For God is All. The Deceiver is God's Unknown dark side, and he too, has a part to play in the divine comedy, as shall be seen.

With corporeality came the division of the divinity into sexes and the dawn of the Reign of Death. But the original unity of the sexes was not entirely obliterated; the Other merely slipped more or less deeply into our ancestor's minds. Nor did we lose our spirits with the Fall into matter; they too became hidden within our Unknown Minds. They survive the death of our bodies and, following a sojourn in the afterlife, reincarnate in a new body.

We can recover our original state of divine unity by becoming aware of the Unknown Mind. Since everything that is rejected from consciousness is encountered in the world, the only way to do this is to live our lives; that, most people manage well enough. But we must also take time to reflect on what the people, objects and events we encounter in the Material Realm represent inside of us, and act accordingly, or we can never become whole.'

'Hold on – everything we reject from our Known Minds is encountered in the world?'

The old man nodded, with the dignity of a sage.

'That would explain why the world always seems to be at odds with our intentions – as if it wished to foil our plans,' I murmured, my thoughts turning to our disastrous voyage.

'Yes, the only certainty is the unexpected. And sometimes, the only way to attain an outcome, is to not want it; but do not try to deceive yourself, to *pretend* not to desire a thing in order to get it, for then you provoke a reaction from your Unknown Mind, and you will either be frustrated or get the opposite of what you secretly intended.'

'Take me; I set sail hoping to find treasure and women. And I wound up in the shack of a hermit, learning about – well, myself.'

The old man chuckled, somewhat ruefully.

'So you see, even The Deceiver's trickery is necessary for our development. Instead of seeing every ache and pain, every disaster, injury, sickness, every fear and desire as a distraction conjured by the Deceiver, they could equally well be seen as warnings or clues from The Enlightener as to the contents of our Unknown Mind. For The Deceiver and The Enlightener are two faces of the same Godhead.'

I had never before conceived of a unified Godhead. As far as I knew, nobody had.

'This is a revolutionary idea!'

'It is not so new as you think. For there was once an empire where the secret religion was the state religion.'

'I am a keen student of history. Never have I heard of such a place,' I said, sceptically.

'Alas, it was buried beneath the waves, thousands of years ago. The gods and their ancestors were once part of the empire's ruling elite. They began as wise rulers but over time, they became venal, tyrannical, depraved and crassly materialistic. But it was their practice of black magic that angered God most of all and brought about the Great Deluge.

However, a good number of the gods used their power and preparedness to survive the flood and exploited the destruction as an opportunity to conceal their mistakes and enlarge their power over the scattered remnants of humanity, by deliberately erasing the past. Ever since, we have suffered collective amnesia concerning our origins, the monad is inconceivable for most and has fragmented into the various pantheons; and the people remain mired in ignorance. But acquiring this self-knowledge is the meaning and purpose of life.'

'How extraordinary!' I chuckled, disbelieving.

'Yes, I know you are sceptical, but ask yourself: does this not explain the commonalities of all the world's religions and languages? The shared belief in a Great Deluge? The mysteriously sophisticated monuments of unknown origin, like the Pyramid of Magirov?'

The Pyramid of Magirov was a vast, four mile-high structure in the land of Khem, across the Olearic Sea. Nobody could explain who had built it, or how; except perhaps Mentor. I began to seriously entertain his doctrine and its implications.

'If the Fall inaugurated the division into Known and Unknown Minds and the Reign of Death, would merging the two into one lead to immortality?'

Mentor smirked at me; but his eyes were grave as death.

'Yes, and all the powers of the gods.'

'Heavens! This is preposterous!'

'I do not expect you to accept this teaching so soon in your initiation. Whether you believe in Atlantea and immortality or no, self-knowledge is our duty; because God is All and we are all part of the Godhead, the more we understand ourselves and unify our Known and Unknown Minds, the more God understands himself.'

I sat and pondered his words carefully. Though they seemed bizarre, I forced myself to keep an open mind, since Mentor had been right about Nero. There was a certain simplicity to it all that was appealing.

'So, the world is just a giant school that exists to teach us about ourselves?' I said, trying to put it into terms I could grasp.

'That's one way of seeing it, yes. By the way, how do you feel now?'

'Well, I'm not mad or suicidal. If anything, I feel a little calmer.'

'Calmness betokens the truth.'

'But can it really all be so simple? The meaning of life, the origin and purpose of man and the world – the great mysteries that have puzzled and confounded the wits of the greatest philosophers since the dawn of time?'

'Just as the simplest explanation is usually correct, complexity is the child of misunderstanding.'

'But there is no proof for what you say.'

'Open your eyes. The proof is all around you. It is also to be met with in your memories and dreams. Does this teaching not explain the nature of reality better than the philosophers do?'

'Perhaps. It is certainly simpler than their ideas and a good deal less far-fetched than the tales of the gods. But I am still troubled by Anima – albeit, not so keenly as before.'

'Take time to ponder my words. Acknowledgement of the Unknown Mind is good; acceptance is better; acting in accordance with its wishes is best of all. Your situation may not be a happy one, but at least it is not urgent. Most men live five lifetimes without understanding such things. But if you understand aright, and act accordingly, your obsession will lessen still further, and may even disappear. And when you attain this state of bliss, you will realise it is more rewarding than any lover.'

'I will do as you say. Though I doubt I can ever become a god.'

'What matters is your will to know. Seek and you shall find.'

And so, taking one last glance at the marvel in the jar, I got up, bade Mentor farewell, and left.

Chapter 14: Identification

It was nightfall by the time I returned to the palace. I went straight to my bedchamber, my mind reeling with exotic new ideas, only to find Helen lying naked in my bed.

'You took your sweet time. I trust you'll make up for the delay.'

Preoccupied with my meditations, I had forgotten all about Helen. But now she was here, with her slender curves, wicked elfin grin and alabaster skin, far from being aroused, I was seized by terror.

I had Persona's awful example before me. What if it was a trap? A means of procuring the next sacrifice for the cult? Even if it wasn't, her very presence here was almost enough to make a eunuch of me. Sobered by this dreadful prospect, I did not feel the least bit inclined towards lovemaking.

'I'm sorry Helen, I got lost in the forest. Now I am dreadfully tired. Perhaps another time,' I said, trying to put her down gently.

'Come to bed, I'll take your weariness away,' she said, spreading her bare legs.

This made me think twice. I stared, rapt, like a rabbit before a snake.

Seeing my temptation, she slipped out of bed and sidled up to me. She whipped my tunic off and kissed me on the chest, the neck, the ear. I stood there, unresisting.

Then the snake around her shoulders hissed, reminding me of the danger.

Recalling the old man's wisdom, I found the strength – or perhaps it was fear – to step back.

'I'm sorry. I just can't.'

She was unaccustomed to rejection; for a second she stood paralyzed, unsure what to do. Then her face twisted into a mask of spite and she hurled her snake at me. I caught the thing by the tail; it bit me in my thigh.

Terrified, I recoiled and dropped the snake. It landed on the floor with a dull thud and writhed monstrously.

I leapt on top of the bed, grabbing a broomstick for protection.

'Don't drop him, you beast!' she cried, somewhat hypocritically I thought, and scooped her darling pet up into her arms.

'Don't throw him at me then!'

She kissed his head, rubbed his scales and glared at me reproachfully. Then she stormed out.

My mind awhirl with anxieties, I consoled myself with the thought that at least if Helen in her spite made a false complaint against me, Anima would get to the bottom of it. Eventually, I went to sleep.

The next morning, I woke feeling strange. I was struck by the softness of my skin against the clean sheets. I often had clean sheets, for I had taken to personally washing them with my clothes at the river.

After breakfast, in which the others seemed wary of me, I stepped into the Hall of the Moon to see Anima sat on her throne.

Seeing my reflection in the throne's mirrored backrest, for the first time I was struck by how similar we looked; we were of the same height and had the same sturdy build. We had the same full lips, thick blonde hair, small nose, long lashes and strong jaw.

But strangest of all, her green eyes, glazed by tragedy and shuttered to the world, were my eyes. There was formidable willpower in those eyes, but it had been cruelly thwarted and turned inward, where it festered as resentment and despair. We were not identical, since her features were more girlish and pretty than mine, but she was my female doppelganger.

Phidias cleared his throat and glared at me. I turned to look at him, still stupefied and a little irked.

'What?' I hissed.

He made a brief kneeling motion.

Then I understood. I was so moonstruck I had completely forgotten. Hastily, I kneeled before the goddess.

Then Helen entered. She hovered beside me as I made my obeisance. I hoped she would pass on by, but she was still there when I finished. I looked up to see her stony little face, her hands on her hips and her serpent rising from her neck.

'Yes, mistress?'

'I'll need you to help prepare dinner.'

'But I'm already working all morning!'

'There's only sixty of us here, and the other men are no help. We all have to make sacrifices.'

She didn't wait for my assent, and stormed past on her way to the kitchen.

Initially, I was enraged. Obviously, she was acting out of spite for the way I had scorned her last night. It was petty and unfair, especially when one considered the risk entailed by embarking on a dalliance with her on this island. What did she want of me – to risk castration and death for the sake of a moment's pleasure? It seemed so absurd.

Then I reconsidered the situation in the light of the Forbidden Wisdom. This could be God giving me the perfect opportunity to integrate my Unknown Mind. For I had always avoided chores. Though I was forced to be the dogsbody aboard ship, that was only for four weeks and I had hated every minute of it and done a fairly poor job into the bargain. I had only begun work in the kitchen as a ruse to poison Nero and stayed on because I was tempted to tumble Helen. At home, my mother had done most of the cooking and cleaning. I preferred to think, to dream as poets dream and in doing so, had neglected my practical side. I could have churlishly ignored Helen's orders, since she had no real authority over me, and I could quit any time I wanted.

But I didn't. I did the extra hours in the kitchen and, after some initial cursing and caterwauling at my own clumsiness, I came to take a perverse kind of pleasure in the work, even elbowing the nymphs aside to take on more than my fair share of chores and growing jealous when someone tried to help me. Helen was distinctly nonplussed at my attitude. She had intended the extra work as a punishment; seeing me revel in it unnerved her. So one day she came up to me as I was chopping carrots and said, 'I need you to tend to my husband in the snake-temple this afternoon.'

'Your husband?' I asked, bewildered.

'Persona. We are married.'

I recalled the horrors of the black wedding and gulped, making a mental note to play dumb.

'Oh. I didn't know. Congratulations,' I said, weakly.

'Thanks,' she said, ironically. 'But he's in a pretty bad way.'

'Is he now? I wondered what had become of Persona.'

'He's had a nasty um, accident. Attacked by a lion. Anyway, he's convalescing now, but he still needs taking care of.'

'Why can't you do it?'

'As his wife, ordinarily it would be my duty to care for him, but tonight we are having a great feast to celebrate the harvest.'

'I see.'

I was peeved at being treated like a dogsbody for so base a motive, when she could have asked any of the nymphs, many of whom had more nursing experience than myself and were more suited to the work by temperament. But then, Anima was a nurse, wasn't she? And as the representation of my Unknown Mind, it was my duty to become more like her. Besides, I was dying to find out what had become of Persona. So I accepted.

I walked across the meadows to the snake-temple. Lucilla, mildly amused at the idea of a male nurse, had agreed to show me the way. As we entered the hall, I was given a nurse's apron with a red cross on the front. Persona was on a different ward to the one we had occupied after the shipwreck; apparently, ours was the emergency ward, whereas this hall was for more chronic cases.

And chronic they were. A bunch of old men, some doddering about on crutches and canes, others drooling vacantly into their porridge as the nurses tried to spoon-feed them. All of them were completely bald, like the priests. The ones who were up and about even wore the orange togas – perhaps they *were* priests? Perhaps this is what became of them when they grew old.

But not all were old. I saw a few younger men, looking rather fragile, Persona among them. He was sat up in bed. His godlike physique had wasted away; he had the thin arms of an adolescent, and his face was pale and gaunt. He smiled weakly when he saw me approach his bedside.

'Hello, old friend,' I said, moved to pity by his predicament.

'Hello Ego.'

'How goes it?'

'Well I'm still alive. Even if I'm no longer a man,' he added, resentfully.

'No longer a man?' I asked, feigning shocked ignorance.

He glanced up and down the ward and beckoned to me to lean closer. I did so.

'I was caught fucking the one they call Helen. At first it wasn't so bad. I got to lie with all the most beautiful women on the island, Anima excepted. They called me "God for a Day." Then they lured me to the sacred grove with the promise of a giant orgy, in which I was to be the only man. When I got there, they were all naked, which was fine by me, but they wore these weird demon masks and carried long wooden phalluses. That set the alarm bells ringing, but I went along with it, since by then I had no choice and still hoped for the mass-fuck of my life. They sat me naked on a stump, lit a circle of fire around me and Helen approached. I still thought – or hoped – it was to be some mating ritual, but as soon as I became tumescent, the other nymphs held me down and Helen castrated me!'

'Egads man! You have my sympathy.'

Persona shushed me and continued, 'After that, they beat me with their wooden phalluses.' He pointed to his broken nose, and the yellow bruises on his head, chest and arms.

'What barbarity!'

'I didn't get it so bad. Look at the other "husbands." Some of them are crippled for life and rendered simple by the beatings. And the nymphs are almost as miserable, for they are condemned to lead the dissatisfying existence of eunuch's wives and must atone for their moment of ritual frenzy by caring for their dotard husbands, feeding, bathing and nursing them for the rest of their days. At least I'll be out of here in a week, to join the other priests in the palace.'

I recoiled in horror.

'So you mean, all those priests in the hall – they are eunuchs too?'

He nodded, grimly.

'Such is my fate,' he said, bottom lip trembling. 'I had such high hopes for my life. I was to be an athlete in the games, a runner. I was popular with the womenfolk and, after a score of love affairs with great beauties, I wanted to settle down with a wife and have children. Now look at me. I am a ruin!' he wailed, and the tears came.

I put my hand on his shoulder. We had never liked each other, but even *I* was moved to sympathy by his plight.

'But why do they maintain these cruel customs, if the nymphs themselves are miserable and dissatisfied?'

He covered his face in shame and shook his head, mystified. After a minute of this, I decided enough was enough.

'Well, Helen has sent me in her stead. I'm to look after you until she's finished in the kitchens. Have you got a bedpan for me?'

And so I emptied his bedpan and walked with him in the gardens. The worst part was changing his bandages. Persona did not want me to, he wanted to wait until Helen returned. But, moved by sympathy and determined to experience the unlived, caring side of my nature, I insisted and was afforded a look at the bloody cauterised stump they had made of his manhood. That image will remain with me for the rest of my days.

I volunteered to work as a nurse during my days off. I nursed not only Persona, but some of the worst cases among the old men, feeding them and bathing them as the nymphs did. I came to appreciate the sacrifice they made for their wrecked husbands, but also to wonder at how such a bizarre custom came to be, for things were not like this in my homeland; there, the man was paterfamilias and when corporal punishment was administered, it was he who beat his children and wife, usually with enough restraint to avoid lasting injury.

I did not see Anima, for she worked in a different ward of the temple. One day though, I caught sight of her galloping in the meadows. Her mount was a black unicorn; a lustrous beast, his legs powerful and sinewy, the muscular flanks shining with sweat. She rode him like a demon and spared him neither bit nor crop.

One day, as I passed the stable, I was seized by a sudden desire to ride. I had never learned to ride a horse; I had an instinctive fear of animals and as we had lost the fields when I was young, the need had never arisen. There were several horses in the stable; this was another of Nero's duties. So I approached one, a calm brown steed, and began to stroke her neck. Nero, seeing my interest, ambled over.

'What's her name?' I asked.

'Destiny,' he said.

'Good name.'

'You want to ride?' he asked, amused.

'Why not?'

Nero smirked. Clearly, he had some derogatory comment he would like to make, but he bit his tongue.

'As you wish. I'll saddle her up.'

I adjusted the left side stirrup to face me and put my foot in there. Then, holding the bridle with my left hand and the saddle with my right, I swung my right leg over her back. I felt a little dizzy at first; I was shocked at how far I was from the stone tiles.

The horse whinnied and reared a little; I leaned forward, holding onto her neck for dear life.

Nero mounted the horse next to mine, a white charger, with consummate ease.

'Having second thoughts?' he taunted.

'No,' I said, summoning my boldness. I had not conquered plague and paralysis only to quail before riding a horse, a thing done by children.

And so we trotted out of the stables. I was slightly unnerved by Destiny; she kept jerking her head and trotting sideways, but Nero told me not to worry.

'The horse absorbs and reflects your anxieties,' he said. 'She's like people in that way. Have confidence and she'll do as you command.'

Then, following Nero's instruction, I gave her my spurs, and we launched into a canter. I used the reins to steer her and threw myself into the thing, trying to adjust myself to the rhythm of her back. Above all, I focused on the ride and refused to indulge in fear.

Slowly, day by day, she got used to me and we became almost of one mind. I came to enjoy the sensation of all that muscle and bone between my legs, an extension of my body, responsive to my every whim, and began to fancy myself a centaur. By week's end Nero had no further cause for condescension and I had no further need of his tutelage; for I was galloping off into the woods, churning the turf, leaping tree roots, swerving trunks and ducking branches like a show rider.

One day, as I rode Destiny back from the snake-temple, I saw Anima riding her unicorn across the meadow. She too, was headed back to the palace. I spurred Destiny and sought to catch up with her. But her mount was too fast for us and in the end, I had to ease up on the poor beast for she was grunting, whinnying and steaming with sweat.

Then it hit me, as I stabled and fed my mare. I no longer wanted to have sex with Anima; in fact, the very idea seemed absurd. In that respect, the old man's teaching had worked. And yet I was just as obsessed with her as ever.

That night, I fell into a deep sleep.

I dreamt I was walking through my chamber in full daylight. I wandered over to the bathroom, took a piss in the pot, and washed my hands in the basin. There was a large, rectangular mirror above the basin. I looked at my reflection.

Anima's beautiful face stared back at me: her thick eyebrows, dull green eyes and shimmering dark blonde tresses were all present and correct in vivid detail. Then I looked down, thinking this a trick of the magic mirror, and my body was transformed into hers; I had her pert breasts, slim waist and wide hips. But I was not shocked or disturbed. Instead, I took inordinate pride in my new identity and began to think myself the best, most intelligent, mysterious and beautiful woman in the world. I said so, as well, to nobody in particular. I felt much more powerful than I had as a man, for beauty in Aeonian men is not esteemed so highly, but in women it has overthrown kings and started wars.

Then I woke up.

Chapter 15: The Blue Flame

For a moment I was wrongfooted by the weirdness of the dream and didn't know what to make of it. But I couldn't really call it a nightmare, for I was quite happy with my new body. Still, it didn't seem right to revel so much in another person's skin and I was left with a vague feeling of unease. I resolved to visit Mentor.

I knocked on the door of his hut. Nobody answered. But I heard a rhythmic banging noise. Curious, I pushed the creaking door open.

Inside, the hut was chaos. Books and papyri were strewn everywhere. I stepped on a loose page with a picture of an uroboros. I leaned down and picked it up. The writing was indecipherable: a harsh, dead tongue. Beakers and alembics were frothing and overflowing onto the boards. Clouds of steam rose into the cobwebbed rafters. But most strange of all, were the little creatures inside the glass jars.

Fascinated and horrified, I stepped closer. They were little humans, stark naked. They had all the same parts as men and women, only smaller; the largest was no more than eight inches tall. And their eyes were black and strangely soulless, like the eyes of fish. They had been placed in separate jars, with one exception: two little men who seemed to be sleeping. One of the creatures made a high-pitched gibbering noise and stared at me expectantly, as if he wanted to be understood. Others ran into the walls of their glass cages, banging their heads and falling down, only to push themselves back up and do it all over again. The human form, without sentience, gave me an uncanny feeling. There was something supremely unnatural about the old man's experiments. I resolved to confront him about them upon his return.

Then one of the little sleepers woke. He stared at his still unconscious cellmate and began to kick him savagely in the head. I was shocked. The victim stirred to life and lunged at his assailant. They went at each other like wildcats; no restraint, no quarter, just pure unthinking animal hatred. I reached out to shake the jar, in an effort to make them stop, but hesitated. Should I really be getting involved in the wars of the homunculi?

Just then, the door swung open behind me. Startled, I swivelled. It was Mentor.

'What is the meaning of this?' he said, storming over with thunderous face.

At first, I thought he was angry at me for snooping around in his absence. But he was glaring at the little creatures. He pushed me aside, picked up the jar and gave it a violent shake. The poor little critters bounced off the sides of the jar and were tossed about as if caught in a whirlwind. The old man stopped. The little men rose, slowly, cradling their sore heads.

'And let that be a lesson to you!' Mentor thundered.

The little folk cringed in terror of their lord.

'Now you see why I put most of the little beggars in separate jars. The others were either fucking or fighting. Three died that way. But these two I'd thought were learning to get along. Apparently not, when my back is turned,' he said, reproachfully, as if the little men could understand his rebuke.

'Where did you get them from? Did you create them?' I asked, with considerable trepidation.

Mentor grunted an affirmative. Then he looked at me and blinked.

'Oh, it's you,' he murmured.

'Of course it's me! Who else would it be?'

He made no answer; he was too absorbed in his alchemical work. He poured a viscous red fluid into the overflowing alembic. The contents settled.

'Is this what you meant by becoming a god? Making little men and putting them in jars?'

Mentor scowled at me.

'I am a mighty and wrathful god,' he muttered. I wasn't sure if this was a jest or no.

'How did you make them?' I was morbidly curious.

'I put my seed inside the womb of a dead horse. And these little beggars came crawling out.'

I was revolted, though considering Mentor's foul mood, I decided not to show it.

'How is that possible?'

'I don't know. Like so much of our natural philosophy, all I know is that I did it and it worked – after a fashion.'

'Why are they so—'

'Stupid? They're half animal. And they seem to be missing souls. Most difficult, obtaining a soul without a woman.'

'What about Clitus? He has a soul.'

'Clitus is dead. Didn't last the week, poor boy. These – *morons*,' he hissed the word with utter contempt, 'represent my next attempt.'

'Attempt at what? What is it you're trying to do?'

The old man turned away from his instruments to look at me.

'Isn't it obvious? I want a child. And, given the prevailing prohibition on reproduction by natural means, I have had recourse to *unnatural* means.'

'Couldn't you just raise one of the nymph's bastards as your own?'

Mentor shook his head, violently, like a stubborn child.

'No. It has to be *mine*,' he said, hotly.

'Alright,' I said, placatingly. I had not expected such rabid vehemence on this point.

'Why are you here?'

'I came to discuss a dream.'

'I have no time for such trifles.'

'Your method. It didn't work.'

The old man looked up from his beaker, angered.

'What?'

'Well, it did, in a way. I am no longer beset by lust. But I am still just as hopelessly obsessed with Anima as before.'

Mentor sighed.

'Why does nothing I do seem to work as planned?' he muttered, half to himself, though he already knew the answer to that age-old riddle. 'Sit down, sit down,' he said, clearing the grimoires from the table.

The door swung open. I looked up. It was an old woman, wearing a peplos and a shawl around her head and shoulders, which gave her a distinctly eastern look. A basket of herbs and berries hung from her right arm. She was not best pleased.

'What the devil have you done to my kitchern, you blustering old fool!' she screamed, storming into the hovel.

'But Aggy dear, there is nowhere else for me to conduct my experiments—'

'Your stupid li'uw men have no place in my kitchen! They should never ha' been born!'

'Now, Agatha, isn't that a little unfair?? Don't the little critters have just as much right to life as you and I?' he said, pleading. I had never seen Mentor so beholden.

'I don't care what you do with 'erm, just get 'erm out of moy kitchern!' she said. Then she stormed over to a jar, picked it up and hurled it into the fireplace. 'Leslie!' Mentor wailed. The jar smashed against the wall and the little man inside burned to death with hideous heartrending shrieks. This set the others off, like infants in a nursery.

I stepped back, anticipating a savage domestic.

'Look what you've done!' Mentor said, more distraught than angry.

I stepped further back.

'Look what *you*'ve done to my kitchen! It's become a hostel for abominations, so it has!' she thundered. Then she grabbed another jar and tossed it at him.

The old man caught the first one. The second jar bounced off his shoulder into the air, and he had to lunge to grab it, but in doing so, he dropped the first, which shattered on the floor. The little creatures, overexcited by their freedom, ran in circles and slammed into each other, like headless chickens.

But the old woman was not done yet. She grabbed a broomstick and smashed it down on the homunculi, squashing them. She hit the old man over the head and chased him out of the door with it. Then she rounded on me.

'I'll be going,' I said, hastily.

She whacked me on the back of the neck as I trotted out.

'Serves you right for encouraging him in his oddments!'

The door slammed shut behind me.

There was further yelling and crashing, inside.

The old man sighed, rubbing his head. She had drawn blood from his temple.

'Who is that?'

He grimaced, cradling his last remaining homunculus.

'Agatha.'

'You live together?'

'Sometimes,' he admitted. He had led me to believe he was a bachelor; again, I thought, what else has he lied about? Was this why he had such a gloomy view of marriage?

'You are man and wife?'

'After a fashion. Come, let's find a safe place for little Timothy here. I know the perfect spot. It's in the hollow of a tree, about an hour's walk from here. On the way, you can tell me of your recent doings – and that dream.'

I did as he asked, while we tramped through the woods. It was good to discuss such things in the open air, with the birdsong and the sunlight filtering through the sighing pines. The homunculus was quiet; he sat rocking in a foetal ball in the corner of his jar, overwhelmed by all he had witnessed.

When I was done, the old man said, 'You have lost yourself.'

'Excuse me?'

'In seeking to integrate your Unknown Mind, you have lost sight of who you really are. Divinity does not consist in imitating others. When I first saw you, with your long hair and nurse's apron, I hardly recognised you; truth be told, I thought you were another nymph come to me with misbegotten child.'

I looked down and blushed. I had forgotten I was still in my apron.

'But you said Anima was the outer manifestation of my Unknown Mind; that I should therefore try to be more like her?'

'Anima represents your Unknown Mind, yes. But in seeking to imitate her and thereby integrate your Unknown Mind, you have forgotten your previous self; what was once your Known Mind is now your Unknown Mind. The two have changed places.'

'Is that not what you wanted?'

The old man laughed.

'No, that is not what I wanted for you. I wanted you to make everything within you Known, not to make what was Unknown Known whilst forgetting what you once knew about yourself.'

'You said nothing of this before; at least, you did not make it *clear*.'

'I told you exactly what you needed to hear at the time. The mind can only absorb so many truths at once.'

I bristled, taking this as an insult.

'I'm trying my best!'

'And you're doing well. By the sounds of it, you've done all the things you have hitherto neglected, resented or least wanted to do. Folk normally only do such things when pressed by sheer necessity. But you have done so of your own free will. That is an achievement,' he said, his voice soothing yet condescending.

'Thank you,' I said, somewhat mollified. 'What do you advise?'

'Anima represented your Unknown Mind, which is a part of you – but so are you; or rather, the part of you that was accepted before but has now been rejected in your desire to imitate her. Just as before she controlled you from your rear, or Unknown Mind, now she possesses you from the front, or Known Mind, by making you identify completely with her, at the expense of the person you used to be. Both approaches are too one-sided. You need to find a way to balance the two. To realise she is you – and not you, at the same time. To absorb some of her essence, her good qualities, whilst remaining true to yourself.'

'That sounds difficult.'

Mentor smiled, as if I had stumbled into a naïve understatement.

'The way is hard and full of ambiguities. It is easy to get lost. But just as the devil is in the details, so God is in the paradox.'

'That is why I turned to you, to be my guide.'

'Guides have their uses, but ultimately, the initiate must find the way for himself, for there is no better guide than one's own experience; and no two ways are the same. What was true for me will not be true for you. Here we are,' he said.

We had arrived at a small pond of greenish water. The surface was dotted with patches of algae. Frogs croaked in the reeds on the periphery. The old man leaned into the hollow of a large beech tree and placed Timothy inside, nestled amidst a bed of leaves. Then he reached inside a hollow log and withdrew a pair of fishing rods.

'Agatha won't let me keep these in the hutment: not enough space!'

'You're a fisherman?'

'I am; I'm also a fisher of men,' he said, with a secret smile, as he handed me a rod. He then produced two worms from one of his many pockets and skewered them on our hooks. He cast his line, slowly, showing me the way. I copied him; my hook landed with a splash in the shallow waters on the far edge of the pond.

'Yank her in a little,' he said, soothingly.

I did as he said.

'Forgive me, I don't see how fishing will help solve my problem?'

'Who said anything about solving your problem? Some of us have to catch our dinner, you know!'

I blushed at my presumptuousness.

'But be careful. There are two kinds of fish in this pond. The silver trout are harmless and good to eat. But the little red fish are poisonous. Eat one and you'll have it coming out of both ends before sundown. Eat three and you're dead.'

'Got it,' I said.

'No, you don't,' he said, smirking to himself.

'What do you mean? What's not to get? Silver fish good, red fish bad.'

'When I speak or act, there is rarely one meaning.'

I pondered this. My brow furrowed.

'I don't see any other meaning,' I admitted, helplessly.

'Perhaps it's my fault. I haven't taught you about symbols and omens yet. You see, in dreams and the world, water represents the Unknown – specifically, Unknown emotions. Fire represents passion, desire, anger, intuition. Squares, circles or spheres represent wholeness. Owls, like Sofia, represent wisdom from the Unknown Mind, which is closely related to magic and the underworld. Children, eggs and beetles represent rebirth. Animals symbolise the bestial component of your Unknown Mind; what you would call your baser instincts; the desire to fuck, fight and kill.'

I heard the screech of a bird high overhead. I looked up and saw the majestic wingspan of a bald eagle.

'The far-seeing eagle, as the creature closest to the heavens, represents enlightenment: the final stage of the process.'

'And fish?'

'Fish in a pond represent the contents of your Unknown Mind. Just as the body is benefited by consuming trout, some parts of the Unknown Mind *should* be assimilated into your Known Mind. And just as the red fish shouldn't be taken into your body, some contents of the Unknown Mind shouldn't be integrated into your Known Mind. Integrate them and they will make you mad, or ill. Persist and you die.'

'So you're saying that parts of the Unknown Mind do not belong in the Known Mind. I thought we had to make everything conscious?'

The old man smirked.

'There are no hard and fast rules, my boy. We live in a world of ambiguity; for every rule, there is an exception. You must integrate the parts that belong to you and separate yourself from those parts that do not, that seek to possess and destroy you, as an alien force.'

'How do I do this??'

'Like I said, the way varies from person to person. But nonetheless, there are certain exercises that prove helpful.'

'Such as?' I felt infuriated by Mentor's reticence. I wished he would just come out and say exactly what he meant. But then he would lose his power over me.

'Imagination.'

'Imagination?'

'Yes, fantasy.'

'You want me to fantasise?'

'When you are in a mood, let it paint its picture, tell its story. Discard all your inhibitions and allow the Unknown Mind to speak; let it set the stage and choose the actors. Then you must respond to the scenario it has presented you with as you would in the real world. The Unknown Mind dominates the dream world. But fantasising in this way enables you to assert yourself and synthesise your co-authors, the Known and Unknown Minds, to reach a kind of compromise. Above all, it is crucial to take the fantasy seriously; not to dismiss it out of hand. If you are overly sceptical, the exercise won't work.'

'But what use are idle fantasies?'

'My boy, the very world is a fantasy, conjured by the imagination of The Creator. And we are his characters, striving to survive, triumph and make sense of it all – to shine His light into the darkness.'

'What?' I was speechless.

'Our fantasies are not so grand. Our thoughts do not create matter as His do. But they can affect it. And they help us to broaden our self-awareness. If The Creator saw fit to fantasise, who are you to sneer at such a practice?'

'Alright. I will do as you say.'

'There is something else.'

'I'm not sure I can take any more wisdom today.'

The old man cackled.

'I insist on telling you, only because I may be absent for a while.'

'Where are you going? We're stuck on an island?'

'That we are, but it is not a small island, and I have business on the far side of it. I mean to hunt and tame the fabled red phoenix.'

'The phoenix?'

'A bird, larger than a griffin but smaller than a dragon, with a plumage of crimson and gold, and a crest of wavering flame. The phoenix is the rarest creature of all; there is only one in the whole world.'

'If that be so, then the breed will surely die out?'

'Not so. There has only ever been one phoenix alive at any given time.'

'This sounds like nonsense to me. How does the bird reproduce?'

'The phoenix is sexless and does not mate. Every 1,000 years, the bird dies in flame and rises, reborn from its own ashes.'

'How is that possible?' I asked, openly incredulous.

'All other creatures are dominated by lust. They breed, die and live on through their offspring. But the phoenix, free of fear and desire, is able to renew itself eternally.'

'And you are convinced this creature is not imaginary?'

'Like all of God's creations, there is a phoenix within and a phoenix without. I have glimpsed it several times from the mountain peaks. The nest must be somewhere on this island.'

'Amazing,' I said, though I remained sceptical.

'Truly. God's imagination knows no bounds. And the next exercise shall stretch yours to its limit.'

'Oh gods, what next?'

'As you separate the you from the not you, you will find that the not you takes on a distinct personality.'

'Anima?'

'Like Anima, but not Anima. For there is much in the Unknown Mind that does not belong to you, but belongs to all humanity; much that was inherited from your ancestors with your blood and the structure of your mind.'

'Are these the "red fish" that should not be eaten?'

'So they are, my boy, so they are. You are a quick study, for one who plays at bewilderment. Anyhow, this personality will eventually become so distinct that you can actually hold conversations with her.'

'Is that not madness?'

'It is, if you cannot keep a cool head and remain detached from what she says.'

'And if you can?'

'Then it is divine madness; and you are saner (and wiser) than the most rational philosopher on earth, for even he has no schema for the irrational.'

'But how do I know this voice is not myself?'

'Let her speak. Judge her afterwards. You shall know her by her words. She will say things you would never say; speak in tongues you cannot speak; know things you could not possibly know. For she is ancient, and you are young. You are to her as the gnat is to us; here and gone in the space of an afternoon.'

'And what are we supposed to talk about?'

'The purpose of this exercise is the same as the fantasising. You must negotiate with her. Reach a compromise. Maintain your own standpoint with firmness, listen carefully and keep your wits about you; be on the watch for trickery and witchcraft and honeyed words, words that might seduce you to madness.'

'You make it sound so perilous.'

'You enter the arena with a million-year-old lioness, my boy. She has seen it all before; every trick in the book. And she knows you well, for she has watched you all your life, yet you have never seen her before. She is invincible, and she wants to devour you. Someone has to forewarn you.'

'I appreciate all you have done for me. Truly.'

'Don't mention it, my boy. An old hermit like myself is glad of the company. And truth be told, for all my tinkering with the laws of nature, I have little else to occupy me.'

There was a tug on my line. I looked to Mentor.

'What do I do?'

'Reel her in my boy, reel her in.'

I did as he said. When I finally wrenched the rod out of the swamp, I was disappointed to see a small red fish wriggling on the end of my hook.

I yanked the fish off; it spasmed and flopped its way back into the pondwater by my feet.

'See, if you didn't know about the dangers of the red fish, you would have eaten it and damn near poisoned yourself to death. It is a valuable lesson I teach. It's getting late. Come, let's go,' he said, setting down his rod inside the hollow log. I did likewise.

I followed him through the forest. But it soon became apparent that he was not taking me back to the hut.

'Is this a shortcut to the palace, perchance?'

The old man shook his head, mysteriously.

'What then?? Whither do you take me?' I said, growing tired and hungry.

The sun had set. The forest was murky; the sky an archipelago of red clouds bleeding into the deeper indigo of oncoming night.

'You wish to become a god,' he said, cryptically.

'Yes?'

He did not answer. I listened to the chirping of the crickets and the croaking of the frogs as we waded through the bog. At last, we came to a small glade in the bower of a towering ash tree with leaves of pale gold. In the centre of the glade, was a small, stone font, crawling with vines. It looked ancient.

The old man led me to the font.

Its waters were still and inky black; I saw the reflection of the full moon and the stars.

'Give me your hand,' the old man said, his voice hoarse with urgency.

'Why?'

'Give it to me.' His eyes blazed beneath the shaggy brow.

I did as he bid me.

He seized my wrist with a sharp jerk and held it out over the font. Then he produced a silver-pommelled dagger, encrusted with jewels.

My heart leapt into my throat. I began to struggle.

'What is this? What are you doing?'

Mentor did not answer. Instead, he began intoning in a strange tongue; a long dead tongue.

'By the light of the full moon, Asgara, I offer this to you that you may reveal the fate of the initiate.'

I struggled to free myself; but his grip was firm as bronze.

Then he slashed my wrist; I grunted. Blood dripped into the pool.

A spurt of blue flame leapt from the still waters.

I stepped back.

'The blue flame of the gods!' the old man breathed.

'What? What is the meaning of this?' I demanded, backing away from him and his confounded firewater, and all his other holy-unholy paradoxes and maddening riddles.

He looked up at me with wide eyes, his face aghast.

'You have the blood of the gods.'

Chapter 16: The Revelation

'What is this drivel? You are mad, old man! Mad, I tell you! Mad!'

'You seek to become a God. You already are one.'

'But this is impossible. I am mortal man born of mortal mother and—'

'Yes? And what of your father?' he asked, eagerly.

'I never knew my natural father,' I admitted. 'I was raised by another, whom I consider to be my *true* father.'

'Perhaps your spiritual exercises – perhaps they have yielded more fruit than we thought,' the old man said, with furrowed brow. 'But I would have thought you too early in the process for such a transformation to occur. Ordinarily, it takes years to achieve the goal. More likely your father was a god or demigod.'

'I wasn't expecting to attain godhood; certainly not so soon, and I half-thought you were lying to me about all that.'

'I do not lie about holy matters.'

'Well, I certainly do not feel like a god. I feel like a fool taken in by the guile of a lunatic!'

'Do not give me less respect than I am due! For there is truth in what I say. The Font of Asgara never lies.'

'If I were a god, wouldn't I have godly powers?'

'Yes,' the old man said, stroking his chin. His eyes roved restlessly back and forth.

'See that raven over there,' he said, pointing upward.

I turned my gaze to a thin branch of the beech tree.

'Yes.'

'Kill it.'

'No!'

'You want proof. I offer you a test. Kill it.'

'How?'

'Will it. Point your finger, if it helps. What matters is the intention – and the belief, without the slightest shred of fear or doubt. You must *believe* you can kill it with a look, a gesture. If I am right, your blood will take care of the rest.'

'Alright, I'll try it, if you'll let me return to the palace afterwards – and kindly refrain from cutting me again!'

'As you wish.'

I stared at the raven, feeling faintly ridiculous. I half-expected the old man to burst into laughter at my apparent earnestness; the whole thing felt like a practical joke, and he was a wily old bugger, perfectly capable of such knavery.

'Do not think. Just will it. Know that the raven is a part of you. Feel what it corresponds to in the World Within. Kill the raven inside and the bird without shall fall as if skewered by an arrow.'

I tried what he said; recalling the world in miniature speech. I imagined the raven inside of me. I empathised with the raven; felt the rustle of its feathers, the twitch of its neck. And then I imagined it falling to the ground with a soft pat; dead of a heart attack. For the moment, I let my critical faculties drop and just believed it would be so.

Then the strangest thing happened. The raven took an unsteady step along the branch and fell. It landed with a soft thud, just as I had envisioned it would, moments earlier.

I turned to the old man, mouth agape. He seemed almost as stunned as I was.

Then I regained my wits, my scepticism.

'A fluke. A lucky coincidence,' I said, but my voice was uneven.

'Do the same with the branch on which it sat. Imagine the branch snapping and falling.'

I imagined a sharp snap, halfway along the gnarled, twisting limb. Then a brief tearing noise and the soft shake of leaves on grass.

And it was so.

'As within, so without,' the old man said. 'You are a god.' For the first time, I saw fear and holy awe in the eyes of Mentor.

I was seized by a strange dizzy feeling, as if I stood atop a shelf of rock on the highest of mountains and longed to return to earth, for my foothold was precarious and overlooked a vertiginous drop.

'It cannot be so. There must be some mistake – some trickery. You deceive me?' I croaked, uncertain and terribly, terribly alone.

'I do not,' Mentor said, with the utmost gravity. 'Even if I wanted to, how could I, without my staff?'

I staggered away, my head reeling. I stumbled on something and landed on my backside amongst the leaves and grass. As I sat up, I realised I had tripped over the branch I had broken. I began to laugh at myself. This was absurd.

'What kind of god trips over a felled branch like a drunkard?'

'More than you'd think; you need only take one glance at the theogony to see the folly of the gods. They are always stumbling over their own miracles. They seem almost like toddlers with the strength of giants.'

'That is true enough,' I said, recalling the tale of Tonos seducing Avropi in the form of a boar, only to be skewered for sport by her husband's hunting party; of Andromachus being killed unknowingly by his illegitimate son. The list went on.

'And, if I am right, you are not strictly speaking, a god; you are a demigod at best, since your mother is mortal.'

'I see,' far from bursting my bubble, this reflection of the old man's served to make the whole thing more plausible, for it is easier to believe oneself a half or quarter-god than a full-blooded deity; after all, the nymphs were one sixteenth part gods, and there were hundreds if not thousands of them scattered throughout the world. 'I broke the branch, did I not?'

'Indeed you did,' Mentor said.

'I suppose you are right. After all, you are the expert on such matters.'

'Indeed I am. But do not look to me for sole sanction. Surely, deep in your heart, this revelation makes sense; explains much about yourself that formerly was obscure. There must have been some sign or portent of your divinity? Something that marked you out from the crowd?'

I considered this.

It was true. I had always felt myself to be different. Superior to others, though they thought me inferior. Had not Nero said he tormented me out of jealousy? And what is jealousy, if not inferiority?

'Sometimes, as a boy, I would predict the future. I told my mother to buy roses when we were in the market. "Why??" she said. "There will be a funeral," I told her. And the next day my neighbour died.'

The old man nodded, sagely.

'Foresight is a gift of the gods, though it is imperfect, and not their exclusive prerogative.'

'And moving objects with the mind, from a distance?' I asked, with a wry smirk.

'Telekinesis is the exclusive preserve of the gods.' The old man chuckled.

I raised my hand; a branch swayed, as if hit by a strong wind, and then cracked.

I began to laugh, the rich, booming, jubilant amoral laughter of the gods; divinity was a heady brew.

Then a thought occurred to me.

'I can use my powers to free myself – and the rest of my crew. We can escape this godforsaken isle!'

My heart leapt with joy and trepidation. For with my newfound power came fresh responsibility; the responsibility to act and act justly. I felt an unbearable burden fall upon me: the burden of agency. For none could hold the gods against their will.

'To do so would be rash,' the old man said, trudging closer.

'Rash?' I sneered, in a booming voice, rich with haughtiness. 'Who are you to question a god?' As I said the words, a tiny voice in my head screamed in alarm. I silenced it.

'I dare not presume to order a deity or even to truck with your grace on equal terms.'

I noted the mode of address, with a satisfied smirk. Your grace. I liked the sound of it. It was pleasing to me.

'But having wandered this earth for many years, I have learned much of the gods and their ways that might be of use to you.'

'Speak,' I said, with a dismissive wave of my hand.

'Godhood is a matter of degree, not kind. Full-blooded Magirovian gods can only be killed by the fires of a volcano. You are a half-blood at best and therefore not invulnerable, especially in combat with other gods such as Anima. But blood is only one of

166

the three pillars of godhood; the others are knowledge, and possession of a red crystal. Without knowledge and the crystal, your powers are but a third part of what they could be.'

'A crystal? You mean the red stone in Anima's wand?'

'Yes. That amplifies her godly powers; and as long as she wields it, she has the advantage over you.'

I pondered this, with a haughty brow.

'So I must seize her wand?'

'If you wish to overthrow her, yes.'

'Why did you not tell me of this before? I needn't have wasted so much time on this island.'

'I did not realise you were a god until now. And only gods can wield the Stones of Destiny.'

'Explain,' I said, folding my arms.

'They were forged in Atlantea, the lost civilisation, during a time of revolt, and used by the gods to increase control over their human subjects. It was the power of one such stone, a thousand times larger than Anima's, that ultimately brought about the Great Deluge and destroyed Atlantea. They were crafted so only those of divine blood may wield them, to prevent humans from stealing one and attempting to overthrow the gods. To a mortal, the only value of such a stone would be in the price it could fetch at market. Since the Great Deluge, some have remained in the keeping of the surviving deities; others have been scattered to the far corners and dark places of the earth, waiting for someone to happen across them.' A faint note of sycophancy had crept into his tone, and he was more forthcoming with his knowledge: eager to please.

'Interesting. And I, as a mere demigod, would be able to wield the power of the crystal?'

'You summoned the firewater; I see no reason why you cannot wield the stone.'

'Thank you, old man. This has been a most enlightening evening,' I said, and made to leave.

'Where goes thou, mighty one?'

'To the palace,' I said, without turning to face him.

The old man ran alongside me, panting. For the first time I saw his age as a source of frailty, rather than wisdom. He seemed smaller somehow, since the revelation of my divinity.

'Stop! I beg you!'

'Why? You have warned me of the danger posed by her wand. Is that not all I needed to hear?'

'No. As you are, she would surely overwhelm you; but if you delay your coup until the completion of the spiritual exercises, your chances of victory will be roughly even.'

'Of what use are such exercises to a god?' I said, though my feet were slowed by some secret hesitation.

'Though you have probably inherited your divinity from your father, go far enough back in the family tree, all the way back to Atlantea, and you will find a patrilineal ancestor who was human, and became a god, by these very means!'

'So?'

'So the wand is one way of enlarging your power. Spiritual fantasies are another.'

'I would rather take the wand. It seems simpler.'

'But you do not yet have the wand: she does. Spiritual exercises will even your odds of taking it from her!'

I stopped dead and weighed his worth with my eyes.

'Though you have deceived me thrice, the greater part of your words have proven truthful – and useful to me. For that reason, I shall heed your counsel.'

'Excellent! You are most wise, grace.'

'The point, old man.'

He rooted around in the pockets of his dirty cloak, somewhat frantically, for a god was staring at him with eyes of impatience. 'Won't be a minute,' he said, with a weak smile. I was not impressed. Finally, he produced a small red mushroom and held it out to me in his hand.

'What am I supposed to do with this?' I said, faintly disgusted.

'Eat it. It will induce a vision and facilitate your faculty of fancy.'

'Can it not be done without the aid of drugs, using only the imagination, as you said?'

'It can. But this way is better; more vivid and easier to believe in. Belief is crucial. When sat at a desk daydreaming, it is all too easy to dismiss the images hovering before the mind's eye as belonging to one's own imagination, and to refuse to take the inner world seriously as a reality in its own right.'

I was about to take one, then I stayed my hand and saw the old man wore a desperate look on his face.

'You first,' I said, sneering.

'If you wish,' he said, with a shrug. He took a bite of half the mushroom and held it out to me.

When I was sure he had swallowed the thing, I took it off him, popped it in my mouth and chewed.

It was strangely fleshy for a vegetable, akin to an orchid bulb or artichoke. Immediately, I felt the drug begin to take effect. I heard whispers in the treeline – sharp, piercing whispers in strange tongues – whispers meant for me.

'Who is there?' I demanded, stepping back.

'Fear not. That is the mushroom's doing.'

'What have you given me?' I said, staring at my right hand, which seemed blurred and doubled. The veins stood out livid blue in the pale moonlight.

'As I said, it will conjure visions that will help you in your quest for knowledge and amplify your power. Just remember; though what you see is not real, to get the most out of the fantasy, you must act as though it is. And if you die in the fantasy-world, the shock of it will kill you in the real world.'

'If you had warned me of this, I would ne'er have agreed to eat your damn fungus!' I growled, lurching forward to take a swing at the mischievous old coot and his cross-stitch of truth and lies.

He lunged aside, howling with laughter, then tripped over a tree root himself. This only seemed to intensify his mirth. He pushed himself up and loped off into the darkness of the forest.

I chased after him.

'Get back here, you crazy old bastard!'

I soon lost his form amidst the dancing, creeping silhouettes of the trees. I was bewitched by strange geometric shapes: triangles, squares, circles, all stitched together in a tapestry like the scales of a fish, wavering and dilating and swirling. Slowly, the shapes became more vivid, and took on bright colours: yellow, red, blue.

Entranced and bewildered by the patterns, I hadn't noticed I had cleared the forest and now found myself in the middle of a barren scrubland. I could see no trees on the horizon, no sign of rivers or streams. Now I was far from water and vegetation, I was in danger of thirst and starvation. I cursed myself; cursed the gods; cursed the god in myself and stumbled on into the night, ranting and raving, beset by sharp whispers and disembodied screams; whither they came from within or without, I could not say; sometimes it seemed as if it were both.

And then I saw it, in the middle of the desert plain.

The Pyramid of Magirov: abode of the Gods. The monument was of awesome, indecent scale; too large to be built by humans. Even the flat top, paved with gold, stretched a mile across. Though it was as wide as it was tall, the pyramid was obviously monstrous high, for wispy clouds passed near the summit. Such a megalith would be blasphemous folly, if it weren't built by the gods themselves.

The gods lived lives of idle splendour in a gold-domed temple on the roof. From the gilded thrones where they sat in council, they had a clear view of the surrounding country and a good part of the sea. The pyramid was split in two, from the top to the base. One half was made of white marble that glowed in the moonlight. The other half was of black quartz. The entire structure was surrounded by a square moat. A large crowd of people gathered at the edge of the moat. I hastened my tread that I might catch a glimpse of what had summoned the crowd, for it was rare for humans to draw so near to the abode of the gods.

Then I questioned what I saw. For the pyramid was in Magirov; and some dim region of my mind still knew and cared that I was in Tyria. So this was the work of the red mushroom? But it seemed so real. I could see the people; each man had his own distinctive careworn face and bedraggled garments. They were like beggars awaiting alms on the palace steps.

I decided it must be a vision but resolved to heed the old man's counsel to enter into the spirit of the thing as if it were real. Given the vivid detail of the fantasy world, this did not prove too difficult.

I approached a stooped, one-eyed old man in tattered rags on the periphery of the crowd.

'Tell me, why are you gathered here??'

171

'We are pilgrims. We were told to come.'

'To what end?'

'To await the birth of a new god.'

'What new god?' I said, seizing him by his filthy tunic.

Fright filled his eye; he shrugged his scrawny shoulders.

'I know nothing more.'

Throwing him aside, I pushed my way through the stinking murmuring masses until I came to the edge of the moat. Here I waited for some time.

Then someone behind me shouted, 'look!'

I turned my eyes skyward.

A red streak blazed through the night. A flaming comet.

The comet was headed towards us. The crowd murmured in fright. A woman screamed. The crowd scattered in all directions. Someone pushed me into the moat. I had to haul myself out, dripping. All thought of the unreality of my vision was thrown to the winds in the mad scramble for life and limb; the panic fear of the stampede gripped me in my innards, the old man's words of warning ringing in my ears. Soon I was one with the herd, outpacing most and jerking my head anxiously over my shoulder. When I was a quarter-mile clear of the pyramid, I turned and saw the comet hurtling to earth out of the clear night sky. Emboldened by distance, I stayed put. I could see the black rock and its smouldering red tail. I stared, transfixed by the fiery vengeance and awesome splendour of the heavens. I knew it was headed for the temple atop the pyramid; and I willed it so. For I wanted to see the old gods dethroned, destroyed, so that something new and grander might arise in their place.

The comet crashed into the pyramid with awesome force; gold tiles flew skyward in a geyser of shrapnel; the earth rocked beneath my feet. Then came the pitter-patter of gold blocks tumbling down the white marble steps of the pyramid. And something else. A giant helmeted head, clanking down, step by step. A limb; a glorious bronzed limb of giant proportions. The leg of a god, dismembered. Were the gods dead? Was such a thing even possible?

Now the danger of the comet was over, I was emboldened to dive into the moat and swim across to the pyramid. The waters were still; bits of marble splashed beside me, but I paid them no heed. I stared up at the pyramid. Vertical miles lay before me; a daunting task; a heroic feat, if it could be done. I looked to right and left. A handful of other bold souls had nursed similar thoughts. They were gripped by the same daemonic curiosity, by an insatiable morbid thirst to look and leer and witness the gods in their death agony.

I ran up the steps, stretching my legs, for such giant steps were not meant for mortal legs. I grew short of breath, panting like a dog. Sweat poured down my forehead and flanks. I ripped my tunic off and discarded my sandals; mortal clothes were only a hindrance to me in the rarefied realm of the gods. I grew light-headed and hungry and felt the strength sap from my legs. My sprint slowed to a canter; my canter to a walk; my walk to a crawl. The others dropped off from exhaustion, dead or half-dead, until I was the only one left.

Then the blood began to run down the steps of the pyramid, gushing rivers of blood. I had to stop and take shelter behind one of the giant steps, huddling beneath the marble for dear life. I was drenched. I tasted the coppery tang of godsblood on my lips, spat it out, drank it for sustenance. At last, the flow abated to a trickle. My progress became even slower, for the marble was slick. I slipped twice, losing my balance and banging my knees on the hard steps. I looked down and saw the moat turned red by the blood of the gods.

It must be near dawn by now, I thought, and yet there was no sign of light on the horizon. At last, near-dead from exhaustion, I slithered onto the flat top of the pyramid, and passed out.

When I opened my eyes, it was to a dazzling light. I squinted and averted my eyes, shielding them with my right arm as I pushed myself up and staggered forward. The remaining gold bricks reflected the light. I stubbed my toe on something and looked down; it was the head of Tonos, large as an elephant's head and handsome as a god: his great shaggy beard like the hide of a mammoth and splattered with blood; his blue eyes shining with divine radiance even in death. I looked back and saw arms and hands and legs scattered all around, alongside bits of comet and misshapen lumps of scorched gold.

Dauntless, I pressed on. Something lay before me. I glimpsed it through spread fingers; the scaled belly of a giant serpent. I considered turning back; my heart quailed at the heroism required to go forward. Then I was seized by righteous indignation. I resolved to clamber over the serpent; I had come too far; I would do battle with monsters, if I must! At that very moment, the snake slithered away, clearing the path for me. I stumbled and the ground slid away beneath my feet. I lurched backwards, for I was teetering on the brink of a black crater. Squinting like a mole in daylight, I struggled to see. In the centre of the crater, sat a child; an infant, probably a boy. The babe was the source of the dazzling light; he was haloed in gold and rays of light spread out from his head as if he were mantled by the sun. His face was smiling and happy. His expression had the divine simplicity and sublime undividedness of a child's soul, tempered by the wily wisdom of a hoary old man. In his right hand was the shepherds crook of the high priest; in his left, the flail of earthly power, wielded only by the emperor himself. On the ground before the child, lay the elongated, pear-shaped tiara of the high priest, encircled by the golden laurel wreath of the emperor; symbols of spiritual and temporal power, hitherto separate, now combined. The child set his crook and flail down and struggled to pick the giant double crown up and set it on his head, for though he was strong for his age, his arms were small and flabby. Frustrated, he stared at me and gestured to the crown. His bottom lip wobbled; he appeared to be on the brink of tears.

'Wear the crown,' he said, in a deep, booming voice that startled me, as it did not belong to a babe in arms. Terrified, I did as the being bid me, picked up the towering double crown and set it atop my head. The weight of it strained my neck muscles. It was precarious and required considerable effort to balance.

Suddenly, the babe's radiance grew dazzling; it burned, as proximity to the sun would burn. I threw my arms up to protect my face and the skin of my wrists sizzled. I recoiled, turned and ran for my life, scrambling up the loose shale of the crater, the heat beating down on my back and threatening to melt my skin. I willed myself to run faster and faster.

'Is that as fast as you can run? Are you a god or no?' came the thunderous voice of the child.

My feet left the ground; I levitated a foot or more above the gold tiles. I thrust my arms out for balance; I felt embalmed in a divine glowing light; the child's halo no longer burned. Soft harp music began to play. The danger passed, the crowds had reassembled and stared awestruck at my flight. Light as a feather and trembling with all the glory and terror of godhood, I glided down the pyramid, increasing my pace. I was headed for a podium jutting out from the steps, roughly halfway down the marble side of the pyramid. My bare feet touched the marble, gently.

Tilting my head back, I surveyed the crowds, haughty as an emperor. Cradled in the crook of my right arm was a tablet etched with archaic pictograms. I knew I had inscribed those pictograms; that this was my Holy Writ and Tablet of Laws. I was unafraid. On the contrary, I felt powerful. The architecture made me feel lordly and divine, for this was where Urmon, messenger of the gods, made his proclamations to humanity in the days of old.

'The old gods are dead,' I thundered, swept away by the grandeur and theatre of the moment.

A collective gasp of terror; a murmur of frightened gossip rippled across the huddled masses.

'Fear not! For I come before you to herald the birth of a new God!'

A moment of awed silence; the crowd stared at me with mouths agape. Then came scattered clapping. The fire kindled; thunderous applause followed. The back ranks hooted and hollered exuberantly.

I held up a hand for calm.

'I speak to you as the Father of the new God!'

As I said the words, I felt a spider roll out of the skin on the back of my neck and saw it land on the marble, to scuttle off into some dark crack of the step. In eerie, perfect unison, the people prostrated themselves before me.

I willed the blocks of broken marble and gold and the fragments of comet into a bridge across the blood-moat.

'Those who are bold may cross the moat and climb the pyramid. The way that was closed is now open!'

A few scattered individuals, perhaps one in ten thousand, rose from the bowing mass to take up my challenge.

The vision vanished, all at once. I found myself stark naked, standing on a rocky outcrop halfway up a scrubby hillside. I shrank back from the precipice and instinctively covered my modesty. I was cold and afraid. My head throbbed, as if from a monstrous hangover. After the heady intoxication of divinity, I felt weak, frail and all-too mortal.

I scanned the horizon. The moonlight afforded me a clear view of the scrubby plain. On the edge of my vision I could make out the dark patch of forest from which I had strayed. It was ten or fifteen miles distant. Sobering up, I prepared myself for an arduous trek back to the palace.

Then I felt a presence behind me.

Trepidatious, I glanced over my shoulder.

Someone was there.

I turned to face whoever it was, ready to fight.

It was a woman. Or rather, a goddess, for she was eight feet tall and had a luminous glow. The skin of her face and arms was smooth and pale as polished marble, yet her eyes were as old as the sea and wise as an owl. At first, I thought she was Anima, for her blonde tresses and beautiful face were the same; but then I realised she carried the spear and wore the red-crested gold helmet of the Goddess Victory. Her tawny peplos and green cloak rustled though there was no breeze. She seemed to have materialised from thin air, for I heard no tread.

'Who are you?' I asked.

She gave me a smile of benign serenity.

'Fear not, wanderer, for your journey is almost come to an end.'

'Pray, fair maiden, identify yourself?' I repeated, urgently this time.

'I am the one you mistook for yourself.'

'The Unknown Mind?'

177

She nodded, serenely. Seeing her like this reinforced the old man's idea of her as a distinct entity; a being not identical with myself. I felt a sudden urge to throw myself into grovelling worship. She had an aura of statuesque indifference and calm about her that soothed my soul and filled me with awe.

'Why hast thou hidden thyself behind me?' I asked.

'You turned your back on me.'

I blushed.

'That was once so. But of late I have sought you and yet still you would not show your face.'

'You cannot speak with one you confuse with yourself.'

'Why dost thou come to me in Victory's garb?'

'I herald a coming victory.'

'Whose victory?'

'Yours, of course,' she said, as if I were being stupid. 'Rejoice, half-god, for your struggle is almost over.'

'What is the struggle of which you speak?'

'The struggle to free yourself; to become who you are.' The voice was ethereal, like harp music, and echoed as if her words were spoken from the depths of a sea cave.

'Say what you will, goddess.'

'You are a god. As such, it is your prerogative to address me on equal terms.'

'As you wish,' I said, deeply flattered, though I did not feel I had earned the right to such an honour; and still half-cringed from her stony numinosity in abject terror.

'I have come to reveal to you the meaning of your vision.'

'So soon? I have not had time to form my own thoughts.'

'You would rather do without my counsel? For I can go as easily as I came.'

'No. Please, speak.'

'The old gods died. They were replaced by a new God. You are the new God. That is why you wore the double crown. That is why the huddled masses worshipped you.'

My mind's eye, still hyperactive from the mushroom, conjured images of gilded splendour: chariots, palaces, endless gardens and grounds, vast harems of beautiful nymphs and mortal women, an empire without limit and a throne atop the Pyramid of Magirov. I shook these seductive fancies aside and found myself naked on a hillside, my teeth chattering from cold, parlaying with a phantom.

'This is madness.'

'This is destiny. Have you not always suspected as much, in the secret hours of the night?'

'Not every idle fancy merits a crown.'

'This one does,' she said, simply.

'But I am not even a full-blooded god. I am a man-god at best.'

'The man-god is more of a god than the full-blooded deity. For God is to be found in the centre, between the Known and Unknown Minds. Is that not the implication of the old man's teaching?'

I nodded, reluctantly.

'Who better for such a role than a half-man, half-god? You stand astride two worlds.'

There was a compelling logic to her words; a divine logic redolent of starry vaults and the vast dome of the aeons.

'Exactly, as half-man, half-god, I stood *between* the people and the new God. The double crown signifies my position between the spiritual and temporal; not as king of all the gods.'

'You will rule the heavens *and* the earth as God-emperor. That is what is signified by your position midway up the pyramid, between the human-world and the god-world. You will combine the power of high priest and emperor. *That* is what is meant by the symbol of the double crown.'

I could not rebut her arguments, so like anyone in such a position, I resorted to casting aspersions on her motives.

'Mentor warned me you would try and seduce me to madness, with words of honeyed poison,' I said, only half-believing it.

'The old man is jealous. He recoiled from the numinous power of the centre, of godhood, because he was afraid of madness. His philosophy reeks of fear; you yourself have thought that he did not go far enough. You are not afraid of madness; you embrace it with the boldness of a lusting youth,' she said, reaching out to caress my arm.

Her touch was cold as marble. But I did not pull away. I stood there, entranced by her beauty and the musicality of her voice.

'That may be. But the old man is wise; he has guided me aright thus far.'

'He has grown timid in his old age. He knew the glory of the divine centre for a single hour in his youth; all his wisdom is rooted in that hour. Imagine how great he could be, if he had possessed the strength to remain a god? He would not be living in a shack, that much is certain. Heed his words, and you will end as just another old vagabond with a beard full of crumbs and a heart full of regret.'

Her words stung me to the quick. She was right. I had nurtured secret hopes of surpassing Mentor; I had thought him a timid equivocal old fool. And there was enough of myself in him to make the dire future she conjured for me ring true.

'This is irrelevant,' I said, hastily, coming back to earth. 'The old gods still reign; who am I to dethrone them?'

She laughed: a musical tinkle like falling crystal.

'The old gods have had their day. They are a religion for goatherds in the wilderness; not the modern man of the cities. Nobody believes in them anymore. Who else is to fill the yawning void they leave in their wake? The people need meaning like water in the desert. They are crying out for meaning in their lives. You sense it; everyone does. You alone can give them their meaning, their new Table of Laws. The vision was the revelation and you were the one chosen to receive it. Who else has such divine powers of imagination and intellect, such heroic will and boldness?'

I barked, contemptuously, if only to cover my glowing pride. Conscious of the danger, I struggled with all my will to maintain a sober detachment.

'Your words are ridiculous. I am captive on an island; I command no armies and have no fortune to my name. I do not even have any friends. I am little more than a pampered slave, and you expect such a pitiful wretch as I to play the prophet; to found a religion and attract a vast following?' I said, with empty sarcasm.

'He who rejects his soul shall be killed by his soul. And he who rejects the world is rejected by the world.'

'What does that mean? Are you a woman or a sphinx?'

'Others rejected you because you rejected yourself. But of late you have begun to accept yourself; particularly, the part of yourself that connects you to the physical world. The part necessary for action. Your divinity is the only piece remaining. Embrace it and the flock shall follow. Why else did the crowds worship you in the vision?'

'It was but a vision; it is air, fancy,' I spat, contemptuously.

'It is well to say that, now you are out of it.'

181

I blushed. Her words were true enough; at the time, *everything* seemed to be at stake, I had feared for my life, for my very soul, for the destiny of humanity and the world.

'It was a dream that saved your life, was it not, in the snake-temple?'

I recalled Anima twined with snakes, the red stone, the exploding buboes. All that was foretold in the inner world had come to pass in the outer world, albeit slowly and in more prosaic fashion. Feeling myself on shaky ground, I changed tack.

'If I proclaimed the birth of a new God and demanded worship from passers-by in the cities, I would be heckled as a lunatic and pelted with rotten fruit.'

'Not all gods proclaim themselves openly; at least, not at first.'

This gave me pause. The mythos was filled with gods disguised as mortals and resorting to subterfuge. I had never before considered such a subtle road.

'You wish to make a mockery of me.'

'Few are those who have looked upon my countenance. I do not waste words on idle jests. The time for trickery and games is past. You have received your vocation. It falls to you to answer the call.'

I trembled before her stone-hard gaze. There certainly didn't seem to be anything remotely facetious about her, unlike my devil, who was brimming with unholy merriment.

Feeling my resistance crumbling before her, I ransacked my memory for the telling detail; the reason not to believe.

'In the vision, I said I was the Father of God, not God himself. You twist my words,' I said, though by this point, my words lacked conviction. I nurtured the secret hope she would prove me wrong with her divine power of reason.

'And who is the child? The child, like everyone and everything in the dream, is spun from yourself, from your own inner world. The divine child is you!'

Her words struck me like a thunderbolt. I recalled the fishing dream; there I had been both Nero and myself; the mirror dream, where I had been simultaneously Anima and myself. Those interpretations had been proven correct by experience and the truth-telling body. Why should this vision be any different? But then I remembered the fishpond; the old man's warning against identifying with the figures of the Unknown Mind. Was this notion a red fish or a silver trout?

Seeing my equivocation, she took a step closer.

'Even if the child were a separate entity, the Father of God is like unto the father of man; his superior in wisdom and power,' she said, running her hand down my abdomen. I felt a shiver of delicious anticipation.

'Not necessarily. The babe could speak and seemed plenty wise to me; for an infant, at least. Imagine what he could do when full grown,' I protested, weakly.

'But he is not yet full grown. He could not even set the crown on his head. He asked you to wear it! Your Unknown Mind begs you to seize power! The people cry out for guidance and fall at your feet! What more sanction do you need?'

I pondered her words, and salivated over her divine caresses, her divine perfection.

'If what you say is true, what is to be done about it?' I struggled to make the words.

'Go to the palace. Tear the silly girl, Anima, off her throne.'

'Will she not turn me into a beast, like the others?'

183

'She could only turn them into beasts because they had beasts inside of them and knew it not.'

'I have a slumbering dog in my breast.'

'But you know it. *That* is the difference.'

'But what of telekinesis?'

'She could use it. But she will not.'

'Why not?'

'She loves you. Propose; she will accept.'

Something loosened inside of me at these words. I had dared to hope it was so; but could it really be?

'How do you know?' I asked, sceptical yet curious.

'As I am within you, so she is without. I am her origin in your mind; that is why we share a countenance. She is my embodiment and echo in the outer world.'

'Assuming she accepts my proposal, what then?'

'Seize power and her wand-crystal. Turn the beasts back to men. Wed the goddess and give her your seed, for she is to be the vessel of the new God; it is out of the conjunction of your semi-humanity and her divinity that your heir will be born. When you have taken your pleasure of her, amuse yourself with the nymphs.'

I gazed into her cold green eyes, shining like emeralds, and beheld her lovely, graceful form. I began to stroke her breasts through the peplos; they were white and cold as marble, but shapely as the real thing, and the nipples hardened at my touch. She was the very image of Anima; only higher, more powerful, and she was telling me all I had dared hope. I had not the strength to dismiss her, to humble myself.

'And then?' I murmured, eyelids fluttering.

'Set sail for Aeonia, where your conquests shall begin. Those who mocked you will humble themselves before you. You shall be the greatest of emperors, the greatest and wisest of men and gods. Your name shall echo down the corridors of history for ages to come. Mothers shall name their sons in honour of you. Husbands shall offer their wives to you, that you may sew your divine seed and spawn a race of godmen to administer your empire. The kings of far-off and unknown lands shall kneel before you as supplicants. You shall rule all the world for eternity, usher in the dawn of a new age, a second Atlantea, greater than the first!'

I was struck by all the glory and terror of godhood. 'I am awed by my mission. How am I to do all this?'

'I shall be right by your side, offering counsel and spinning what you mortals call luck. I ask only one favour in return.'

'Name it,' I mumbled, half-sensible.

'Think of *me* as you ride your queen.'

I smirked and closed my eyes, savouring every word, every touch.

'I will.'

'And whatever hardships you may encounter, remember: I love you,' she breathed into my ear and gave me a squeeze.

On the brink, I opened my eyes, that I might behold her sublime form during the climax.

She was gone.

Chapter 17: Mounting the Dais

She was gone. But in her place was a small bush on the sandy hillside. There was something strange about that bush. I leaned down to inspect it. It had broad, ovate leaves and bell-shaped purple flowers, streaked with red. I gasped, awestruck.

The belladonna Sagittarius.

Had the goddess left the poison shrub there, to give me the idea? Or had it been there before she appeared? Either way, it was clear what I must do.

I grabbed three sprigs, looked to the west and saw the first grey hint of dawn and the white gleam of the distant palace. I stumbled down the hillside, looking for my peplos and nurse's apron. I could not find them.

As I staggered the wilderness, naked as a mad prophet, a plan began to germinate in my mind.

In the depths of the forest, I happened across a stick; five feet long and relatively straight and sturdy. I picked it up, for I had a use in mind, and made straight for the palace.

It was mid-morning by the time I arrived. As usual, the doors were open. Covering my modesty with my free hand, I tried to sneak through the vast entrance hall. I made it half-way up the marble stairs when a voice called out, 'Where the devil have you been? And why are you naked?'

I spun around; on the far side of the mezzanine stood Helen.

'I was out hunting in the forest. I got hungry and um, ate the wrong mushroom. Next thing I knew, I was naked on top of a rock in the desert. Imagine my surprise!' I said, with good humour. There was something lordly, rich and velvety smooth about my voice now, which I noticed for the first time.

She shook her fair auburn head, unamused.

'You missed the Feast of the Full Moon. The goddess is not pleased.'

'The goddess deigned to express an opinion of me? I was of the mind she had forgotten me entirely, so did not think my absence would be missed,' I said, a hard edge of tempered bronze creeping into my voice.

'She was most insulted. For the Feast of the Full Moon is sacred to her; she is goddess of the moon, among other attributes.'

'I thought Melea was goddess of the moon?' I said, insolently. I had been emboldened by my newfound divinity.

'Deities can share a celestial body!' she shrieked.

'As you say,' I said, shuffling away, smirking at her agitation.

'You are expected to apologise to the goddess and make an offering, to atone for your absence!'

'And what does the goddess wish me to offer?'

'Five deer.'

'That will take some time.'

'Since you were gone hunting it was assumed you would return with something. It seems we have overestimated your prowess with bow and spear,' she said, guessing that I had already deposited my weapons at the stables, or lost them in the wilderness. She turned primly to leave, nose in the air.

I gazed at her with eyes of contempt. 'We shall see,' I muttered, darkly.

Finally, I made it back to my room, where I was able to drink an amphora of water and devour a hunk of bread and cheese before crawling into bed. I heard a faint giggling noise, coming from behind the walls. It sounded like the laughter of maidens. Perhaps Doloma, whose room was next to mine, had seduced a nymph or two. How, I could not say, for he was frightfully ugly, but women were curiously forgiving in that regard, provided the man had confidence. Then I heard it again; it was clearly a child's laughter. I shrugged my shoulders, attributing it to the lingering influence of the red mushroom and promptly fell asleep, utterly exhausted by my travails in two worlds.

I woke to find the afternoon sun blazing into my eyes, through the open window. I had not thought to close the shutters when I left and was too exhausted to notice upon my return.

Then I heard it; the giggling. It could no longer be dismissed as an illusion of the mushroom, for it was clear as day. I swung my legs out of bed and pressed my ear to the wall.

Someone was whispering and rustling about in there; I heard children's voices. I shuffled along the wall, keeping my ear pressed to the stone. The noise seemed loudest at the segment of wall beside the mirror.

Curious, I knocked on the wall.

A hushed silence. They knew I was onto them and were playing dead.

I knocked again.

The wall was hollow here. It was of wood, not stone, and thin wood at that. I could break it down, with the right implement. I donned a peplos and was about to find a hammer to batter the wall with, when I was seized by a sudden impulse to look behind the mirror.

I lifted the mirror away from the wall and set it down on the bed. As I suspected, there was a secret door, made of wood, concealed by the mirror. I turned the knob and pushed it open.

Sunlight splashed into the darkness, revealing a small secret room, no larger than a closet, leading onto a narrow passage. Huddled in a nook, were a boy and a girl. They couldn't be older than six.

Their skin was pallid, and their eyes were beady and squinting, as if they had never seen the sun before. They wore browned, dusty old rags and reeked of shit; I saw a pile of festering dung in the corner.

'Hello there, little masters,' I said, unsure why I addressed them as Mentor had his homunculi. 'Fear not, for I mean you no harm.'

But they were not afraid. That was the strangest part. They grinned at me, impishly, as if I had caught them at a childish game.

'You found us!' the elder lad said, distinguished from his sister by his height. Both children had shoulder length brown hair.

'You win!' said the girl, giving me a gummy smile.

'What's the game??'

'Playing hide and seek, silly.'

'Who told you that?'

'Mummy.'

'And who is mummy?'

'Agnes. She works here.'

I recalled the busty red-headed nymph who had asked Helen to cover her hours in the kitchen so she could see to her husband.

'I know your mother. But tell me, did she say why you should hide here?'

'She said it was a game!'

I let them out of the nook and gave them some of my water and the leftover scraps of my bread. They bolted it down like wolf cubs.

'Stay here,' I said, and ran downstairs.

I found Agnes in the kitchen. Luckily, Helen was not there. The other nymphs glared at me. Evidently, I was *persona non grata*. I did not care; I found their scorn fatuous and amusing.

'Agnes, come with me.'

'What do you want?'

'A word, in private.'

'The goddess awaits her apology in the Hall of the Moon,' she said, stony-faced.

'I will get around to it.'

'She is not accustomed to waiting.'

'Then it'll be a new experience for her. Speaking of new experiences, I found your children behind my bedroom wall. Care to explain?'

Her eyes darted. The other nymphs were looking, but they could not hear. She grabbed some provisions and stormed from the kitchen, murmuring her excuses to the others.

'Mummy!' the two children said, as she entered my room. They ran over and hugged her. 'Did you bring any food for us?'

'I did. There you go, little ones,' she said, setting the venison, bread and water down on the floor.

'What is the meaning of this cruelty?' I demanded, with stern eyes of reproach, when the children were out of earshot.

She blushed and grimaced. Her eyes widened and her tone was pleading as she said, 'I had to hide them. I just had to!'

'Why?'

'Please don't make me tell.'

'You can tell me, or Anima.'

She sighed. Her shoulders slumped.

'Are you familiar with the customs of this island?'

'If by that you mean the barbarities in the grove, then yes.' I was past caring about maintaining the secret of the black wedding.

'My children are bastards, by two men; both God for a Day.'

'You wanted to save the boy from castration?' I guessed.

'I wanted to save their lives!' she said, tears flowing from her hard, jaded eyes. 'Only a certain number of boys are permitted to grow to manhood and become priests and only a certain number of girls are needed as nymphs. The remainder are sacrificed in the grove, to the goddess Melea. Drowned, in a tub of water. It is known as the black baptism. What else was I to do? At least this way I can feed them with scraps from the kitchen! They are alive; though it isn't much of a life I have given them! A wretched shadow existence!' She broke down and sobbed into her hands.

'Mummy? What's wrong?' the elder child said, during a rare glance up from his feast.

Hesitantly, I placed a comforting arm around her shoulders.

'You did the best you could. You were placed in an impossible position,' I said, soothingly.

I had misjudged Anima. Even having witnessed the black wedding, I had not thought her capable of ritual child murder. And yet she had surprised me once again. Was there no limit to her evil?

I was not afraid. Seeing these helpless innocents gawping solemnly at their crying mother, I imagined Anima curtly ordering their lives to be snuffed out. Righteous anger rose in my heart. Someone must put an end to this madness; since the others could not or would not confront the witch-queen, it fell to me. I would sooner die than tolerate such depravities, for to meekly obey the whims of a tyrant harmed body and soul; this much I knew beyond doubt. My right hand tightened to a fist.

'Rejoice, Agnes, your suffering has come to an end.'

'What do you mean?' she asked, looking up at me with bleary bloodshot eyes.

Just then, there was a knock on my door.

'Take the children and hide in the secret room,' I whispered, ushering her and the little ones inside and closing the door on their frightened faces.

I replaced the mirror, scurried across the chamber and opened the door.

It was Doloma. His wrinkled, bearded face was twisted into a scowl.

'What the devil are you up to?'

'Just sleeping.'

'The goddess expects an apology. For your sake, I suggest you make it sooner rather than later. I have never seen her so angry,' he said, barging past me and into the room.

I smirked.

'What's this, eating on the floor now? You spend too much time with that half-wild madman,' he said, at the sight of the children's food.

My heart lurched when I saw the trail of breadcrumbs leading towards the wall.

Doloma saw it, too.

'What have we here?'

A belch.

Doloma froze. He turned, facing the wall.

'What is going on in here? Do you have a nymph tucked away here somewhere?' he said, a wry grin on his ugly face.

'Keeping her to yourself, are you?' He wagged his finger at me and crept over to the wall.

'Nothing of the kind. There are rats in the walls. Perhaps you heard them.'

'I've never heard a rat belch! Nay, your vermin is surely human,' he said, knocking.

He turned to face me; his eyes narrowed.

'A hollow wall.' His grin was knowing, conspiratorial.

Then he thrust his fist through the wood.

The children screamed, through their mother's hands. Their mother screamed. I ran over to stop him. Doloma pushed me aside and battered away at the wooden wall until he saw them, huddled in terror.

'You're harbouring an illegitimate family?' Doloma asked, puzzled.

'I haven't been here long enough to sire children, you fool!' I thundered.

'Whatever it is, it reeks of rule-breaking. And you know the penalty for rule-breaking,' he said, grabbing his balls.

'Have a heart, man! These children would be killed if the others knew. They are illegitimate.'

Comprehension dawned in Doloma's jaded eyes.

'I see.'

He considered the ramifications. Then he looked back up, his gargoyle face bitter with malice and fear.

'That is *most certainly* forbidden!'

'The witch who runs this island is cruel without limit. She respects not the laws of gods or men. I mean to overthrow her. Join me, and I shall make you my lieutenant,' I blurted.

'She is a goddess. She *is* the law here. She has the wand, three beasts, countless snakes and sixty helpers. Who are you to challenge her?'

'I am half a god myself; and I know of what I speak,' I said, with a hard-edged voice and a countenance of stone.

'You know nothing. You are a fool, driven to lunacy by the ramblings of that hermit. And soon you are to be a eunuch – or a corpse,' he said, making hastily for the door.

I stepped in front of him, blocking his way.

'Show some respect to your future ruler!' I said, my eyes dark with hatred.

'Out of my way, madman!' he pushed me aside.

I saw red. I pounced on him like a lion and sank my teeth into him and jerked my head, ripping out the side of his throat. He gasped in horror, like a fish on land, and tried to scream, but I shoved my hand down his mouth and tore out his tongue, for my strength was tripled. The woman and children looked on in horror; Agnes was too stunned by my sudden savagery to even think to cover their eyes.

'You shall speak no more threats or lies!' I hissed, grabbing Doloma by the back of his neck and frog-marching him over to the basin, filled with my dirty bathwater. I dunked his head underwater. He writhed and wriggled but it was of no moment. I held him under until the water was red, and he stirred no more. When I withdrew my wrist from the water, I noticed the serpent and rose tattoo I had received upon my arrival at the palace was smudged and starting to wear off. This was curious, for I had washed my arms countless times before without any fading.

I staggered out of the bathroom and into the chamber, my mouth and my right arm up to the wrist covered in blood.

I covered the hole in the wall with the mirror.

'Stay here. I will come and get you when it's over,' I said, to Agnes and her children.

'When what's over?' she asked, but I did not tarry to answer her.

I grabbed my stick, and the kitchen knife I had taken to kill Nero, and made for his room, down the corridor. He was usually to be found there, in the late afternoon, between feedings.

'Good gods!' he said, startled by my blood-spattered appearance, as I stood on his threshold.

'Why thank you.'

'What? Wh—'

'I need to talk to you,' I said, barging past him.

He saw my knife and stick and glanced at me, warily, staying close to the door.

'I do not come to attack you. I need your assistance.'

'With what? Recovering your wits?'

'I need you to grind this down,' I said, producing three sprigs of belladonna, 'and feed it to your predators with their meat.'

'Why on earth should I do that?'

'I mean to mount the dais and seize Anima's wand, so that I might turn the beasts back into men. I need them docile for my ascent.'

He stared at me, disbelieving. Then he barked with laughter.

'You really have gone mad!'

'On the contrary, I am more rational than I have ever been.'

'Assuming I agreed to this far-fetched scheme – what's in it for me?' he said, sobering up now he saw that I was serious.

'As the new King of Tyria, I will make you my general. You will be in command of my army.'

'What army? A few beasts, eunuchs and nymphs?'

'I will use Anima's wand to turn the beasts back into men. They followed you before; they shall follow you again.'

This got his interest. He had rued the loss of his power, ever since the shipwreck.

'That's all well and good. What makes you think she won't turn you into a pig before you get to the third step?'

'I am a god. I have powers of my own.'

Nero barked with derisive laughter, though I could see the lunatic solemnity of my face made him scared, for no one is so bold as to be unshaken by the unpredictability of madness.

Sighing, I waved my hand at the clay cup on his table. It smashed against the wall, spilling wine everywhere.

He turned to me, mouth agape.

'Did you just—'

I showed him the palm of my hand. A gust of air made him stumble backwards, but he kept his feet.

He raised his hand in submission.

'Alright, alright. You've made your damn point! There's no need to be a bully!'

I lowered my hand, grinning at the Unknown irony of his statement. But I was disappointed; I thought myself stronger. Evidently, my Unknown Mind was right to leave me the belladonna.

'So what if you can fart with your hands? I'll scream and draw the others if you try it again. I'll not get in your way, but I'll have no part in this mad scheme of yours.'

'You forget,' I said, stepping toward him, slowly, 'if I should fail or be subdued, under questioning I will reveal your penetration of the sacred grove and your tawdry affair with Lucilla.

Our fates are bound,' I said, my voice filled with the warm glow of power.

'You're right, our destinies *are* intertwined. Hate me and you hate yourself. Kill me and you kill yourself! You wouldn't dare denounce me!' he said, animal terror filling his dark, handsome eyes.

'Why shouldn't I? If my coup fails, I would have nothing left to lose, and one thing is for certain; I owe you no loyalty. Give it up; I have you, quite literally, by the balls.'

His eyes darted. He was thinking of a way to slip out of my net.

'It's for the best,' I said. 'Do you really want to stay here, mucking out the stables all your life and living under a tyranny? Sooner or later they'll catch you and Lucilla, then you'll join the ranks of the eunuch-priests. A worse hell for one such as you I cannot imagine.'

'True,' he admitted, still thinking.

'And I know you. You want your crew back, don't you? A man like you does not feel alive without someone to swindle, bully or beat.'

Hatred flashed in his eyes; but he bit his tongue, out of fear.

I realised my mistake, almost instantly; I needed to take a different tack. A gentler tack. 'If I succeed, you are free to do as you please. Go where you wish, mad pirate. Take your crew to the high seas. Kill, fuck, pillage, burn, steal. Do what you will – provided it doesn't come back to me, I don't care what you get up to,' I lied, for I had no intention of permitting such wantonness. 'Do we have a deal?'

I extended my hand. It hovered there, expectantly.

'No,' Nero said.

My stomach lurched. How could he refuse?

But then he smiled. 'No. I meant we're blood brothers. We do it like this,' he said, producing a knife from his pocket and slicing his palm with it.

'You brought a knife, too?' I raised my eyebrow.

'Just because we work together, doesn't mean I trust you. I'd advise you to take the same attitude, but I think you've already learned that lesson – so well you've forgotten several others, but no mind.'

We clasped hands and grinned at each other.

'Feeding time is in half an hour. The belladonna will have taken effect an hour from now. That is when I shall mount the dais.'

I placed a brotherly hand on his shoulder and left the room.

I spent the time in my chamber, whittling my stick into a spear with the kitchen knife. From my window I had a clear view of a sundial in the garden, which I used to keep track of time.

'Is it safe to come out?' asked Agnes, through the wall.

'For you. The children stay.'

Agnes stepped out, blinking as her eyes adjusted to the light.

'I need you to go down to the kitchen and start a fire.'

'What? Why?'

'I need the nymphs to be distracted while I mount the dais and seize power.'

Agnes' mouth fell open.

'You're mad!'

'I am a god.'

She stared at me, blankly.

I sighed. Evidently, a demonstration was necessary.

The mirror was ten feet away from me. I knocked it over with a wave of my hand; it shattered, loudly.

Agnes knew not what to make of this. She stood there, frightened and bemused.

'I will make this easier for you: you have nothing to lose by aiding me. If I fail, and you were careful in the kitchen, none will suspect you, for I shall not denounce you.'

'And if I do not help?'

'Then my coup will fail, and your children will sooner or later be discovered and drowned, even if Anima fails to break me under torture. You cannot play hide and seek forever; that they have lasted so long is a minor miracle, attributable only to the mercy of the gods. You know what I say is true.'

After her nerves had settled, Agnes had to admit that I was right. Hands trembling, she kissed her children goodbye as if she may never see them again and headed down to the kitchens. I had instructed her to start her fire when I entered the Hall of the Moon.

When my spear was finished, I went into the bathroom and plunged my right hand into the basin up to the elbow. When I withdrew it, the tattoo had faded some more. Now the snake was barely discernible. I wiped and scrubbed it off with my fingers.

When the hour was up, I braced myself for the fight of my life, and headed downstairs.

I entered the Hall of the Moon. A shaft of sunlight illuminated the dais just in front of Anima's throne. The beasts slumbered and lounged on the steps, which was not unusual; I still did not know if Nero had held up his end of the bargain.

The nymphs and priests were gathered on the black quartz semicircle below. They turned and stared daggers at me – a ripple of alarmed whispering ensued at the sight of my spear. Nero stood close to his beasts, to the left of the dais' bottom step. I saw him gulp with terror.

I was not without trepidation myself. My heart throbbed in my chest; the task before me was immense. To overthrow a goddess was heroic madness: the stuff of myth and legend.

I halted in the middle of the semicircle, but I did not make obeisance.

'Kneel!' Phidias squeaked, on my right.

I ignored him.

A murmur ran amongst the nymphs. Helen motioned for me to kneel. I grinned at her, using impudence to cover my terror.

For the first time since my arrival in the palace, Anima looked right at me. She wore her silver tiara, rose garland and the diaphanous white peplos I had come to loathe. Her green eyes were cold as death.

'What is the meaning of this insolence?' she said, her voice wrathful and piercing.

I stared right back at her, baiting her with my silence. I wanted to give her a taste of her own medicine; I wanted to rile her.

'Kneel! Kneel before your goddess!' she commanded, losing her temper.

It had worked. I did not kneel. I stepped forward, spear in hand, defiance burning in my eyes.

'I am not your slave!' I boomed, in my rich, lordly baritone.

Her mouth fell open. She was speechless; paralysed. None had ever defied her. None had ever broken her spell. She knew not what to do.

I heard a scream. Fire had broken out in the kitchen. Half of the nymphs ran to douse the flames, and a few of the more enterprising priests left the hall to help. So far, so good.

I approached the beasts on the steps of the dais. The wolf and tiger did not rouse themselves. It seemed Nero had kept his end of the bargain, though I had given him little choice. Only the lion rose, on unsteady legs, and managed a feeble roar.

Feeble or no, my bowels plummeted with dread; for I was about to enter the arena with the King of Beasts.

I raised my spear. The lion lunged forward, hurling a paw at my knees – I hopped backwards on nimble feet. The lion roared and took another swing at me. I sidestepped, but his paw caught my shin, drawing blood. Enraged, I thrust the spear at his face and ripped open the wet, glistening snout. The lion growled and reeled aside. Blood dripped onto the quartz. Pressing my advantage, I dived in and struck again, piercing the flank and twisting the spear, a cruel snarl on my face. The lion writhed, trying to free itself, but I withdrew the spear and stabbed the beast in his shoulder, opening up a huge livid gash. Already enervated by the poison, the lion retreated, swaying drunkenly. Then he collapsed on the floor, stewing in his own blood.

Anima, shocked at the vulnerability of her throne, waved her wand at me, somewhat frantically.

I felt something grip me in the innards; a terrible primordial hunger-lust, a desire to pounce and kill and rip. Hairs began to grow on my arms and chest. Terrified, I snarled and roared with the depth of a tiger. I recalled the words of my Inner Woman; had she tricked me? Lured me into a trap?

She had not. The transformation went no further. I was conscious enough of my bestial nature not to be vulnerable to such spells. I grinned at Anima; she was utterly confounded.

Recovering her wits, she waved her wand again, and murmured an incantation, but not at me; no, for the red stone was aimed toward the west wall.

I pressed forward.

Then I heard a growl and the pitter-patter of fast-moving paws. I swivelled. A white wolf bounded in from the entrance hall. The priests and nymphs darted aside in terror, but the beast only had eyes for me. Finding her own pets unexpectedly docile, Anima had summoned a friend from the forest.

The wolf circled me, warily, snarling and snapping its jaws. I could see the raw light of hatred in her eyes; the froth on her black lips. She was a big brute, too. Terror scrambled my wits; for a moment, I knew not what to do, and the wolf advanced on me.

Then the words of the old man came to me: 'Know that the raven is a part of you. Feel what it corresponds to in the World Within. Kill the raven inside and the bird without shall fall as if skewered by an arrow.'

Staring into the yellow eyes of the brute, I was overwhelmed by compassion, understanding, love; I saw the wolf as a mere embodiment of the bloody-minded hate within my own breast and I thought of all the anger, all the rage and fury at Nero, at everyone who had mocked, bullied, beaten and derided me. And then something strange happened. The wolf shrank, until it was a yapping little dog and even this got smaller, metamorphosing into a bee. In a curving arc of shocking velocity, the bee shot right into my ear and buzzed and wriggled its way into my brain. I reeled, clasping my head with both hands; the buzzing was deafening but worse still was the pain of the bee crawling through my mind as if it were a honeycomb. Sensing weakness, the nymphs advanced on me.

At last, the pain ceased. The bee had stopped moving and I was able to act again. Indeed, I could barely feel it. Taking advantage of the moment's respite, I walked up the steps. The nymphs backed off.

The cobra rose to its full height and was able to stare me in the eye. I stared back, unfazed; I felt his will snap, and the serpent fell to the floor and slithered away, hissing. The last barrier between myself and the goddess was removed.

Anima was still shocked. She raised her wand to throw me back, but it was too late, for I was on her, grabbing her delicate wrist and wrenching the weapon from her grasp. 'Oh my God,' she said, eyes widening as the severity of her underestimation dawned on her. The nymphs gasped in horror. To them, this was sacrilege. I did not care. Anima's eyes flashed with hatred; she bared her teeth like a tigress. God, she was beautiful. The mirror image of my soul. I kissed her.

Those full red lips were warm. After a moment's paralysis, she returned my ardour. A heavenly glow suffused my body; my thoughts ceased; instinct took over. Her arms closed around my neck, her tongue darted into my mouth and, carried away by passion, I lay her down on the marble before the crowd and tore off her peplos; she tore off mine. The supple alabaster perfection of her body lay before me. The spectators stood in awed silence as I prepared to make love to a goddess.

Chapter 18: The Mirror-Throne

Conscious of the crowd's leering eyes, I picked her up and, still kissing, stumbled through the veil, down a passage and into a dingy candlelit room. I set her down on a large, soft bed; her bed. I caught but a quick glimpse of a cage in the corner, which seemed strange, but I only had eyes for her. All the same, I kept hold of the wand for the duration; even at the height of our passion.

When our lovemaking was finished, we lay beside each other in her bed.

'Why do you have a cage in here?'

'In case the animals prove troublesome.'

This seemed a reasonable enough excuse. And yet, I did not believe her.

'Why did you ignore me?' I asked, as she ran her fingers across my chest. I had been yearning to ask her this for months.

She chuckled, softly.

'That was only a pretence, you fool. Since our first kiss, I was beset by strange new feelings; they terrified me. I prefer to be alone, you see.'

'But you have changed your mind?'

'I am of two minds. I am a goddess and want to remain aloof, to preserve my power, for a husband would be king co-ruler and my experience of men has been terrible. But another part of me does not wish to be worshipped as a goddess and has yearned all these long years for someone to treat me as a woman.'

'What of Iambus?'

'Iambus was a drunken fool.'

We chuckled.

'I should really go and tell the nymphs and priests not to worry,' Anima said.

'You'd better put some clothes on first.'

'And you.'

She went to her bathroom to wash and dress. My mind turned to more practical matters. The worries flooded in. I donned my undergarments and peplos and prepared to return to the Hall; to get a glimpse of what was happening out there. I half-expected to be greeted by a wall of angry faces and kitchen knives.

As I opened the door to the corridor leading through to the Hall of the Moon, I saw Mentor stood but a few inches in front of me, bedraggled and covered in grass, his eyes bloodshot and half-crazed.

I started at this fearful and unexpected sight.

'Mentor? Were you listening to us?'

'That's not important,' he said, coyly, 'what is important is seeing through what you have started!' he hissed.

I grimaced.

'I had planned to seize power, but now I don't know if there is any need,' I demurred, my head aswim with thoughts of Anima's tousled blonde hair and lovely pale body.

The old man balked.

'A poem, one can leave half-finished – not a coup! Can't you see man, this is victory or death!'

I hesitated. Fear gripped my heart.

'Right now, they're panicked and bewildered, like a herd of sheep beset by a lone wolf. They've seen you turn a dog into a bee and deflower their goddess – now is the time to act!'

'What do you suggest?' I said, intimidated by the gravity of the situation.

'Imprison Anima – put her in the cage! I will draw a magic circle around it, so she cannot use her powers while she's in there.'

'But—'

'But what? You *love her*? Don't be so naïve,' he spat, contemptuously, with all the bitter cynicism of age. 'She tried to grab for her wand, you know, when your back was turned.'

I stared at him askance.

'You *did* watch! You satyr!'

'I was watching out for *you*! That woman kills children. She castrates men for sport. She has to be secured or she'll turn on you the first chance she gets, and have you sacrificed in the grove!'

'I see your point,' I said, thinking. She was a monster, of that there was no doubt; but she was a beautiful monster. I was torn.

Seeing my equivocation, Mentor hissed, 'Look, no final decision need be made today; if you lock her up you could always let her out again, though it would be the height of folly. But wouldn't you like to have the choice?'

I stammered and blithered.

'Right now, you've got a she-wolf by the neck – throw her in the cage!' he hissed, cutting me off.

In the bedroom, Anima groaned, 'Ego? Where are you?'

'How should I do it?' I whispered, panicked.

'You're alone. You need reinforcements. You have the wand – turn the beasts back into men. With their help you can cage her and cow the others!'

I nodded, glad of his clear thinking in a time of peril. Though a god, I still feared like a man.

'Announce you are their new king and god.'

'Just announce it? Won't there be resistance?' I asked; I couldn't believe such a crude ploy would work.

'Bluff – say you have all 18 men at your command. The nymphs and priests could not see what you've been doing behind the veil; for all they know you've been using your time productively, not rattling away like a satyr. In times like these, all you have to do is act like you're in charge, to be in charge; everyone else is so confused that one focused liar can take power.'

I recalled my historical studies; it was usually so.

'Right. Then what?'

'Make the bluff into a self-fulfilling prophecy. Get the rest of your crew; turn them back to men. Impose martial law. Threaten extrajudicial death to anyone who challenges your regime.'

'Isn't that a little harsh?'

'A little harshness now will save much harshness later! Do this now and the thing is bloodless.'

'But what about Anim—'

'I will watch Anima and Nero in your stead. Go! Go! Speed is your salvation, go!' he said, pushing me toward the purple veil – and my confused public.

The fire in the kitchen had been extinguished and all were present in the Hall of the Moon, chattering nervously, with worried looks on their faces. Everyone stared at me.

I pointed the wand at the bleeding lion and willed the form of Macro out of the beastly carapace. It did not work as I expected. The man came out of the animal like a butterfly emerging from chrysalis; I saw a face and yawning mouth press itself against the hide. Then he burst forth from the belly of the beast, widening the hole for himself, in a ghastly parody of natural birth – as if the spectators were not stunned enough by the day's circus. It went much the same with the wolf, the tiger and the snake. The men were all bewildered at their sudden blood-soaked rebirth but seemed to possess a dim awareness of what had transpired. Or at least, they sensed I was their deliverer, for three of the four obeyed my orders; and the other, Macro, obeyed Nero.

I felt a presence by my side. It was Anima. She made no objection to the metamorphosis and beamed at me, radiantly, her eyes shining with affection, which made what I had to do next all the harder.

'Nero, there is a cage in the room beyond the veil. Place Anima inside,' I said, quietly.

'Ego? What is this?'

I was unable to meet her gaze.

'I thought you loved me?' she asked, crestfallen.

I felt a pang of guilt ripple through my abdomen; but I held fast to my decision, for I knew in my heart it was necessary.

'Anima, you are a remarkable goddess, but you are also a murderess and a castrator. But fear not; my yoke is soft, and my judgement shall be just,' I said, largely for the benefit of the audience.

Nero and the other three men advanced, warily; Macro had retained the wounds he suffered whilst a lion. Eyes blazing with scorned wrath, she rounded on Nero and thrust her palm at him; he was blown off his feet and the others stumbled backwards. I pointed the wand at her – she flew into the far wall with a thump and smacked her head on the marble. She was conscious but concussed. I stared at the wand in wonder. It was more powerful than I expected; the effect of the telekinesis was quadrupled. My four goons, after gawping at me in amazement and helping Nero up, escorted the dazed goddess to custody. I felt guilty; I had hoped this could be avoided. Fortunately, the nymphs were too stunned by my sacrilegious power to avenge their fallen idol.

As she was about to pass through the veil, I said, 'Halt!'

I approached her and took the silver tiara off her lovely blonde head. I forced myself to look her in the eye as I did so. Though silent, she exuded pure malice; I could feel it; taste it. I was not overly concerned, for I was the victor.

Then I placed it on my own head and sat on the Mirror-Throne before the awed spectators. My head swam with confidence; I had bested a goddess and seized the throne! Such things were unthinkable a mere two weeks prior. I had come a long way and was damn proud of it.

'I am your king and god now. I have eighteen men at my disposal, most of them armed,' I said, bluffing, for as Mentor pointed out, they knew not what had transpired in my absence from the hall. 'Of my divinity you have had ample demonstration. I wish for a smooth transition of power and have no desire to embark on a witch-hunt. Many of you were complicit in the crimes of the old regime, but fear not: I shall show clemency to all except the worst perpetrators of the horrific crimes I myself have witnessed.' The acoustics of the Hall were magnificent; my voice carried with the deep eloquence of a master orator in the Agora of Aeos.

'And to you priests, I say, you are free! You need no longer cringe in terror before your womenfolk. Men and nymphs shall henceforth be treated equally. Therefore, all the old laws are abolished. Until a new table of laws has been drafted, anyone caught attempting to free Anima, to plot my usurpation or revolt against my rule shall be executed without trial.'

A gasp amongst the crowd. I smirked, enjoying my newfound power, and my ability to wrongfoot my audience. They really had no clue who I was, or what I was capable of, and it frightened them to death.

'This, however, is an emergency decree, in place only until the most egregious wrongdoers have been routed out and sentenced. You are to remain here until further notice.'

Leaving Nero in charge of the hall, I made my way to the stable.

'That was good; very good. You are a born orator. Who'd have thought it?'

I turned around. It was Mentor, leaning on a pillar in the passage.

'I am terrified,' I confessed.

'You don't look it. That's all that counts.'

We pressed on. At the stables, I returned the sheep, oxen and pigs to their human forms.

Theodotus was naked and covered in the blood of the sheep he had been. I asked him what, if anything, he remembered from his spell as an animal.

'I remember the voyage and shipwreck. Everything after that is blurry and vague, like a dream. I get bits and pieces. Mostly eating, sleeping and shitting.'

I laughed. 'I don't expect your life shall change much, now you're human,' I said, with cruel humour.

He laughed along, out of fear.

'You've changed, Ego,' he said. 'I scarcely recognise you.'

He was right. No longer the nervous smooth-cheeked youth who had set sail, I now had the weather-beaten face, full beard and commanding aura of an ancient prophet. Though I was still fearful, it now took a coup to make me scared, whereas a bee would have sufficed back in Aeonia.

I armed my men with spears and hunting bows before leading them to the kitchen, where they grabbed knives. We returned to the hall and I ordered them not to let anyone leave – by force, if necessary.

Now there were eighteen of us, and they could see as much, I told the crowd they were free to go, with the reminder that any rebels would be executed without trial. I thought the threat superfluous; the coup was complete, for the nymphs and eunuchs were stunned into obeisance by the sheer audacity of the thing. It was unexpected, inconceivable; and that is precisely why it worked.

That night, my sleep was troubled.

I dreamt Anima was leading me into her bedchamber, running on ahead of me, dropping her clothes one by one until she was naked. She turned and giggled and beckoned me with her finger, then disappeared inside.

I followed her into the chamber. Mentor stood there, wearing Anima's white peplos. She was gone; though there was a pile of skin and blonde hair left in a crumpled, bloodless heap on the ground, as if it were a costume the old man had discarded.

'What are you staring at?' Mentor said. 'Don't you know, the wisest of men wear women's clothes?'

Then he approached me, a wanton glint in his eye. I was terrified; I saw Mentor as a father figure, not a lover. I turned and ran. Then I woke up.

Needless to say, I did not get back to sleep.

Chapter 19: Poison

'What do I do now?' I asked, feeling unequal to my deed.

'You've done well, my lad, but the task is only half complete,' said Mentor, puffing on his pipe.

It was the day after my seizure of power. Mentor and I were exploring the palace. For it turned out the palace was far larger than I originally thought; we had only been using one of *four* wings, all arranged in a cross formation around a central fountained courtyard.

Presently, we were pacing a corridor in the east wing. Mentor was looking for a kitchen, that he might continue his alchemical experiments free from the prying eyes of the nymphs.

'Half-complete? But we have carried off the coup!'

Mentor shook his head and smirked at my naïvete.

'You are still outnumbered. There are forty nymphs and twenty priests. If they all revolted, you and your men could not withstand them – certainly not with kitchen knives! And as long as Anima is still in play, there is hope for would-be rebels.'

'How do we crush out that hope? Stabilise our regime?'

'Thoroughly discredit their former leader.'

'Anima?' My gut churned with unease.

'Yes. We can't kill her, since she's immortal. Even if we could, you'd make a martyr of her and your subjects would hate you forever. So investigate her. Produce evidence of her litany of crimes. But the sacrifices and castrations won't be enough, for the nymphs participated in those; having known nought else, they

believe such things are normal – nay, right and proper! I fear it will
be a giant's labour to bring them round to our way of thinking.'

'What then?'

'You must find something that discredits Anima even in the
eyes of her supporters; some secret treachery against her people.'

'What treachery?'

'The foul rites of the sacred grove are not what they seem.
Melea does not accept castrations and human sacrifice: only
animals. She is a benign goddess of fertility, tide and agriculture.
Make no mistake, they worship a demon on this island, for whom
Melea is but the mask.'

'What demon?'

The old man scoffed.

'How am I to know? Countless demons accept such
sacrifices. We must find out – and prove our charge!'

'Where am I to find such evidence?'

'This is a state, albeit a small and peculiar one. There must
be archives somewhere.'

'There is a library. Helen said so.'

'Perfect. If we cannot prove our charge, we can at least use
the pages of the *Theogony* to prove Melea does not accept human
sacrifices. Where did the nymph say it was?'

'The east wing.'

'Right, it shouldn't be far then.'

We came out into a vast hall, like the Hall of the Moon,
only utterly derelict. A herd of deer grazed on the weeds. Seeing
us, they raised their heads in unison, and darted off. A pond of
scum filled the bottom corner. Ivy and brambles dangled from the
oculus in the middle of the dome. The mosaic tiles were weather-
damaged and covered in mud and moss.

'Why have they let it fall into such a state of disrepair?' I asked, bewildered. It seemed the height of folly to let all this splendour go to waste.

'I imagine it's a simple matter of practicalities,' said Mentor, putting away his pipe. 'There are only forty nymphs. It's easier to maintain one wing than all four, and they only need the one. However,' he said, stooping down to wipe moss off the mosaic tiles under our feet. It depicted the sun god Rai riding his chariot.

'There may be theological issues at play,' he said, giving me a sidelong look.

'You think they abandoned it because it honours a male god?'

The old man shrugged his shoulders.

'Who knows? It's possible.'

Then he waded through the swamp. Reluctantly, I followed him. The algae clung to my legs; there were dead rabbits and live frogs in the fetid green water.

We came out in an abandoned kitchen. Mould covered the ceiling. There were rabbit droppings on the marble floor. Weeds sprouted betwixt the tiles. Ivy crawled in through the windows, a long crack lined the ceiling and the surfaces were filmed with a thin layer of grime.

The old man checked the clay oven and the pots.

'Yes, this'll do nicely,' he murmured, distractedly.

'Still intent on crafting abominations?'

'With a kitchen like this to work in, and some privacy from that blasted harridan, my next creature shall be the prince of abominations!'

I remained silent while he opened the storage chests and ransacked the broken pots.

'And what if Anima is found guilty?'

'What do you mean, *if*? She certainly will be,' the old man gave me a sharp look.

A rat leapt from a chest and landed on the floor. The old man cursed and gave chase.

'How do you know? I am the judge.'

'If there's insufficient evidence, forge it,' the old man said, running after the rat, which had scurried under the rotten dining table.

'Are we really sure this is necessary?'

'Absolutely.' He was breathless now; his hands were on his knees.

'What would *you* do with her?'

'We needn't decide such matters now,' he said, wiping the sweat off his brow, having given up the chase.

'I wanted to marry her, you know. Part of me still does.'

'You still might.'

'Even though she be my prisoner?'

'Why not? All marriages are prisons.'

'I need counsel, not jests.'

'Many wives of kings have been *actual* prisoners. It is the custom of a thousand years in Khem.'

'It is cruel!'

'It is no more than she did to you and I!' he thundered, with such extraordinary booming volume, the ceiling cracks deepened. 'Holding us on this godforsaken island against our will, when we desired to range the wide world!'

'You want revenge.'

'Damn right I want revenge! And so would you, if you were honest with yourself, and your wits weren't scrambled with lust. In separating yourself from her, you have fallen a prey to desire once again; so much so, you endangered your coup, and your very life just to take your pleasure of her. That is *not* the path of wisdom.'

There was some truth in what he said.

'Either she's my prisoner or my wife; not both,' I said, hotly.

'Better she be your prisoner, then, or *you*'ll be the one in a cage,' he said, shrugging.

After he had finished poking around the kitchen, we looked at the library. Vast shelves stacked with yellowed, cobwebbed scrolls and mouldy bound books. After much searching, we found the state archives.

'There's five hundred scrolls here!'

'I know. We'd better get started!'

After five hours of fruitless and tedious inquiry, we found a list of the priestesses involved in the ritual castrations and black baptisms. Though there was no mention of Anima, Helen's name recurred more than any other as the presiding priestess.

'This shall be most useful.'

'You want to punish Helen?'

'Absolutely!'

'Aren't you afraid they'll revolt?'

'You arrested their queen and they did not. Who cares about the kitchen matron?'

'And what of her punishment??' I asked, once again.

'That is for you to decide. But this list doesn't discredit Anima; we have yet to even implicate her in the rituals.'

'We must keep looking, then.'

After another two thoroughly boring hours, we returned to the Hall of the Moon for dinner. To get there, we had to cross the central courtyard.

The courtyard was square and contained three circular pools: one with a white marble centre surrounded by a circle of black quartz, itself ringed by white marble; one with a central black dot surrounded by white marble encircled by black quartz; and between these, a pool of grey stone tiles with white and black serpents intertwined around a red staff. All three pools were connected by small, gurgling channels.

'Interesting pattern. I wonder what it means??'

The old man barked with laughter.

'Wouldn't you like to know,' he muttered.

I thought this a strange thing to say, but let it pass. I had grown accustomed to Mentor's 'oddments'.

We were pacing down the corridor, when Mentor stopped dead.

I turned and stared at the strange old man, quizzically.

'What's wrong now?'

He seemed to be insensible. His eyes were glazed, in a kind of trance.

Then he looked at me, panic-stricken and gasping.

'You must appoint a taster!'

'What?'

'You heard me. A taster.'

'Why?'

'To taste your meals, damn it!'

'You're worried about poison?'

'The nymphs prepare our meals. They hate us; especially you, the profaner of their goddess! You must have the priests prepare the food in future. Select them in random quotas of six – and have two of your men detailed to watch them while they cook!'

I nodded. 'A wise precaution. I'll make the changes tomorrow.'

'My dear boy, those were the last words of Argo the Ripper!'

'He was a usurper!'

'So are you!'

I sighed.

'Alright, I'll hire a taster for tonight, since the meal is already cooked. Tomorrow, we make the priests cook under guard. Agreed?'

The old man gave me an odd, frightened look, as if he thought I was trying to entrap him.

'You are god and king here. You alone make all decisions. I can but offer counsel, as your humble servant.'

'Nonsense. I don't know what the hell I'm doing half the time! If it weren't for you, I'd be dead or castrated by now!'

'Not at all. Not a bit of it!' the old man objected, terror raising the pitch of his normally gruff voice.

Strange, the way power made people react.

Macro was to be my taster, since he was more loyal to Nero than I, he was already wounded from my spear-thrusts, and I still held a grudge against him for battering me without cause aboard ship. If there was any poison in my fish, I would not miss him. I sat at the head of the dining table, waiting impatiently for him to finish chewing the meal the nymphs had served.

His chewing was damnably slow! And getting slower. And his face was turning pale.

'What's the matter?' I asked, seized by terror. 'Is it your wounds?'

He groaned and doubled over. Then he looked up at all our tense, expectant faces and laughed. The others joined in, hesitantly.

'Very funny!' I said, nonplussed.

Then, still giggling, he popped a mushroom into his mouth. Another groan from Macro.

'The jest has gone stale,' I said, haughtily.

But this was no jest. His stomach roiled like an angry sea; they could hear it down the far end of the table. I rose from my chair to seize hold of him. Then he launched a torrent of red vomit, with such force it pushed plates and cutlery off the table. The nymphs, priests and crewmen alike screamed, rose from their seats and stepped back from the table. Macro turned to look at me; his eyes were bloodshot, terrified. The veins stood out on his head and neck. I tried to lower him to the floor. Someone kept screaming.

'Nurses! Help!' I bellowed.

But it was too late. Macro expired with a long gasp; his eyes frozen in an expression of confused horror.

'He's dead,' I said. 'Poisoned.' I looked for Mentor, who nodded gravely. Terror pierced my soul. The poison was meant for me. Then came a wave of anger; *the poison was meant for me!*

'There will be an inquiry! The wrongdoer shall be punished by death! Do not fight a dragon unless ye be prepared to *burn*!' I shouted, to cover my terror, for I had escaped death by the narrowest of margins. I summoned Mentor and we retreated to the dais.

'Thank you, old man. You saved my life!'

'Think nothing of it,' he said, waving my praise aside. 'I am only glad that you are still alive!'

'What thinkest thou?'

'There must be blood.'

'Agreed. Anima is behind this; they would not dare try to kill me without her sanction, given the uh, favour she showed me,' I seethed.

'No. Not her. Not yet. To kill a goddess is no easy matter, and we must needs have proof to show the masses first.'

'Who, then?'

'The nymph, Helen. She is the kitchen-matron, is she not?'

I nodded, swallowing a lump in my throat.

'And we know she is the chief castrator and killer of children.'

'Yes,' I said. My blood was up; I was scared and angry and wanted to lash out. My life depended on their fearing me and they did not.

'Have her executed. Publicly. Right here, in the Hall of the Moon.'

'Now?'

'Yes, now! Tomorrow may be too late! They need the fear of god – by which I mean you – put into them immediately!'

'Right. You're right.'

My head blazing with red-hot fear and loathing, I stormed back into the dining hall.

'Helen!' I boomed.

Nobody stepped forward.

'Where is the nymph Helen?' I demanded, grabbing a knife off the table and approaching Agnes.

'She ran out the kitchen door, your grace.'

I cursed.

'Nero, Mentor, Matrochus, with me! The rest of you, stay here and watch these nymphs!'

I ran. I ran as I had never run before in my life. I knew well the exit of which Agnes spoke, from my days as a kitchen hand. I was out of the door like lightning. The others could not keep up.

I saw a white shape, about two hundred yards ahead, close to the treeline. I sprinted across the lawn so fast I practically glided. My legs pumped a furious pace; looking down, they were a blur, which meant I was a blur. Realising my divinity had given wings to my feet! My breaths were even and smooth, I hardly felt my leg muscles at all. It felt as if I could sustain this hare-pace for hours, without breaking sweat! I saw her, ahead. She was pitifully slow. I bore down on her like a wolf chasing a rabbit. Before she knew it, I was on her.

I dragged her back into the Hall of the Moon, cursing and sweating and pleading, her hair tousled, and threw her onto the quartz floor. Mentor emerged at my side, with the timeworn scroll proving her involvement in the murders. I pointed at her and said, 'this nymph is guilty of child murder and castration. I saw her castrate a man, a crewmate of mine, and I now bear witness against her.' I took the scroll off Mentor. 'This scroll testifies that she presided over the murder of forty-three children. The sentence is death.' I nodded at Nero, who whispered in Matrochus' ear.

'No. Nero, *you* shall carry out the sentence!'

Nero gulped. He saw what I was doing.

Reluctantly, he walked forward. I passed him the knife.

'Thank you, brother,' he said, bitterly.

Then he approached Helen, slowly. Her face was distraught; she backed away from the dark-eyed terror with the blade.

'Stop! Please!'

'Tell us who gave you the order to murder those infants, and I'll commute your sentence to drowning,' I said, haughty and sovereign.

Her eyes darted toward the dais. She broke down in thick sobs.

'I received no order. I *gave* the order!' she said, lips moving through snot and streaming tears.

I nodded to Nero. He advanced.

'Please! I beg you! Can't you see he's using you as his cat's paw? His executioner?'

Nero leaned forward, placing a tender hand on her bare shoulder, and breathed in her ear, 'My brother knows what I like.'

And then he stabbed her in the neck, the stomach, the chest, the blood splashing freely, a crazed demonic lust in his blood-bespattered face, Helen gasping and screaming and clawing at him feebly, the blood shooting from her neck in great pulsing squirts.

There was a long wailing croak. With a last baleful blue-eyed glare in my direction, Helen expired on the cold tiles.

'Dinner is to be made again, with fresh ingredients,' I announced. 'Matrochus, Nero – watch them as they work! If anyone tries to poison us, kill them.'

My men saluted. I conferred with the old man in the passage outside Anima's room. I had a nasty feeling she might be behind this. I had been avoiding her, sleeping in my old room; part of me was still ashamed at my actions, which smacked of betrayal. Anger gave me courage. The confrontation could be delayed no longer.

Leaving Mentor to oversee the disposal of Helen's body, I stepped into the candlelit darkness.

She was there, in her cage, wearing her transparent white peplos, braiding her blonde locks; the very image of loveliness. She looked up at me. Her eyes were cold.

'You know why I am here,' I said. It was not a question.

She made no answer. That infuriating silence again.

'Someone put poison in my dinner. Fortunately, I employed a taster beforehand, and he took my place in the underworld.'

I watched her face for a reaction. There was none. Only stony resentment.

'I know nothing of this. You have locked me in this cage; how could I place poison in your food?' she said, sullenly.

Then she turned back to her mirror and continued braiding her hair.

'Your meals are served by your maid, Livia. You must have given her instructions.'

'Why do you think the nymphs are incapable of acting on their own?'

'The nymphs worship you. They saw us – together.' My voice cracked here. 'They would not dare move to kill me without your sanction, for fear of incurring your wrath.'

She turned to face me.

'I heard a woman screaming out there.'

'That was Helen. She was executed for murder, by the laws.'

'The law mandates that I appear before the accused as ju—'

'The *new* laws!'

Another sullen silence, pregnant with wrath.

'Why did you lock me in this cage?'

I was taken aback by the directness of the question and the hardness of those emerald eyes.

'I told you; you are a criminal.'

'You are,' she said, staring at me evenly. I recalled our conversation in the pavilion. Xanthus.

'Your crimes are graver and more numerous,' I said, defensively.

'I knew nothing of the supposed child murders and the priests all *wanted* to be eunuchs, that they may take holy orders.'

'You lie! You hate me and want to kill me!' I yelled, moved to anger by the very evenness of her tone.

223

'The body does not lie,' she said, rising to her feet. Then with a single shrug, the peplos slipped from her body, revealing her divine, curvaceous form. 'Your body did not lie yesterday.' She swayed towards the bars of the cage.

I stood, transfixed by her loveliness.

'That was yesterday. Since then I have incarcerated you. You are accustomed to being goddess and queen here; I have usurped your throne and you hate me for it.'

She pressed her nose between the bars. Our lips were inches apart. I drank in her heady, fragrant scent; the creamy skin with its youthful sheen, the plump round breasts, those brilliant phosphorescent eyes, shining with supernatural wisdom and power, piercing me to the quick, seeing through my kingly facade to the frightened quivering lustful adolescent within. I stared into those green eyes, helplessly entranced.

'Lay with me,' she said, simply.

'Here?' I croaked.

'My body does not lie, either. If I hated you, you would know.'

She reached out through the bars of her cage. I hesitated, snatched my hand back.

'It's alright,' she said, soothingly, as if I were a frightened animal.

I felt a strange calmness come over me; my will to resist evaporated as I stared into the fathomless depths of those luminous irises.

I let her touch my hand – my left hand. In the right I kept a firm hold of the wand.

'That's it,' she said, gently. Then she guided my hand to her wetness and began to moan and quiver, all the while staring at me, drenching me with such horrible desire.

I could take no more.

I removed the key from my pocket and unlocked the cage. As I did so, I could scarcely believe it; it was as if I were watching myself from outside, acting under the impulse of a will other than my own.

She caressed me. Kissed me. It was a long, deep kiss, full of passion. She placed my hands on her behind. Dazed and besotted, I let go of the wand to grip her more tightly.

Her eyes alighted on the wand on the floor, with sudden intentness; it whipped through the air and returned to the hand of its mistress. She rapped me across the face with it; I reeled backwards, bleeding from the brow. She pointed it at me and muttered a guttural curse in a harsh tongue.

Nothing happened.

She stared at the wand, aghast. Then, looking more closely, she saw: the red crystal had been replaced by a mere ruby.

Bleeding from the cheek, I pulled the red crystal from my pocket and grinned at her. Acting on Mentor's counsel, I had not trusted her. Nor had I trusted myself with temptation. I had been right not to, on both counts.

Her face was stricken with horror.

Then my eyes turned black and I jerked the crystal.

She began to choke. Red marks appeared on her neck – hand marks – my invisible hands. Her eyes bulged, her face went red; the veins stood out on her head and neck. I twisted the stone again. She wheezed for air that would not come. Mentor had said she was immortal, but she looked pretty mortal to me.

As I gazed into those dying, desperate eyes, I saw another eye, a third eye, peering at us from a hole in the wall at the rear of her cage; the grey eye of Mentor.

Chapter 20: The Wizard Behind the Veil

The eye blinked and withdrew. There was a sudden rustling behind the wall; a bang, a stumble, a muttered curse.

My gaze returned to Anima, on the brink of death; death at my hand.

And suddenly I saw it all. The dream – I guessed what it might mean: Mentor within Anima. Mentor *behind* Anima.

I loosened my invisible stranglehold.

Anima sagged to the floor, coughing and spluttering and gasping for air.

'Did he tell you to poison me?' I demanded.

She looked up at me, stunned.

'Who?'

'Truth may go unpunished. Feigned ignorance will not,' I said, my voice sharp as daggers.

'He said you were going to have me executed tomorrow. That you were going to execute many nymphs involved in the rituals and make the others your concubines.'

'I never said nor intended such a thing. That is why you tried to poison me?'

'It was not poison,' she admitted, sheepishly. 'It was a sedative. I ordered the maid to give you a triple dose, since you are obviously some manner of god.'

'It was enough to kill my taster,' I said, bitterly.

'That was not my intention.'

'But you did mean to kill me, once you had me sedated? After some sort of show trial?'

Her mouth squirmed. 'I suppose I should tell you, since you'll find out anyway.'

'Tell me what??' I demanded, raising the red stone threateningly.

'The idea was to drag you sedated to the sacred grove. There we would sacrifice you to Melea.'

I glared at her.

'I'd almost prefer it if you had tried to poison me to death!'

'I'm sorry. I would never have done so, if I didn't think my life and the lives of a good number of my nymphs depended on it. Now they are expecting a sacrifice tonight.'

'You'll have to call them off!'

'I'll do my best. I need to think about how to approach them, without it seeming like I'm acting under duress. But how did you guess Mentor was turning me against you?' she asked, bewildered.

'A dream.' I smiled, recalling her telling me the value of dreams in the snake-temple. How simple-minded I was back then. 'And I saw him spying on us, through a hole in the wall.'

'What has he been saying about *me*?' she asked, touching the sore skin of her neck.

'That you were sure to try and poison me: hence the taster.'

'Before that. Was it his idea to have me imprisoned?'

I nodded, ashamed at my naïvete.

'He said you would have my balls and my life at the first opportunity. He pointed to your record: your crimes.'

She sighed. Her face turned morose. Suddenly, she looked ten years older.

'I committed those crimes on *his* advice. He told me that I had to sacrifice the children, else the harvest would be insufficient for the island's swelling populace, and the excess would starve to death. Drowning seemed the kinder choice.'

'That is nonsense. You could clear the forest; sew more seeds.'

She shook her head.

'No. It wasn't that. You see, at first, I disregarded his counsel as inhumane. But when we refrained from castration and drowning illegitimate children, the crops withered and died. There was less food and more mouths to feed. Dozens died from starvation – half our people! He told me we had angered the demon Medoc, the tutelary deity of this island, by denying him sacrifices. Medoc had withered our crops in revenge.'

'And you believed him?' I asked, incredulous that an intelligent woman, let alone a goddess, could be deceived by such fairy stories.

'You did, too,' she said, reproachfully. Then she cast her eyes down in shame. 'The next year, faced with the destruction of our community, I assented to the sacrifices and the castrations as necessary evils for our continued survival, concealing the ugly truth about Medoc behind the façade of Melea worship. And the harvest improved.'

I pondered her words. My rage at Anima abated. She was no wicked witch, after all; she was a gullible puppet of a wicked wizard. As was I. I became furious at the old man and my own stupidity. Then, all of a sudden, I felt a horrible tickle in the back of my throat. I coughed; it was dry, like a cat hacking up a furball. I heard – and felt – a horrid buzzing and crawling in there. I choked, spluttered and coughed.

'Are you alright?' Anima asked, making her way toward me. Still wary of her, I raised my hand dismissively.

It was coming further up my gullet, whatever it was. And then, with one giant meaty cough, a black ball flew out, across the room – and took flight. It was a bee; the bee that had been a dog. The bee that had flown into my ear.

Anima stared at me, astonished.

'That's not even the most remarkable thing that's happened today,' I spluttered, between coughs.

When I recovered, I said, 'It seems we have both been deceived; Mentor has set us against one another to enlarge his own power. It seems probable, in light of his conduct, that *he himself* burned the crops.'

'I am not a fool. If it was so I would have suspected arson. The crops were withered and rotted from within, not burned from without.'

'I see,' I stroked my chin. 'Mentor is an alchemist, a black magician, a necromancer. I have seen him create homunculi and bring the dead back to life, albeit for a few days. He is more powerful than he lets on. It would not be beyond his powers to wither a few fields of grain.'

'Not at all,' Anima agreed. She looked devastated, as she realised the magnitude of her error.

'I am curious what other lies he told us. He claimed to be a hermit, a bachelor – and then I see he is living with an old woman!'

Anima laughed uncontrollably.

'He is no bachelor. He is my father!'

My jaw fell open.

'The woman is Agatha?' she asked.

I nodded.

'She is my mother.'

I sat down on the edge of the bed and put my head in my hands. I let my guard down; it had become apparent that Anima was no longer a threat. The spell of love-hate that drove us together and apart was broken and we were left to face the desolation wrought by our naïvete.

'He said you seduced him – that you bewitched him into being his prisoner here on the island.'

Anima laughed, again.

'The latter part is true, for I needed his counsel; or rather, I thought I did, after he supposedly saved our harvest with his wise words. Though it appears the bewitcher was also the bewitched,' she said, ruefully.

'I feel such a fool.'

'How do you think I feel?' she asked, hotly. 'At least he only tricked you into one murder; and that was not without cause. I have the blood of innocents on my hands; dozens of innocents,' she said, her eyes moistening with sorrow for all those wasted lives, all those wasted years.

Suddenly, I rose from the chair, animated by cool fire. I was not going to let the old bastard get away with it.

'Have you any idea where he is?'

She nodded.

'Some. There are secret tunnels in the walls. He uses them to move around when he wants to communicate with me. They lead to a small room hidden behind a purple banner in the central courtyard. That is the only way in and out of the tunnels.'

'Come on,' I said, dashing out of the room. Anima stopped to don her white peplos and ran after me.

We soon reached the central courtyard.

'That's the one,' she said, pointing at a purple banner, hanging from the wall.

I whipped it aside.

Behind the veil was a small candlelit room with stone walls. The old man stood over the blood-stained corpse of Helen, waving his gnarled old staff, holding a jar in his left hand and gibbering in strange tongues. A transparent dark wisp was floating out of the nymph's head, and the old man opened his jaw wider than humanly possible to suck it all in. He was devouring her soul.

Terrified, I flicked the wand.

The old man was wrongfooted and stumbled over the far side of the room; the soul slipped from his mouth and dissipated into the air like smoke. He turned to face us, his grey eyes startled and full of wrath.

He dropped the jar and jerked his staff in our direction.

I felt a wall of air hit me – my feet skidded backwards on the floor. I looked left, and saw Anima holding her hands up; having anticipated the attack, she was creating an invisible protective shield around us.

The old man shimmied his hips; something round and black fell from his pocket and landed on the floor in a puff of smoke. Anima and I stepped back, coughing and spluttering at the acrid stench. When the smoke had cleared, he was gone.

'He's gone up the stairs!' Anima said, running after him.

I followed. We went through a low doorway and into a narrow, winding stone stairwell.

We sprang up the crumbling, uneven steps three at a time. Our youthful bodies soon caught up with Mentor. He turned and faced us, blind panic in his grey eyes. I thrust the wand at him; he flew backward and smacked his head on the stone wall, leaving a bloody smear. Desperate and dangerous as a cornered animal, Mentor flicked his wand and yelled the guttural spell, 'Urguulu!'

I was tossed backward, like a doll caught in a hurricane. I slammed into Anima, who was directly behind me on the narrow stair. We tumbled backwards, bruised and battered by the hard steps, until finally we came to rest in a tangled heap. Then the stones of the wall ahead of us burst open. Groaning, we staggered to our feet and wafted the dust-haze aside, to be confronted with a wall of rubble blocking our path. Anima turned to me, her face caked with dust. She was bleeding from her swollen lip.

'Give me the wand!'

I hesitated. Was this a trick?

'Give me the wand, I know a spell to clear it!' she demanded, thrusting her hand out expectantly.

I held it out. She snatched the wand off me and flicked it backhanded at the rubble; the wall magically reassembled itself, brick by brick, the fragmented masonry fitting back together with astonishing rapidity.

The resulting structure was not stable.

'Run!' she yelled.

We sprinted past the buckling, flaking wall, which collapsed when Anima was but two paces past. We continued tearing up the stairs, animated by mad hatred for the black magician whose evil knew no limit.

Finally, we emerged through a wooden trap door onto the roof of the tower. It was square, with battlements on every side. Mentor stood in the centre. Cackling madly, his eyes glinting with boundless malice, his wizened face contorted into grotesqueries of hatred, he thrust his staff at us and yelled 'Dushkoo!'

A tongue of flame licked from the tip of his staff. Anima, having understood the incantation, yanked me back downstairs by my peplos – I felt a waft of terrifying heat on my cheeks and nose, but the fire missed me and set the wooden trapdoor ablaze. Anima jabbed the wand at the trap door; the hinges creaked, groaned and snapped with a jangle. The flaming door levitated a foot above the level of the roof. She jerked her wand left, in the direction of the old man. There was a strangled yelp. We rushed onto the roof, to see what had happened.

Mentor lay flat on his back, pinned beneath the heavy trap door. His brown robes were dancing with flame and hc had dropped his staff. His bony, obscenely wrinkled old hand groped for it. I thrust the palm of my hand in his direction, meaning to push the staff away; all it did was create a waft of air that blew out some of the fire and dislodged the trapdoor, freeing the wizard to grasp his staff. The door was launched at us, with lightning speed. I ducked, instinctively, but it was not aimed for me. I looked over my shoulder; the door was flying off into the forest that surrounded the palace. Anima was unharmed, for she had dodged the projectile in time.

Then the old man, now on the far side of the roof, did something very strange. He stood muttering to himself, apparently in a trance, clasping his staff with both hands. The fair-weather wisps strewn across a mostly blue sky coalesced into towering storm clouds, swirling overhead in a vortex. Anima jabbed the wand at him. It was to no avail. 'He has created a shield around himself,' she muttered. Then, eyes still closed, Mentor raised the staff above his head.

His eyes opened, gleaming with pure sadistic delight.

'Zorimaaahn!' he bellowed, in the deepest voice I had ever heard, a supernatural voice harsh and terrible as a thundercrack.

Then he slammed the base of his staff into the stones before his feet. At the same instant, a bolt of lightning leapt out of the deepest blackness, dazzled us all with its blue fire and struck the roof.

A crack darted across the stones, running right down the middle of the tower. Anima pulled me back, towards the battlements, and screamed 'Naaamiroz!' at the top of her lungs. This seemed to arrest the crack's progress and the force of Mentor's spell turned back on itself; the cracks reversed and spiderwebbed toward him. The entire midsection of the tower crumbled into a hollow abyss; Anima and I remained on a narrow, rectangular pillar of teetering stone. The pillar threatened to overbalance at any moment. Anima stepped forward, then backward, trying to keep the balance.

The old man looked on, a sadistic smile playing on his chapped, puffy lips.

He pointed the staff leisurely, as if in no hurry to bring about our demise.

I saw a loose battlement stone behind him. I hadn't the wand, but I had some power without it. With the fingers of my right hand, and an intense concentration of will, I waved the stone toward me – it flew loose and caught the old man in the centre of his back; he stumbled forward, toward the crack, and dropped his staff into the yawning abyss. He flailed his arms, leaned backward and managed to step back from the brink.

Cursing me in the foul, guttural tones of a dead tongue, the old man made a sharp, piercing whistle. I continued to help Anima by manoeuvring on the teetering pillar. Then I looked up and saw the majestic wingspan of a golden eagle descending from the stormy sky. The bird was headed straight for me.

Seeing those long wings spread, those sharp black talons aimed at my face with intent to rip, I was gripped by primordial terror. I was done for. I had not the space to dodge.

Then I recalled the raven; I had killed it with ease. The eagle was bigger, but if I could do enough to at least stun the bird and take the sting out of its attack, I might yet survive. I threw my mind into the eagle; imagined its clear, far-seeing vision, the wind rustling through its feathers, the finely-honed instincts of the hunt – and then saw it landing on my outstretched hand, ready to obey the will of its new master.

And it was so.

The eagle flapped its wings, slowing down, and landed smoothly on my right index finger. The bird was glorious and terrifying: large, living motion perched on my delicate little hand, placing itself at my disposal – but the eyes were sharp and questioning, as if to say, 'are you really fit to command one so majestic as I?' The yellow, scaled feet tightened, cutting the blood supply from my fingers. I winced in pain. I could hold the bird no longer and was terrified that it might decide at any moment to peck my eyes out.

I flicked my wrist, flinging the bird's considerable weight at the old man.

The bird flapped off, bearing down on Mentor, intent to kill.

Mentor's eyes widened in horror; he had not seen *this* coming.

The eagle attacked him with its talons; Mentor cringed and covered his face, but his arms were scratched by talon and beak. He backpedalled, on the defensive. Then he tripped over the battlements and fell backwards off the roof. I heard a hoarse wail of 'Mesephania!' as he fell, then a dull thud as his body hit the grass.

Suddenly, a gale blew at us from the storm cloud. Squatting low, we were able to avoid being blown off, but the rectangular pillar on which we stood tipped far to the rear; we were going down!

'No,' I said. 'No!' I roared, the blood pounding in my head, and I directed all my will to survival. In the few moments remaining before death, I turned around, scooped Anima up into my arms and jumped from the pillar. To my amazement, we did not fall; we hovered in mid-air as the pillar fell and smashed crumbling against the earth. I gasped with giddy laughter, scarcely able to believe my plan had worked. Anima looked up at me, astonished. We wavered in the wind and suddenly lurched down a few feet. I buoyed my faith with the example of my levitation and thus slowed our descent to a glide. I aimed for a patch of grass away from the fallen tower. The ground was oncoming, faster than I would have liked. I bent my knees, bracing for impact.

We landed hard. My feet smacked terra firma and I crumpled with a strangled yelp, dropping Anima, who rolled on the grass. Groaning, she stirred. I had a terrible pain in my left ankle but was able to lift my head and move my legs. At least I wasn't crippled again.

Anima pushed herself to her feet and helped me up. I grunted with pain. Then she scoured the grass for her wand and found it in a weed patch. I tested my ankle; a bolt of pain lanced up my foot and into my shin. I winced. I tried again. It was just about able to bear weight.

'It's not broken,' Anima said. 'Just badly bruised and twisted.'

Heartened by this knowledge from the greatest physician I had ever met, with Anima's arm around my shoulder I staggered around the far side of the ruined tower, giving the broken masonry a wide berth. On the way, I saw Mentor's staff amidst a pile of rubble. Anima scrambled over the rubble to hand it to me, so I could use it as a walking stick. I noted the ugly, misshapen rock enclosed by wooden fingers at the top of the staff and thought this a curious device for so powerful a mage.

Then we saw him. A tattered, frail figure swaddled in scorched brown cloak, dead to the world.

'Is he alive?' I asked.

As if in answer, the old man stirred. Groaned. Opened his eyes.

I thrust the staff in his face, balancing on one leg. Anima directed her wand at him. Our faces were grim and full of recrimination.

'Oh God,' he wheezed, 'have I got some explaining to do.' Then he passed out.

Chapter 21: The Black Wedding

I pretended to be asleep as the nymphs carried me by stretcher to the sacred grove. I could see the white glow of moonlight through my closed eyelids and feel the heat from the nearby torches on my bare skin. I daren't open my eyes by even a crack, for I was supposed to be sedated. I had been stripped to a loincloth, as was customary. I could hear their feet crunching over the fallen leaves, hear their laboured breaths, smell the faint odour of their sweat. Agnes and Mytilene were the lead stretcher bearers; Lucilla and Crysethis brought up the rear.

Suddenly, I heard the hoot of an owl. A rustle of feathers, a springing branch, and a wet splash on my bare chest, scattering as far as my chin. I was unable to suppress a grunt of disgust.

Lucilla stopped dead. I could feel her eyes on me. The others stopped too.

'What is it?' demanded Agnes.

'I could have sworn he just grunted.'

'Nonsense. The goddess put him under a potent sleeping spell; enough to kill a normal man, as her herbs killed the brute Macro!'

'All the same, what's the harm in binding his hands and feet? I mean, just in case,' Lucilla said.

'He shall remain unbound,' came a stern, queenly voice. Anima.

'But mistress—'

'Do you question my power?'

'No,' Lucilla said, sheepishly.

We moved forward again. I breathed a gentle sigh of relief.

After the old man's fall, one of the crew, Sphiro, had come running to us from the treeline. In our absence, the nymphs and priests, in a last-ditch attempt to save their queen, whom they believed I was about to murder for the attempted poisoning, had revolted and succeeded in occupying the palace. There was an affray; the crew were forced out of the palace by sheer numbers and retreated to the forest to find sticks and sharpen them into spears with kitchen knives in preparation for an assault.

Anima and I concocted a plan and informed the rest of the crew via Sphiro. We decided it was best if we pretended that Anima had succeeded in knocking me out with a sleeping spell. This would allow us to play along with her planned black wedding, using myself as bait, to draw all the nymphs into the circular glade of the sacred grove. Because of the ritual taboo on men witnessing the ceremony, the thirty-nine nymphs would be separated from the twenty male priests, reducing the number of potential hostiles we must confront at one time. Instead of castrating and sacrificing me as planned, Anima would announce the abolition of the ritual, I would awaken, the symbolic tree stump would be burned to ashes, and the men could emerge from the treeline and surround the nymphs with wooden spears. Anima thought that, of those nymphs who were willing to disobey their queen, only a small number would be prepared to risk a confrontation when surrounded by eighteen fully armed men – with two gods at their backs. Anyone who resisted would either be impaled on a spear or killed with pyromancy, for Anima had brought her wand *and* Mentor's staff. The plan was good, and I knew it was likely to succeed, though we were outnumbered – provided Anima stuck to her word. Everything hinged on her cooperation. Our alliance was fresh and fragile as a newly hatched chick, so I was placing a great deal of trust in her.

At last, I was set down on the broad stump, and the women made their circle around us, preparing to ignite the ritual fire-circle. I sensed Anima stood over me. I heard her unsheathe her jewel-encrusted, ceremonial dagger, said to be carved from a meteorite. I felt the sweat trickle down my armpit. My heart hammered away in my chest. She was taking her time. There was only a short interval before the others turned around and held me down on the stump for the ritual murder; because I was a demigod, the castration would take place only once I was dead, as a precaution. For a frenzied second, I wondered if Anima had double bluffed us or was having second thoughts. Was she going to stab me after all?

I opened my eye a crack. Anima stood before me: masked and stark naked, her face, breasts and muscular thighs smeared in blood, the dagger in her right hand, the wand in her left. She was a fearsome sight; peril lanced through my bowels. The nymphs had finished laying the kindling around us. Once Lucilla lit the fire, our men would be unable to attack the nymphs and I would be trapped alone with them all inside the magic circle. What was Anima thinking? She had already left it too late for comfort, since a single spark could see us cut off from our reinforcements.

Then Anima winked at me through the eye slat of her red demon mask. She flipped her mask off and waved her wand. All the women's clay masks shattered at once. They turned, shocked, to face their goddess. I thanked the gods, stood up and grabbed the staff at Anima's feet, levelling it at the nymphs.

'The black wedding ritual is abolished!' Anima boomed, stern and queenly.

The nymphs raised their wooden phalluses uneasily but were too stunned and confused by Anima's sudden about-face to make a decisive move.

I cupped my hands and hooted like an owl.

On my signal, seventeen men armed with spears emerged from the shadows of the treeline. Their faces were smeared with black mud and they wore nought but loincloths. They were every bit as primordial and fearsome a sight as the nymphs.

'From henceforth, there shall be no castration, no sacrifice, no child-drowning. Those cruel days are done!' I thundered, emboldened by the sight of reinforcements.

The women were incensed. 'Profaner! Kill him! Chop off his cock and burn it!' came the frenzied cries of the hubbub. Lucilla started towards me, fondling her phallus menacingly.

I raised my staff, signalling for the men to advance. The nymphs hissed at the approaching men; a chilling, collective hiss. The men were not cowed. They raised their spears.

I prepared to roast Lucilla alive. I had practiced pyromancy before feigning unconsciousness and was quite impressed with the results; part of me relished the prospect of revenging myself upon that cruel nymph.

Anima stepped between us.

'Stop! I am your goddess! I instituted the black wedding; I have the power to change the customs of this isle as I please! And I declare, this barbaric ceremony must end!'

A ripple of confused murmuring passed amongst the nymphs.

'But what of Melea? Will she not be disappointed? And will her wrath not be terrible?' asked Lucilla.

Anima laughed. I decided to let her speak, since they respected their goddess more, and my words had only served to rile them.

'The sacrifices were never dedicated to Melea. Melea is a benign deity of fertility and the harvest. She demands no human sacrifice.'

A collective gasp of astonishment.

'Then who were we sacrificing the children to?'

Anima sighed.

'No one.'

Another confused murmur.

'For you see, ladies, your queen has failed you. I was tricked into creating the black wedding and black baptism by a wicked wizard, who promised us bounteous harvests and ample food in exchange for sacrifices. It was he who destroyed our harvests, not Melea.'

'You mean Mentor?' asked Lucilla.

Anima sighed.

'It was he.'

'But why?? Why would Mentor have us do such things?'

'That is what I mean to find out. Ego and I have defeated him in battle. He is wounded and in our custody.'

By now the blood of nymphs and men alike had cooled considerably and few were still in the mood for a fight; most were confused by the revelations. Everything they had believed in was revealed to be a pack of lies.

'Do not be disheartened. The cessation of the rituals shall be no loss to us. In truth, it shall be a boon. Think about it. Would you not rather have healthy vigorous husbands, able to share in your labours, than invalids and dotards who serve as a constant reminder of your guilt? Would you not rather let your illegitimate children grow and flourish, instead of drowning them before they see their second summer?'

The women considered her words. It was a lot to take in, but already they could see the obvious logic of her arguments.

'But what shall we do? With – the men,' asked another nymph, with a coy glance at the muscular half-naked spear-wielders who surrounded them.

'Go, set down your snakes and phalluses and speak to the men as equals, as humans.'

'But how shall we wed, if not by the black wedding?' asked a small nymph with long black hair.

'Things are different in the lands beyond the sea. There, the weddings are white, not black. Man and wife are bound by rings and vows,' she grasped my hand and gazed at me tenderly. 'Ego and I declare ourselves married, and the consummation shall be an act of love, in the privacy of our palace, not ritual violence, committed beneath the stars like animals! The goddess has spoken!' she said, striding forward with me at her side.

The nymphs parted for us, slightly awed.

Even I had no idea we were to be married! Let alone that the declaration was to be made by her, in so dramatic a fashion.

'I don't suppose there's any chance I could have time to consider your proposal?' I jested.

She slapped my thigh.

When we reached the edge of the glade, we turned and watched. The nymphs and men had followed our example. They had paired off and begun talking, laughing and joking. A few couples were even making for the privacy of the trees. All appeared to at least be willing to get along.

Except for a small clique of three nymphs, who remained aloof and refused to fraternise with the men, meeting their greetings with cold sneers and harsh words.

'It is well,' she said, smiling at me.

'What of those three?' I asked.

'If only three grumble at the reform, it has gone better than expected.'

We proceeded to the palace with a detachment of ten armed men, who were reluctant to leave the nymphs. This was sufficient to cow the priests, who accepted Anima's changes meekly. Anima retrieved two ruby-set golden rings for our ceremony, and I told Phidias some basic Aeonian wedding vows. He recited them monotonously, I kissed Anima, and we were man and wife.

We made love in the bedchamber; and again, in the central pool of the courtyard, the pool of stone where the serpents met.

Chapter 22: Truth Enough to Choke On

'How is he?' I asked.

'Better. He was sitting up earlier, and his spine is almost healed. He will be out of bed by tomorrow,' answered Anima, in her nurse's apron emblazoned with the red cross.

'So soon?'

She nodded.

'He is immortal.'

'Now I see where you get it from.'

She smiled, sadly.

'It is my gift and my curse to be my father's daughter.'

It was the morning of the following day. We were standing beside a pillar in the snake-temple. The ward was empty except for the old man and a few insensible, long-suffering dotards still reeling from their black weddings. The old woman, Agatha, was sat at Mentor's bedside, feeding him porridge. The wizard slurped it down horribly through his puffy, chapped lips. Agatha sneered in disgust.

'I'll let you get away with your beastly table manners just this once, since you're injured an' all.'

'Thank you, my dear,' the old man croaked. 'You're too good to me, you know that?'

The harridan's wrinkled face cracked into a sentimental smile.

'Aw, stop eet! Yer just sayin' that to get me inter that bed with yer!'

The old man grinned sheepishly.

'Nonsense, there's only room for one: unless you were to go on top!'

'You old lech! I knew it!'

'I readily confess my guilt!'

They giggled together like lustful youths. I saw Anima shudder in disgust.

I stared at him. Out of his brown rags, he was a mighty creature. The fur-blankets came up to his navel. The shoulders were incredibly broad and the muscles beneath the slack skin and large, hairy nipples were taut. I was also struck by the size of the man, laid out like that. His massive feet hung off the end of the bed. I was over six feet tall and hadn't had such a problem during my sojourn in the house of Esklepios. His stoop concealed it, but Mentor was nearly seven feet tall!

'That's not all you're guilty of, is it?' I said, stepping forward into the rectangular patch of sunlight beside the old man's sickbed.

Mentor turned to me, a look of sad grandfatherly contrition on his face.

'My boy—'

'Don't *boy* me!'

The old man was about to snap back at me, then held his tongue.

'As you wish – your majesty,' he said, with uncharacteristic meekness. 'I shall explain it all. But first, could you give me some wine?'

'No. You may drink the truth-water though,' I said, passing him the skin. Anima had prepared a special, god-strength concoction, using the old man's herblore against him. Unbeknownst to him, his bandages had been lined with the truth-herbs too, while he was unconscious.

He sighed, wearily.

'Very well, you are the victor, after all,' he said, and took a long swig.

'Speak,' Anima said, her face stony.

'Yes, daughter, I am so very sorry—'

'Speak!' I interjected, pointing the wand in his face.

'Well, apologies are in order, for I am responsible - though only in part, as shall be seen – for all that has happened to you two so far in your respective journeys. Anima, I bewitched you, isolated you from men, and tricked you into committing horrible crimes.'

'Medoc – he's not even real, is he?' she demanded.

The old man swallowed, staring at his daughter with eyes of fear.

'No.'

'Then why? Why the sacrifices?' she demanded, stepping toward him with balled fists. I placed a restraining hand on her shoulder.

'The truth is, I wanted to keep you safe – keep you to myself,' he admitted, sheepishly. 'I am grown lonely in my old age and you are a jewel of a daughter!'

'That could have been done without slaughtering countless babes in arms!'

Mentor shook his head. Tears welled in his baggy, bloodshot old eyes.

'You're right. I wanted control of this island! I had you castrate the men and kill the infants to keep the numbers down, specifically the number of able-bodied male inhabitants.'

'Why?'

'Isn't it obvious? To prevent rebellions from breaking out. Ever and anon it is the men who stir up trouble in the state; the men who mount rebellions, turn assassin, and commit most of the crimes! Women are on the whole far too clever to go around plotting such nonsense. I thought if I kept the men down, your throne – and my occult power – would be secure.'

'And yet it was a woman who helped bring you down,' Anima said, stonily.

'Yes, I underestimated you. Please, daughter, forgive a poor old fool!'

'We have not heard it all yet! Once your confession is complete, only *then* can we can talk about forgiveness!' she said, arms folded.

'You placed her on the throne so that she could take the brunt of any such rebellion, while you were safe under the guise of Mentor the Madman – Mentor the rambling old fool. Isn't that so?' I asked, jabbing the staff in his face.

'Alright, I admit it, I'm a stinking misbegotten coward who hides behind his own daughter! Are you happy now, high and mighty king!' he said, with real bitterness. 'The truth is, I hate to rule. I hate to deal with people – mortals and gods alike. I hate and fear them and they hate me! I much prefer the seclusion of the forest, with my alchemical books and my alembics—'

'And your abominations!'

'Yes, those too. For they are no idle hobby!' he said, waving a long, bony index finger. 'Oh no!'

'What are they then?' I asked, unconvinced.

'They are attempts to bring a new God into being. A mighty God that may overthrow the old gods and reign in their stead!' he boomed, grand and oratorical once more. 'The people hate the old gods; they are corrupt and venal and steal their daughters and take sacrifices without gratitude! While mortals fester and starve they wine and dine and fuck away to their heart's content atop their lofty mountains and pyramids, living in idle splendour and decadence! I hate the old gods and would rip their world asunder if it meant I could rule in their stead – even if via the proxy of a god-child!' he thundered, tears streaming down his jowls.

'Why do you hate the old gods?'

'You see, I was once of their number. But I was born a mortal man.'

'A mortal man?' I asked, intrigued. For all his talk of gods and demigods, I had never stopped to ponder Mentor's bloodline.

He nodded, gravely.

'It is so. I was among the first wise men to leave the shackles of humanity behind and elevate myself to the rarefied air of godhood through sacred wisdom. I was fortunate enough to be born into a golden age, where the knowledge, far from being forbidden, was actively taught in the academies. Even so, only a tiny intellectual and moral elite were capable of reaching the highest levels of spiritual attainment. I established contact with the other new deities, first telepathically, then in person, and we conspired to seize power in the state. It was no difficult thing, given our abilities and the freedoms we enjoyed at the time. But as the centuries and millennia wore on, the gods grew corrupt. They lost interest in bettering mankind and thought only of their own pleasures and prestige. I counselled them, warned them of the danger; but they were grown haughty and refused to listen. The Great Revolt followed; thousands of men were killed, a god, and three demigods.'

'There were demigods back then?'

'Oh yes, for the gods in their lust had lain with the daughters of men and broken the purity of their cast. It was an immortal, Astarxes, who led the rebellion. He was executed, along with countless mortal followers, when we put the revolt down. We threw him into a volcano: the only way to kill a full-blooded god. It is a strange and horrifying thing, to kill a god. They take days, sometimes weeks, to die. His cries could be heard for a month afterwards, rippling down the black valleys,' he said, shaking his head ruefully. 'I tried to persuade the gods to mildness and clemency, but after seeing their brothers and sisters killed, they wanted blood. Afterwards, their restless, boundless minds turned exclusively to the problem of power. Thus began the Age of Building. Grand monuments, new chariots and mighty weapons were constructed, and a race of homunculi was spawned, and trained to guard us against an increasingly unruly humanity. For the homunculi were soulless, void of free will and did our bidding like disciplined hounds. But, like dogs, they were bestial in their cruelty and occasionally unpredictable. That is why the gods have refrained from bringing them back, after the Deluge.'

'And you wish to resurrect such horrors?' I asked.

'The homunculi were bestial, yes, but some of the overseers were monstrously intelligent, with wits to rival a demigod, and the greater part were industrious workers; being soulless, they didn't need sleep. Lacking manpower as I do here in my exile, of late I have sought to use the gods' old weapons against them. For how else am I to raise an army?'

'What other weapons do you speak of?'

'The red stones,' he said, his face terrifyingly grim and haggard. 'They were mined, fashioned and consecrated by the great smith of the gods, Heaston, in his mighty forge Drimulpir, which lay in the deepest bowels of the earth. All this was done at the behest of a mighty god named Archon the Dread, a materialisation of the demon Zorimahn.'

'If the red stones possess such power, why do you then have such an ugly, plain stone set in the crook of your staff?'

'That stone,' the old man said, nodding at the tip of the staff, 'is a fragment from the ruins of the Great Temple of Atlantea. I visited the site, when the waters abated. I took three stones in all, but the others were lost during my travails. It holds twice the power of a red stone, though it was rejected as misshapen by the builders of the temple, *and* by the shipwrecked crew I set to building the Palace of Sun and Moon on this island, so I decided to keep it for myself.'

'*Men* built these halls?' I asked, staggered.

'With the help of my telekinesis, yes, and the power of the Stones of Destiny.'

'But these stones were used to keep the masses in line?' Anima asked.

'The crystals powered our cities and chariots, but could also be used as weapons, to eradicate any rebellious cities or regions; once, we destroyed an entire planet colony for refusing to pay tribute!' He shook his head in shame at the folly and pride of the gods.

'Your civilisation spanned multiple planets?' I asked, aghast.

'Oh yes, for love of matter had made us mighty. Sacrifices were made to Zorimahn The Deceiver, every manner of perversion was indulged in his name, and in exchange he spoke through our greatest sages, giving us the knowledge necessary to extend our dominion to the stars! *He* was the one who showed us where to mine the crystals that became our principal energy source. But the stones were a curse, I tell you! A curse!' At this, he broke down weeping.

Agatha placed a tender hand on his broad, muscular shoulder and he clasped it greedily, unashamed at his tears.

He went on: 'There was a rebellion, in the south. The god Archon, who had become our world-emperor, tried to use his giant stone to quell the humans. But something went wrong. I know not what. An accident, most likely, for too much labour had been entrusted to mindless homunculi. The result was the Great Deluge. Half the world was submerged beneath the waves; a giant wall of green water devoured all in its path; cities were engulfed and wasted; billions were drowned! But we gods in our *foresight and wisdom,*' he said the words with bitter irony, 'had prepared against such an eventuality. We retreated in our chariots to the high and dry places, the mountains and deserts safe from the flooding. Some demigods were consumed by the consequences of their own monstrous pride and folly, but alas, we are a hardy, cunning race and to the detriment of humanity, the greater part of us survived.

After the flood, a council of the gods was called on the Pyramid of Magirov, for Magirov and the surrounding desert plateau had remained largely dry. I wanted to spread the sacred wisdom and the forgotten knowledge of harvest, building and drainage. For we gods had hoarded it to ourselves and grown proud in our splendour! Our power had corrupted us, rendered us exploiters and destroyers of humanity. I wanted to give humanity the chance to join us on our pedestal, to rebuild Atlantea anew, without the glaring inequities and resentments of the old empire. But alas, the other gods got wind of me sewing my seeds and spreading my word...They feared that if even *they* had not the moral strength to control their powers, lowly *mortals* would surely fail the test and destroy the world anew in the ensuing cataclysm! This is what they said, though naturally, they also wished to keep humanity ignorant that they may maintain their stranglehold on

252

world-power. So I was tried, in Magirov, and they banished me to the farthest chasm of the underworld for a thousand years! I was bound with ropes. By wile and trickery, I managed to escape, for I had ample time to plot,' he chuckled, bitterly. 'I provoked my gaoler, the five-headed dragon Smolnir, into burning me – yes, I burned, but so did my bonds! I was free! But I needed someplace to recuperate from my burns and escape the gods' watchful eyes, and so I exiled myself to a remote isle in the Olearic Sea, a helpless onlooker to the thraldom and misery of the world they have re-created!

Here, on the deserted isle of Tyria, I healed myself with the sacred wisdom and had a passing merchant ship wrecked on the rocks, that the crew might swim ashore and help me in my labours. Together we constructed the snake-temple, dedicated to Esklepios. Then I set about building myself a palace, with marble and quartz quarried from the isle's green mountains. But I grew lonely in my paradise. Yes, even I, Mentor the Hermit, grew lonely! So I created a storm that blew a local fisherwoman ashore. I healed her wounds and took her into my palace and made her my wife.'

Anima glanced suspiciously at her mother.

'Were you involved in this?'

Agatha gawped at her daughter.

'Involved in whut?'

'Keeping me here, against my will?'

The old woman grumbled and grimaced.

'I lurned long ago there's no sense in loyin' ter you. Aye, I didn't want you to leave the oisland neither. I didn't care for power or nuthin', but I wanted to keep you here. You're my little gurl – cain't have you wanderin' the wide world in your slinky little peplos! You'd be raped!'

'I'm a goddess, mother – I can overpower any man!'

253

'It's not the men that concerned me – it's them blasted Magirov gods! Horny beggars they are, and, goddess or no, they don't ask nicely when they wanna take a gurl to bed!!' she said, bottom lip quivering with motherly devotion.

'You are just as craven as he, crone,' Anima said, contemptuously

'Watch her mouf, yang laydy!' Agatha snapped; she slapped her daughter, reflexively. Then she came over all contrite. 'Though mayhaps I desurv yer reproach.'

'And what of me?' I asked.

'You? Ah yes, *you*,' said the old man, with a secret smile. 'You want the truth, do you?'

'Yes!'

'Above your peace of mind? Above all else?' He raised a shaggy eyebrow.

'Yes!'

'I shall give you truth enough to choke on, mighty one!' Mentor said, cackling.

'Enough crooked words!' I boomed. My countenance was of thunder.

'Have it your way,' he said, as if his hands were clean, now he had tried to warn me. 'Well, you see, I built a ship for the priest Phidias, the boldest of that sorry bunch of old maids from the merchantman, and sent him and a small crew across the Olearic Sea.'

'So the priests were once merchants?'

'Some of them. Others were lost fishermen. Over the centuries, we've had more than a few castaways wash up on our shores.'

'Why does Phidias think you a mere herbalist, if he saw you build the palace with your mind? Or did he lie to me?'

'Do not blame him, for he knows no better. Anima cast a spell on the early castaways; made them forget themselves, and my powers.'

'Why?' I asked, staring at Anima, though I feared I already knew the answer.

'It is hard to rule if you admit there is one greater than you in the kingdom, and your subjects remember their true home lies elsewhere. Isn't that right, daughter?'

She blushed and stared at the floor.

'Anyway, where was I? Oh yes. Phidias and his crew had set sail. I ensured they had propitious weather. He reached Aeonia and found Nero, offering gold and the promise of more. Nero, avaricious as he is, accepted. He voyaged here and stayed with us for three years before returning home.'

'So that is why he was entrusted with the position of beast-master!? He was no stranger at all!'

'No, no stranger at all,' the old man repeated, with a wry grin. 'For he is my son!'

'Wait – if he is your son. And he and I are brothers—'

'I am your father.'

My mouth fell open.

'No — no, it can't be!' I gasped in horror, as if physically struck.

'It is.'

'Then that means—'

'Anima is your half-sister,' the old man said, grinning sadistically through his thick beard.

I stepped away from Anima and scrutinised her face; my countenance, only female – that explained it! It was family resemblance!

'How —'

'Allow me to explain,' the old man said, holding up a huge hand. 'Before Anima's confining spell was laid upon me, I was travelling in Aeonia, disguised as a vagabond. I wished to judge the mood of the people; whether the time was ripe to incite a revolt against the resident deity Xarcas. I needed a place to stay for the night and your mother's house was the nearest. Your father was away, fighting in the war – I invoked the law of hospitality and she obliged me,' he said, with infuriating innuendo.

'You bastard!' I shouted.

Mentor raised his eyebrows, suggestively. 'No, I'm afraid that you are *my* bastard.'

I jerked the staff at him. The hand of death tightened around his throat, leaving red marks.

'Don't give me truth-water if you don't want the truth!' he said, choking. He was still grinning, though his face was red as a beetroot.

Anima placed her hand on my arm.

'Don't. Let him finish. *Then* he shall be punished!'

I released my stranglehold and rounded on her.

'Did *you* know about all this? *Sister*?!'

'She was privy to the plan to draw you here, since by then Phidias would never have set sail without her sanction, but she knew not that you were her half-brother. And, may I say, she is taking it a good deal better than you!' the old man said, coughing.

'Yes, you are! Altogether too well!' I fumed, casting a sidelong look at my long-lost relation.

'I was raised a goddess. It is common amongst the gods for cousins and siblings to wed, since there are so few of us and we have a sacred duty to keep the bloodline pure.'

'Yes, it is very dangerous to spread the blood – very dangerous indeed. A race of half-breeds sprung up in Atlantea and caused all manner of trouble. We appointed them kings and governors, but they often abused their power. For they had the power of gods twinned with the weakness and stupidity of men! They were an embarrassment to us all with their corruption and rapaciousness and proved devilishly resentful of their fathers' yoke. When they rose up in revolt, they were fiendish difficult to quell, for they fought like gods!'

'I am a half-breed! So is Anima!'

'You are different. You are *my* children. You have inherited my wisdom and temperance.'

'Wisdom! It sounds as though you were a blundering old fool who did nought with your prestige but wreak havoc and fail to avert catastrophe!' I thundered, my face reddening.

'Silence! I may be your prisoner, but I am also your father! As such, I deserve respect and a fair hearing! For I am ancient and have seen many worlds come and go!' he said. A frightful coldness settled across the room; the sun disappeared behind a cloud.

'Very well, old man. Tell me why it is that you, in your boundless godly wisdom, saw fit to encourage me that I might fuck my half-sister!' The hatred laid heavily upon me, like a desert curse.

'I did a sight more than that,' Mentor said, shamelessly. 'Through proxies, I paid Nero to lure you aboard ship. I instructed him to make your life a nightmare of torment and misery; I even told him how to turn the others against you. I spread the pestilence aboard ship and appointed that godawful hacklimb ship's doctor – for *I owned* the ship! I summoned the storm that wrecked you near Tyria and broke your back. Only then did I educate and embolden you to fuck your half-sister. So you see – I am the architect of all your woe!' he shouted, his thick lips curling back in sadistic glee, as if he was scarcely able to repress a bout of gummy laughter.

257

'You lie!' I thundered, as bulls and demons chased each other around my mind.

'I tell the truth! I can do nought else, thanks to the herbs – and even if I could lie, your sister would know it, for she has the gift.'

I roared, consumed by blind fury, and jerked the staff; a dragon's tongue of flame shot from the ugly stone. Before it could lick Mentor's face, a splash of water shot from Anima's wand, extinguishing the fire. The red stone was pointed at my chest. Her face was stony and forbidding.

'Let the old man speak! For it is more than the riddle of your life that he reveals! And I too, have a right to know!'

'Listen to your sister; she is your superior in age and wisdom,' Mentor said, grinning.

'Gah! What is the meaning of it all?! Did you work all this mischief merely for your own amusement?' I screamed, staggering away and clutching my head.

'The meaning? You know the meaning, my boy! You were put through the torments of the damned – trials that would crush lesser men – indeed, most men. You were forced to do the impossible – to overcome broken spine, plague, starvation, thirst, guilt, grief, the tyranny of your half-brother, the wiles of your Unknown Mind and even your own humanity – that you would be wise and strong enough to consort with a goddess!'

'No one can control so much!' I laughed, hysterically. 'This is preposterous!! You are mad!'

'Not as preposterous as the notion that you, a wastrel who lived off his mother's charity, could be wise and strong enough to elevate himself to the lofty heights of royalty and godhood!' he said, scornful in the fire of his wrath. 'Come, be honest – do you really think you could have got this far by yourself!' the old man said, with a patronising smile.

'I did not consent to be the plaything of an evil god!' I thundered, my voice grown hoarse with shouting. 'Have you no respect for human dignity? For human freedom?'

'Oh, but I did not act without consent. Like everyone you have encountered on your odyssey and in your life, I am merely an externalisation of some secret force within your Unknown Mind.'

'Do not cloud my head with your damned jargon! Speak plainly or die!' I yelled.

'I have not done anything to you that you did not really want!'

'No!' I cried, my voice breaking like a weak pubescent, for I knew in my heart he was right.

'Yes! You willed it so! Admit it! Say it!' the old man demanded, sitting up in bed.

'No,' I said, my face twisting in grief as I slumped to the floor.

'Enough! Leave him be,' Anima interjected.

The old man lay back, palms raised.

'Why *us*?' she asked, somewhat shaken, though trying not to show it.

'I sought the conception of a new God,' he said, simply, as if nothing could be more noble.

'What – our incest is to create a new God?' I asked, stunned.

'Yes,' the old man said. 'For you are both demigods, with a divine father and mortal mother. The resulting offspring will be a half-god born of half-gods; a thoroughbred demigod. For God lies in the centre between opposites – male and female, Known and Unknown Mind, human and god. For this reason, the human-god is

259

more of a god, is more *central* in the grand scheme, than a full-blooded deity such as myself. But there are other considerations, of a more spiritual nature.'

'What does that mean?' Anima demanded, trying her best to keep her voice level, though she was burning with rage and morbid curiosity.

'At the dawn of time, you two were one. Then, with the Fall into Matter, you separated into male and female halves, but throughout your various lives you have always been together, fighting and loving, complementing and contradicting, whether as mother and son, father and daughter, husband and wife – and now half-brother and half-sister. Your unknown family relation, combined with your shared spiritual history, made you perfect embodiments of each other's Unknown Minds – contra-sexual doppelgangers, if you will – and thus created ideal conditions for obsession – for love – and for self-knowledge.'

'Self-knowledge?'

'Oh yes – you were thrown together that you might see yourselves – from the outside, then the inside. All of these elements – blood, spirit and wisdom – were prerequisites for the conception of the god that quickens within your womb as we speak!'

'How can you be so sure?' Anima asked, clutching her abdomen instinctively, and not without trepidation.

'The first time you fornicated, I was performing a sacrifice, in the secret tunnel behind the wall; a rabbit was killed, silently.'

My anger was spent; I was hit by a wave of nausea. The old man, my birth father, revolted me.

'You must be a demon, that you are so depraved!' Anima said. She had remained even-tempered hitherto, but at last she could hold her tongue no more.

'Easy, daughter, I did only what was necessary for the age!'

'You did what was necessary to satisfy your own depraved appetites and your all-consuming lust for revenge!'

'No! You misunderstand me. The god in your womb is prophesied to one day overthrow the old gods and end their reign of cruelty and injustice, ushering in an age of freedom and plenty for humanity – just as Ego here is prophesied to overthrow the tyrant of Aeonia!'

'What?' I asked. I could not take much more. The blood was gone from my face; I felt as if I was going to vomit.

'All the kings of Aconia trace their lineage back to me, just as all the kings and aristocracy of the world have some measure of godsblood, descended as they are from the original race of half-breeds. Well, there is an ancient and well-known prophesy, made by the Seer of Alesia, that during a time of civil war, when a usurper sits the throne, the rightful king will return to Aeonia from across the sea with the Stone of Destiny.'

'Wait! There is civil war in Aeonia?' I asked, bewildered.

'In your absence, the King of Aeonia was assassinated by his chief bodyguard Myconas, who assumed power as the tyrant, Thraxa the Cruel. A civil war rages between the royalists and the tyrant's followers. Famine and plague ravage the land. Your mother suffers – she has the forgetting sickness!'

'Forgetting sickness!' I grew frantic and light-headed.

'Yes, she is very ill. Your aunt does what she can, but she has her own family to think of. Your mother spends her days wandering the market, lost. Sometimes she cannot even find her way home and must throw herself on the charity of strangers. All this while soldiers burn and pillage the land!'

'You lie! It can't be true! Can it?' I turned to Anima with the terrified eyes of a child.

She nodded, gravely, and placed a hand on my shoulder – a sisterly hand.

'So you see, you *must* return! And soon!'

I fainted.

Chapter 23: Inner and Outer

It wasn't long before I came to, on the cold marble floor. Agatha and Anima helped me up and I took the bed next to Mentor's. I sensed sharp words had been exchanged with the women, for his manner was altered. He no longer seemed sadistic and superior; instead, he was fatherly and contrite.

'I'm sorry, my boy.'

'Sorry for what?' I groaned, my head pounding.

'Sorry you had such a hard road to tread.'

'You do not regret your actions?' I said, thickly.

He shook his head.

'No. For no other road would have led you here, and I can see the glorious bounty that awaits us all at road's end.' At this, his features misted over in blissful serenity.

I considered asking about this bounty, but decided against it.

'Such an end would justify any road,' he continued, allusively. 'But I always knew you would prevail. That you would triumph and overcome all the challenges I sent your way.'

'There was a risk I would be killed or castrated. You cannot foresee *everything*,' I said.

'That is true. We can only be certain of our fate once it is accomplished. But in my heart, I always suspected you were too wise to miss the mark – or rather, your will was too strong, for the intellect is merely the child of the will. I *wanted* you to see through the glitter-haze of your half-sister's bewitchment and take the throne.'

Anima bristled at that. Against my will, I felt a glow of pride. Did that mean I was father's favourite?

'But you never thought I would see through you, too, right? It never crossed your mighty mind that the wisdom you gave me could be turned on its promulgator?' I said, with a defiant grin.

Mentor frowned.

'I hoped you would be so seduced by the powers I *awakened in you*, that you would mistake them for your own. Few men who work miracles can resist the temptation of thinking themselves superior and getting drunk on the wine of their hauteur. But you proved wiser than I thought.'

'If I am so wise, why did I have to be tricked into doing your will?'

The old man thought before answering; he was a crafty devil, of that there could be no doubt.

'If you had known Anima was your half-sister, would you have lain with her?' he said, bushy eyebrow raised.

'No!' I cried, revolted.

The old man shrugged.

'You have your answer,' he said, as if my supposed bigotry justified any deceit.

The old anger stirred in my breast, but I let it slumber, for I was drained and wearied.

'I feel so stupid. I thought myself a bold and powerful king, but in truth, I was merely your plaything,' I said, bitterly.

'I could only manipulate you into this position because it was your fate. I merely administered what heaven had already decreed. Should I have failed to bring you so far, you would have got here by a different road.'

The old man's words had the ring of truth about them. It was a strange truth, consoling yet disheartening.

'Do we have *any* free will or are we entirely shackled by the law of Fate?' I asked.

Mentor sighed. He looked at me, shrewdly, and said:

'A man was fated to reach the end of a road. He could have walked there directly but he did not, because he knew not his fate: he never asked. One day, he was beset by bandits and dragged to the end of the road behind the horses of the bandits. Therefore, we are free only to embrace or resist our fate.'

I considered his words carefully.

'So I could have spared myself and everyone else the shipwreck if I'd only set sail for Tyria from the very beginning?'

'Theoretically, yes. In practice, no.'

'What does that mean?'

'You didn't know where Tyria was.'

'And if I had?'

'You didn't know your fate or understand how life works.'

'I do now. Does that give me the capacity to choose?' I asked, wondering whether I should return to Aeonia and fulfil Mentor's prophecy or not.

The old man shrugged.

'*If* you are no longer asleep, you may give the charioteer a rest and take up your own reins.'

'What a burden you have laid upon me!' I wailed.

'It is hard to drive yourself, but it is harder still to be a passenger, for the charioteer is half-blind and is wont to choose the longest and bumpiest of roads to the destination.'

'So if I do not go to fulfil the prophecy voluntarily, I will be forced by bitter circumstance to return to Aeonia?' I asked, despair creeping into my voice.

Mentor nodded. His face was grim.

'You cannot seriously believe this sophistry? After all the lies he has told?' Anima asked, horrified.

'It is not sophistry!' The old man objected, heatedly. 'A sophist would tell you what you want to hear; I do the opposite.'

'Exactly, you seek to make us feel miserable and helpless, that we might resign ourselves to your will.'

'Fate is rarely desirable; that is why so few go to her willingly. You cannot blame me for that!'

'And who are *you* to tell us our fate?'

'Perhaps it *is* sophistry. I don't know. I need to get out of here,' I said, lifting myself out of bed and stumbling across the temple, careful to avoid the snakes on the cold floor. I'd had enough madness and truth for one day.

Outside, the birds were tweeting. It was a sunny day with fluffy white clouds scattered across a deep blue sky.

Anima appeared at my side.

'This changes things between us,' she said. It was not a question.

'Yes, it does.' I was still unable to look her in the eye, since we had been told of our hidden relation. Of all the old man's revelations, that is the one I never doubted, for it explained so much. 'We should annul the marriage.'

'Why?' she asked, dismayed.

'Well, don't you want to?' I asked, astonished. 'I *am* your half-brother.'

'I told you; it is normal, customary even amongst gods for brother and sister to wed.'

'I may be a god, but I was raised mortal and *I* keep mortal customs,' I said, with an air of moral superiority.

'Well, in any case, there are no annulments in Tyria,' she said, defensively. 'Though if you are adamant, as king I suppose an exception could be made for you…' she trailed off, her lovely face clouded with care.

'What? What is it?'

'What about the child?'

I scoffed.

'You said it yourself: the old man is a liar. He lies like he breathes. Chances are, there will be no child.'

'But what if there is?'

I turned to face her. She looked anguished.

'What would you want to do with it?' I asked.

'I would raise the child to be our heir.'

I was speechless. I hadn't thought that far ahead, though on reflection, it seemed quite natural Anima should wish to raise her own flesh and blood and secure the child's future. I had only just learned to take care of myself and felt unspeakable dread at the prospect of fatherhood.

'Wouldn't it be a lot of work, taking care of a dependent child?'

'I've been doing it for years.'

'Oh, and where are these children of yours?'

'All my men are children.'

'Are they really so infantile, or did you make them so?' I asked, wryly.

'Well, one of them grew up. Though sometimes I wonder,' she said, grinning at me.

Her smile was like a beam of sunshine in the midst of a storm.

We laughed. The path narrowed between flower beds: roses and hyacinths.

'You know, I have another dream to tell you of.'

'Really? It's been quite a while since I heard your last one.'

We strolled down the gravelled, cypress-lined path. Memories of our early talks here in the gardens of Esklepios came flooding back to me; the snakes lay silent in the grass.

'Oh, there have been many since then. No, I tell you of this one, because you featured in it.'

'Did I now? Is this appropriate to tell your half-sister?' she chided, mocking my mortal inhibitions.

'Not really. But we are past inappropriate, aren't we?'

She giggled. 'I would say so.'

Briefly, I felt the old desire stir again; then I crushed it mercilessly under the leaden weight of taboo.

'Well, in the dream, you beckoned me to your bedchamber.'

'So far, so incestuous.'

'But when I got inside, Mentor was stood there.'

'What next? Your half-brother??'

I gave her a playful nudge.

'The old man was wearing your peplos, and your skin and hair lay discarded on the floor.'

She stopped dead, serious all of a sudden.

'I know, it is strange,' I said, a little ashamed. 'But it would not be a dream if it was not strange.'

She remained silent.

'What do you think it means?' she asked, finally, in a mousy voice.

'Well, the dream helped me to realise he was manipulating you – controlling you.'

'*And* you,' she said, defensively.

'Yes, and me. But I suspect there's more to it than that. What do you think?'

268

'You have interpreted the dream on the external level. But there is an internal level.'

Then it all fell into place.

'Oh!'

'What??'

'You represent my Unknown Mind – particularly my Inner Woman, right?'

'I think my – *our* father made that clear.'

'And he said that he was an externalisation of something in my Unknown Mind, too. Something male in character.'

'Yes.'

'Well, in the dream, Mentor was *within* you; under your skin. You were effectively his puppet; he was acting *through* you. What if, just as Mentor manipulated you in the outer world, my *Inner* Woman has her own Unknown Mind? Her own inner opposite? An Inner Man – an Inner Mentor, if you will.'

'That makes sense. Everything has its opposite. Opposites are the structure of reality.'

'And just as I was possessed and controlled by my Inner Woman – via my obsession with you – my Inner Woman was possessed by her own Unknown Mind, her Inner Man, her own inner opposite.'

'Yes, and as the outer manifestation of your Inner Woman, I can tell you I do have an Inner Man whose character and designs correspond pretty well to Mentor in the outer world,' she said, regretfully. 'While I was unaware Mentor was deceiving me and my Inner Man possessed me, they were able to manipulate me – the one from the outside, the other from within – by making me think badly of you; for evil thrives in darkness. That is why I wanted to kill you: I believed Mentor and the Inner Man when they said you hated me and plotted my demise, when really, it was *they* who sought to undermine my throne, and you were merely their unsuspecting puppet.'

I bridled silently at that last epithet, but bit my tongue, since I had called her the same.

'The turning point came when I made you aware of Mentor's trickery,' I said, seeking to restore lost pride.

'Yes, by making me aware of the trickery of Mentor, you made our alliance possible. Because he was controlling me *through* you, my gaoler, and you *through* me, your bewitcher. As soon as I was no longer ignorant of his malign designs, he could no longer bewitch me – because then I could see through his lies.'

'And as soon as I saw how he had misled you and misrepresented your intentions, his spell over *me* was broken as well,' I said. 'Only then, could we at last recognise our common foe and our common interest in overthrowing him. But all this is external; the play of shadows on the cave wall. There was a parallel process going on *inside of us*; and Mentor could only control us because he represented something or someone within ourselves that we were not aware of – until now. You could call that someone your Inner Man, and the Inner Man of my Inner Woman.'

'Yes, that sounds right. I only sought to control you because I was unaware Mentor and my Inner Man were lying to me about you, the former by poisoning me against you, the latter by making me see his evil in you. He flooded me with suspicious *thoughts* of you. Usually I feel more than I think – the old man would say this makes thinking my Rejected Stone.'

'But you are not stupid; far from it, you are the most intelligent person I have ever met, save perhaps Mentor, and we bested him.'

A snake lay across our path, basking in the midday sun. It may have been asleep, for it did not stir, even as we drew near.

'My thoughts are not weak compared to the thoughts of others; I just prefer to feel, to empathise. Hence my thoughts come largely from the Unknown Mind, and my Inner Man. This Inner Man made my thoughts of you suspicious, deprecatory and malicious; made me think you a murderous idler, and a lowly mortal, not fit to consort with a goddess such as myself. These critical thoughts were used by the Inner Man to keep my natural sympathy suppressed; to strike it down mercilessly and make me cold and cruel towards you.'

'The Inner Man of my Inner Woman played me against you by means of emotion: chiefly, anger,' I confessed. 'Probably because I am not good with feelings; I prefer to suppress them. Even after my indoctrination in healing magic, which did much to improve my awareness of hidden emotions, I still think better and more often than I feel.'

'Mentor and the Inner Man exploited our weaknesses, our Rejected Stones.'

I nodded. The snake slithered away, letting us continue along the path.

'He made us seem dangerous and hostile to each other because of our differences; because my strengths are your weaknesses and your strengths are my weaknesses. Since my feelings are mostly hostile and angry, and you are a feeler, he made me *think* that you bore me ill will,' I said, lost in a labyrinth of abstract thought, yet determined to find the fountain in the centre.

'Since my thoughts are mostly critical or scheming, and you are a thinker, my Inner Man made me suspect you of unbecoming hauteur and malign designs.'

'Meanwhile, the positive sides of our thinking and feeling went unappreciated.'

'And our commonalities remained unknown or suppressed, driving us to distraction and conflict.'

'And what – nay, who – was it that made us akin?' I asked, seeing how the pieces fit together.

'Mentor.'

Rabbits frolicked on the grass.

'*He* was our unknown commonality; our missing, hidden link. Now we *know* we share a father, we no longer obsess and distract one another with desire – I hope,' she said, with a mischievous smirk.

'You desired me to distraction?' I asked, astonished. 'I was under the impression you either hated me or were completely uninterested.'

'You were mistaken,' she said, staring at me with an ambiguous expression in her placid green eyes.

'You didn't show it!'

'You didn't show much of your desire, either.'

'I wrote you love poems!'

'That was your job! A job *I* gave you! That should have been a clue to you!'

'I ranted and raved at you – and you ignored me!'

'Just because the waters are still, does not mean they are shallow.'

'You maddening sphinx!' I said, exasperated.

She shrugged, grinning.

'Some mortal women veil their hearts and play tricks on their men. Why should goddesses be any different?' she said, with a secret grin.

'They aren't. They're just better at it.'

272

She laughed. 'My desire is more controlled than yours I think, which has something of the Unknown Mind about it – something wild.'

'Whatever gave you that idea?' I said, with a roguish grin.

She giggled and blushed. The memories of last night came flooding back – quickly followed by the shame of having done these things with my half-sister.

'Though we cannot be lovers anymore, I hope we can remain close,' I said, growing serious.

Anima stopped dead.

'Of course. I love you,' she said, her eyes welling with tears.

'I love you too – sister,' I said, uneasily, taken aback by the words I had never thought I would hear from her lips.

We embraced. Her grip on my back was tenacious, and when she finally released me, I saw she was still crying.

We came to the pavilion and sat down on the bench, overlooking the snake-temple: site of my resurrection.

After a long silence, in which I pondered her wish to stay married and her concerns about having a child, I said: 'I would be prepared to remain married, with two conditions: we do not sleep together, and we keep our relation secret.'

Anima shrugged.

'Done. Though I see no need for secrecy. All the gods are related, and there would be scandal here if I married anyone *but* a god.'

'Yes, but—'

'Out of respect for your mortal sensibilities, I shall hold my tongue when I am with my handmaidens.'

'Thank you.'

'It is good to talk to you again – now the serpent does not lie between us.'

'Yes, it is not so uncomfortable, without the desire. Not that I didn't find our previous discussions fascinating, but being near you, it felt so —'

'Strange. Stifling.'

'Yes, exactly. Like there was an overwhelming tension – inside.'

'Well, now we know why.'

'We do indeed.'

We sat there, silently, watching the breeze sway the canopies.

'What are we to do with the old man?' I asked, at last.

Anima frowned.

'We cannot kill him, since he is a god, and there is no volcano to hand. We could keep him prisoner—'

'But?' I asked, reading her mind – for increasingly we were of one mind.

'What if he's right?' she said, her green eyes frighteningly earnest.

'About the prophecy? About his new God?'

She nodded, afraid.

'Then we would have need of his counsel,' I admitted, reluctantly. 'The safest course would be to incarcerate him in the cage, once he is recovered.'

'When he is recovered, the cage could not hold him. I got out, and I have only half as much godsblood, and a fraction of his learning,' Anima said.

'One of us would have to watch him, always. We could take it in turns.'

'That sounds irksome in the extreme. I have no desire to waste half my life standing watch over a blithering dotard.'

'Me neither, but until we can come up with a better solution, I see no alternative,' I said.

'I suppose you are right.' She sighed resignedly.

Chapter 24: The Unknown Bird

'There is something else that has been troubling me,' I said.

Anima and I were walking the forest paths, beneath the groaning canopies of copper beeches.

'Yes?'

I told her of Mentor's mushroom and the ensuing vision in the wilderness: the Pyramid of Magirov, the flaming comet, the death of the gods, the giant serpent; the divine child in the crater with crook, flail and double crown; how I had taken the crown and announced that I was the Father of the new God on a pedestal halfway down the marble side of the giant structure; and the sudden appearance of a bridge across the blood-moat.

'That was quite the vision,' she said, faintly amused. 'We use the mushrooms sometimes in the snake-temple. We reserve them for those who are distempered but not completely mad.'

'Yes – I would not feed them to the mad.'

We came to a glade in the forest. The fragrant grass was dotted with dandelions and the swaying maroon leaves shimmered in the sunlight.

Out of a clear blue sky, I saw an eagle soaring high overhead – past us. I had always been fascinated by eagles, and I thought it may be the bird that Mentor had summoned on the tower – the one that had placed itself at my command – so I ran to follow its descent. The bird landed behind a cluster of tree trunks.

The eagle had changed as I lost sight of it. It was now a strange bird I did not recognise, perching on a low-hanging branch. It was about the size of a goose and had grey wings and tailfeathers, a bright yellow belly merging into a long white neck surmounted by a small white head with a tiny black beak. As my pace slackened in awe, the bird hopped down from the branch and ran over to me on swift, webbed feet.

Something about the bird's demeanour made me unafraid. Its beady black eyes were gentle. I let it approach. The bird came right up to my knees and lowered its neck, expectantly, as if it wanted to be stroked.

I gave the slender white neck a stroke, then the bird scooted past me, its task completed, and flew off into the spotless blue sky.

I turned to face Anima, who had remained rooted to the spot.

'What was that?'

She thought carefully before answering.

'I have never seen nor heard tell of such a bird before.'

'Was it the fabled yellow peacock?'

She shook her head.

'Peacocks have brighter and larger feathers.'

'Was it then the phoenix that Mentor spoke of?'

'No, the bird was too small.'

'A golden goose?'

'It was yellow, white and grey, not gold. And the beak was small and black, not large and orange as with the goose.'

'Did you think it transformed from the eagle, or was it a different bird?'

'It transformed. It is the next symbol after the eagle.'

'What comes after the eagle in alchemy?'

'Nothing. The eagle is the embodiment of spirit freed from matter.'

'Then it represents something new.'

'Yes. And birds are thoughts. As an unheard-of creature, the bird portends a thought nobody has had before. A thought meant only for you.'

'Yes, it wanted to be touched by me. Once I stroked it, it flew off.'

'It is a good omen. We should resume our discussion,' she said, earnestly.

We continued our walk through the fallen leaves; autumn had deepened, and the canopies had shifted from pale yellow to golden brown and burnt orange.

Anima said, 'How did you interpret the vision in the desert?'

'I thought it meant I was the new God. I was seduced by a vision of loveliness with a heart of stone into thinking so. That I was to have spiritual and temporal power and be the new king of gods, as signified by the double crown, my levitation, and the adoration of the crowd.'

'That is not what was said, in the vision.'

'What?'

'In the vision. You said you were the Father of the new God. Not the God himself.'

'True.'

'And the forbidden wisdom has it that the god with no name lies in the centre between Known and Unknown Mind. The black side of the pyramid represents the darkness of the unknown mind; the white side, the light of consciousness. You were not in the centre of these opposites; the child was.'

'Yes. I was halfway down the marble side of the pyramid – the side facing the huddled masses; the side facing humanity. So I am to be a waystation between humanity and the new God of the centre? A bridge, if you will?'

'That would explain your positioning. And the bridge over the blood-moat. You erected it with telekinesis?'

'Yes, it seemed so. So I am to be a bridge between humanity and the new God – a sort of prophet or half-god, delivering a revelation inscribed on a stone tablet,' I murmured, trying to make sense of the vision. 'Someone who builds a bridge, that a few bold souls from the huddled mass might cross over and join me on the platform equidistant between humanity and the centre-god.'

'If the old man is right, and the new God, because of his centrality, is more a true embodiment of the All than a full-blooded god such as Tonos, then as the Father of the new God, you constitute half of his nature, just as I do. Perhaps I was halfway down the black side of the pyramid, though you didn't see me.'

'But then what of the double crown? The crown of high priest and emperor combined? It was on *my* head.'

'It means you are to be a conjunction between spiritual and temporal; heaven and earth; humanity and the gods.'

'But the infant had the crook and flail: traditional regalia of the emperor of Khem. The crown belonged properly to the infant. I was merely lent authority by the babe, at *his* urging,' I admitted, though only with reluctance.

'If the old man is right, and our child is to be the new God of Gods, then he will be unable to assume such dire responsibilities immediately. A regency will be required, until the babe attains maturity.'

'You think I am to be that regent?'

'If you are wise – and resist the lure of the centre. For you were burned by proximity to the new God in the crater. Only when you distanced yourself from the centre, were you safe from the harsh glare of the burning light.'

279

'The second sun.'

'And you were mercury to the new God's sun, mediating between earth and the celestial light.'

'I see. Yes, it makes sense.'

'Do not be carried away by fantasies of grandeur. All of this is only possibility; what may come to pass, if you are wise and fulfil your destiny. Nothing is set in stone.'

'Yes,' I said, feeling a little deflated. 'Do you think this is the "new thought" heralded by the bird?'

'It would be quite the coincidence if it wasn't…'

We fell silent, lost in thought as we trekked uphill amongst the stone pines. Through a gap in the trees we saw the bright blue sea. The late afternoon sun shimmered on the face of the rippling waters. Listening to the softly sighing surf breaking on the rocks, serenity settled over me with the lightness of a new-woven mantle. We continued walking along the ridge of the scrubby hill.

Further down the coast, past a rocky promontory, we saw the men hard at work logging trees for the new ship.

'You are dead set on going back?' Anima asked, her voice filled with dread.

'You heard the old man's prophecy.'

'He lies,' she noted, simply.

'Even if he lied about my mother, I must return to see whether he lies or no. And the men are anxious to see their families again.'

'I understand. This is not your world,' she said, gravely.

There was a long silence as we trudged along the scrubby ridge between the creaking stone pines. Then I took my sandals off and we went down a sandy slope to the beach. The sand felt pleasantly warm between my bare toes.

Nero was the labourer's overseer; he lounged in the shade of a palm while the others chopped the stone pines down with axes. He grinned when he saw me and rose to his feet.

'How goes it?' I asked.

'Slow.'

'Might go faster if you helped.'

'Marginally.'

'What of the driftwood?'

'We used what was on the beach, but it is only one quarter of the wood required.'

'Could nothing be salvaged from the shipwreck?'

He shook his head.

I cursed and stared bitterly at the small heap of wood planks and broken beams that lay mouldering on the beach, encrusted with barnacles.

'We sent a couple of divers out, but they were unable to find anything. To look any further out to sea, we'd need at least a rowboat, for the waves are dreadful choppy near the whirlpool. Then there is the kraken to consider – none dare swim near that beast of the deep.'

I frowned at the distant headland of Tyria, the islet Menoa, and the narrow fjord that lay between them. When the ship was built, we would have to pass through the fjord again, because the current and winds pushed in that direction, Menoa was too sheer and long to sail around in the face of those winds, the surrounding waters were full of concealed jagged rocks, and this was the only beach on the island: the rest of Tyria's coastline was cliff.

'So, logging it is.'

'Logging it is,' Nero repeated.

'When do you think the ship will be complete?'

'Five months, minimum.'

'So long?'

'It's a lot of work for nineteen men.' Persona had recovered from his castration and was chopping a fallen trunk with an axe.

'Even if two gods pitch in?'

'Your power is only really any good for heavy lifting; at the end of the day, the wood must be fashioned by hand into beams and planks. I doubt you will significantly expedite our work; the gods were never much for labouring.'

I smarted. Nero still knew how to make his words sting.

'Very well.'

'We wouldn't set sail until the spring, anyway. The seas are too stormy in winter,' he said, in an attempt to placate me.

I shrugged and bade him farewell. Anima and I trudged back up the cliff, toward the treeline.

When we returned to the palace, the Hall of the Moon was in turmoil. Priests and nymphs were running scared. The kitchen was empty; nobody was preparing dinner. Sphiro, the blonde lad of the crew who had helped us plot our ambush in the grove, ran toward me, breathless.

'Sphiro, what is the meaning of this chaos?'

'It's Mentor, king – he escaped!'

My stomach lurched. I had dreaded as much.

'How did this happen? I set four men to guard him!' I thundered, though in my heart I knew the blame lay at my door for leaving my post.

'And I drew a second magic circle!' Anima said.

Mentor represented a most thorny and insoluble problem, for as a full-blooded god he could not be killed. Even if he could be killed, neither of us really wanted to do the deed, since he was our father and had been as much a helper as a hindrance to us; a dreadfully ambiguous purveyor of corruption *and* enlightenment.

We had kept him incarcerated in Anima's old cage, while we decided what to do with him. But he was only truly secure when presided over by a god armed with a Stone of Destiny. So it was that every day and night for the past month Anima and I had taken turns to watch the old man's cage. Since neither of us wished to have our discussions overheard by the wicked wizard, we had been unable to speak plainly all this time and had been forced to send written messages via courier. Because we were co-rulers, there were several urgent matters that demanded discussion, and a face-to-face meeting could be put off no longer. Besides, we had both grown weary of watching the old man through the long moonless nights and listening to his prophecies of doom in Aeonia, for though we knew to take his words with a pinch of salt, they nonetheless filled our minds with buzzing drones of care.

'When I entered the room, I found all four men fast asleep on the floor. They looked as if they had dropped where they stood; for some had bruises on their heads and arms. When I finally succeeded in rousing them, Alios said that the wily old god just sat there on the floor meditating; making a low, droning chant. They'd told him to stop but he ignored them.'

'His voice sent them to sleep,' Anima said. 'He has practiced such trickery before.'

'Damn!'

'Where is he now?' I demanded, my choler rising. I had been itching to revenge myself on the old man; now my Unknown Mind had furnished the opportunity, I meant to take advantage of it.

'In the kitchen – the old abandoned kitchen of the Sun Wing.'

'What the devil is he doing there?'

Sphiro shrugged.

'Most of the men are there now, but they daren't approach, for fear the wizard might put a curse on them.'

Anima and I took up our wands and raced across the central courtyard to the Sun Wing. The fetid pond had been drained and the floor cleaned; I meant to take up my throne there, so Anima and I could have a throne each, and make full use of our palace.

I could see five men, armed with spears, blocking the threshold to the Sun Wing kitchen. They were peering around the doorframe like nervous children, murmuring in hushed voices.

As I drew closer, I could see the old man and Agatha pottering around the kitchen, erecting alembics and jars and firing the clay ovens. The men stepped aside for me and Anima, looking profoundly relieved that Mentor was no longer their problem.

'What's this? Are you going to cook us dinner?' I asked, staff held at the ready.

The old man did not cease his restless activity. He did not even turn to look at me, so distracted was he by his kitchen work. All he said was, 'Making another homunculus. A *better* homunculus.'

'You have escaped,' Anima said, stonily.

'How else was I to set about conducting my experiment, since you declined to hold me in the kitchen as I asked?' the old man grumbled, as though badly done to.

I looked at Anima.

'What should we do?' I hissed.

She shrugged. She was just as perplexed as I was.

What to do with a meddlesome old god?

'Alright old man, have it your way,' I said, finally. 'You have the freedom of the palace. But if you cause further trouble for us, by all the gods, I swear I will exile you to the waves on a raft!'

'Fat lot of good that would do you; I would merely swim back to shore when your back was turned,' he mumbled, vaguely amused. 'In any case, I accept the clemency, though it is not within your power to grant it, and shall not betray your trust, since I am only concerned with my experiments.'

'Why do you insist on continuing to make stupid little men??' I asked, bewildered.

'With this kitchen at my disposal, and the resources of the palace, the next one will be anything but stupid, I promise you that,' he said, with disarming confidence.

'You have not answered the question. Anima will have the child you tricked us into conceiving. Is not one "new God" enough?'

The old man turned and looked at me, a shrewd grin on his mouth and a canny glint in his grey old eye.

'Nothing is certain in this life, least of all that we expect.'

'You suggest the child will be stillborn??'

'Not at all,' he said, seriously. 'This is just a contingency, my boy, that's all.'

And so we left him to his work.

Chapter 25: Two Godchilds

The winter passed slowly. One day, the old man began covering up his giant jar with a purple veil whenever any of the guards entered the kitchen to see what he was doing. When questioned, he said he had created a homunculus, but his creation was 'not ready' to be shown. I thought he spoke the truth; given his previous embarrassing failures, the old man wanted to ensure this homunculus was 'a good brew' before unveiling him.

On the third day, we were allowed to see Mentor's creation. Anima, Nero, the old man's four guards, Agnes the nymph and I were gathered in the Sun Wing kitchen.

Mentor was feverish with excitement. Though his hair was scattered, his beard full of the detritus of hastily scoffed meals and his robes dishevelled, his face was radiant, and his wizened skin glowed like that of a new mother. He was surpassed in the lustre of his skin only by his daughter; as her belly swelled with new life it had begun to emit a soft golden glow, which could be seen even through her peplos.

'Ladies and gentlemen, behold, your new deity,' Mentor whipped off the veil, 'Hector the Homunculus!'

The creature in the jar was male, naked and small: he stood no more than three feet tall. His arms and legs were thin and short, though perfectly proportionate and lacking the puppy fat of infancy, which suggested he would not grow any taller. Despite his limited stature, Hector's face twinned the smooth skin of a new-born with the surliness and shrewdness of an old man. I did not like the look of him: his eyes were shiny black, like beads of jet; and his small, lipless mouth was set in a smug grin.

The old man reached down into the jar, grasped Hector's tiny hand, and lifted him out onto the kitchen table like a child.

'Hector, be polite. Introduce yourself,' the old man said, chidingly.

'Greetings,' Hector said, in a deep, confident voice that should not have belonged to a new-born – even an artificial new-born.

'Hello,' we all mumbled, more awestruck by him than he was by us.

'How does he know how to speak?' I asked, unnerved.

'I've been teaching him a few words these three days past, that his unveiling might be the more impressive,' the old man said, hastily. 'He's a quick study – damn precocious!'

The old man scooped him up in his arms like a babe and sat down at the table. He dandled Hector on his knee, staring at his creature with besotted eyes. Agatha presented them with a dish of fish guts.

'Is that healthy for a new-born?' Anima asked.

'Hector is no ordinary new-born. He is a little man. And besides – he loves them!' Mentor said, beaming. 'Watch him eat!'

And so the wizard fed the little man on his knee the slimy entrails of fish. The strange creature gobbled and slurped the stringy offal like a goat; I saw he had a full set of sharp little gnashers, which bit the old man's finger when he wiped a blood smear off Hector's tiny mouth.

'Ouch! Hector!' the old man said, a look of betrayal on his face.

'Sorry,' the being said, smirking impishly. 'I thought you were fish guts. You smell no different!'

287

Mentor glared at him sternly, and for a moment I feared for Hector's fledgling life. Then the magician burst into raucous laughter. The others joined in, astounded by the creature's precocity.

'That's nothing. Hector, tell them where you are?'

'On the lap of a dirty old bastard!'

More laughter.

'No, which island, you rascal!' the old man gasped, delighted.

'Tyria, in the midst of the Olearic Sea.'

'And what is the world's tallest structure?'

'The Pyramid of Magirov.'

'The capital of Aeonia?'

'Aeos.'

The others applauded, cooing over his intelligence. Seeing I did not join in the adoration, Hector grinned at me. I felt a shiver run down my spine. It was like gazing into the eyes of a baby crocodile.

'Where Ego's mother is slowly dying,' he said, quietly, with a sick little smile.

I rose from my chair, filled with instinctive hatred for the little beast.

'Easy there, Hector meant no offence,' the old man said, concerned. 'Did you, my son?'

'Of course not,' he said. Did I detect a trace of irony? The cynicism of adulthood in the small body of a three-day old being was terribly uncanny. I looked down; the knife was in my hand. I had no recollection of picking it up. I sat back down.

'If I'd meant to be offensive, I'd call him a mongrel. And the twat over there,' he said, jerking his head dismissively at Anima, 'a filthy child-murdering bitch who eats cocks for lunch.

The incestuous union of these curs will give rise to an even worse abomination than I. It shall have two heads, three cocks and four cunts!' the little fiend cackled, slapping his tiny knee with unholy mirth.

'Hector!' the old man admonished, growing concerned now. 'That is not how we behave at table! Apologise at once!'

'No!'

'Hector!' the old man thundered, his face grim and haggard.

'Make me, you perverted old sodomite!' the little man said, with a shrill giggle. The magician was stunned into speechlessness.

With that, Hector leapt from Mentor's lap, grabbed a steak knife, which looked like a sword in his tiny hands, and ran around under the table, slipping between our legs like a boisterous little dog.

'Ouch!' said Agnes. She pushed her chair back and saw blood running from a stab wound in her shin.

'Hey!' yelled Sphiro, Mentor's chief guard.

The little shit was running around stabbing us all!

He came to Anima next, feinting towards me before stabbing her in the calf and scrambling up onto her knees. He held his blade aloft, ready to plunge into the ripeness of her round, glowing belly.

Horrified, she smacked him backhanded in the chops; the homunculus flew across the table, knocking over bowls and knives and falling to the floor with a dull thud. He lay insensible on the ground, twitching his little limbs and murmuring in his troubled sleep.

'How dare you assault the deity!' Mentor thundered, rising to his full formidable height.

'He tried to kill my baby!' Anima protested, pushing back her chair and rising. 'I had every right to defend the unborn life you also call God!'

The two gods glowered at one another. The room darkened; the sun passed behind a cloud. The atmosphere became so poisonous with divine wrath I could have sworn the air was tinged with green smoke. Anima raised her wand. Swallowing my fear, I took up my staff and prepared to defend my sister-wife.

Seeing he was outmatched, Mentor shook his head and ran over to Hector's comatose form. Light returned to the room.

'He is not to be allowed out of this kitchen,' Anima said, firmly, and left.

***

Months passed without any trouble from the old man or his little horror. Though occasionally banging, crashing and yelling could be heard from the kitchen, it did not spread to the Hall of the Sun, so I let it pass. And that was my mistake.

Finally, on the winter solstice, four months to the day after our wedding night, I was sitting next to Anima on the dais of the Hall of the Moon, discussing the harvest with the priest Phidias, when there was a loud splash. I looked down. The floor around the Mirror-Throne was wet. Wet and inky black. Anima's eyes widened in shock. Her water had broken.

We rushed her to the central fountain of the courtyard, for Mentor had insisted the god be born there and only there. Seeing no harm in this odd request, we had assented. Lying in the shallow water of the circular pool, Anima's breathing grew frenzied and shallow.

'Isn't this a little premature?' I hissed, to Mentor. It had been four months to the day since Anima and I had coupled in this very pool.

'We've been over this,' he said. 'It goes this way sometimes with demigods. Full-blooded immortals are born within days of conception! It follows that a half-god should have a middling gestation,' he said, though his voice cracked with anxiety.

Anima's face was pale. Sweat ran down her neck and shoulders. She groaned again.

'Don't just stand there, you fools! Get the sisters – Flora and Nora!' Anima shrieked, deliriously.

'Where are they?' Mentor asked.

'The snake-temple! They are my best midwives! Go!'

I gave her one last lingering look and then I dashed across the hall, through the main door and into the night. I'm sure some of the older priests never even saw me, so fleet of foot was I. I must have appeared little more than a blur. By the time I reached the meadow, I was bounding along like a deer in flight; indeed, I passed a herd of deer trying to run away from me. They sprang off to my left.

I trampled the flower beds of the gardens and crashed through the doors of the snake-temple.

'Flora! Nora!'

The two sisters came running from the old priests they were tending to. They were both buxom brunettes with large noses.

'Yes, majesty, what is it?' Nora said, clearly exhausted from a long day's work.

'Anima! She's in labour!'

Without further ado I swept Nora up in my arms and dashed off, flying back across the meadow, my pace hardly diminished by my squirming, shrieking burden. I glanced behind; Flora was running along as fast as her short legs would take her. I passed the shocked priests once again, brushed past the purple veil, skidded along the marble-floored passage on the soles of my feet and came out in the central courtyard, heart hammering in my chest, sweat pouring from my head. I set Nora down and she began tending to her goddess.

I was just in time. The glow in Anima's belly had intensified; it was like the noonday sun reflecting off the marble façade of the palace. Then a shaft of bright light shot out of her, dazzling us all. Nora was blinded; she had to shield her eyes. The shaft widened as the head emerged. We were now all of us blinded. I covered my eyes. Nobody was left in any doubt that we were witness to the birth of a god. It was like watching the sun rise over the mountains.

When the light had abated enough for me to take a look, I saw the child was out, lying in water polluted by blood and afterbirth, the limbs tangled with the umbilical cord. Anima had passed out; she was so pale and stricken that I worried she might be dead.

Rushing to her side, I stroked the wet hair back from her sweat-soaked head. She stirred and groaned. She lived! Thank God!

Then I looked to the infant. Nora sliced the umbilical cord and swaddled the baby in cloths, for it still glowed, though not so brightly as before.

The baby was content. There were no tears, the face was serene, and the eyes were strangely knowing.

'Father,' it said, in the high, garbled tones of an infant.

My mouth fell open. How the devil did the child know how to talk? It had never heard a word spoken in anger! Unless it had been listening to us, in the womb…

Then, as if amused by my reaction, the child gurgled with infantile laughter.

Mentor knelt down before the child, bowing his shaggy grey head in an act of supplication. The infant reached out to touch him on the crown and started pulling his hair, but Mentor was too reverent before the new God to show anything more than the merest flicker of annoyance. At last, he rose to his full height and gave the baby his wizened old finger to nibble on. The infant turned its mouth away from the proffered digit and shook his head no.

This only made Mentor even more besotted.

'Goo-goo!' he said, growingly increasingly silly, 'goo-goo!' He stroked the baby's cheek and got a reluctant smile in return, which fairly made his day, for he cackled with laughter. Watching them, I thought the infant more mature than his grandfather.

'He is so divinely precocious!' the wizard exclaimed, clapping his hands together jubilantly. 'My greatest creation!'

'*Your* creation?' Anima cut in. 'And what am I, a mere breeding ewe?'

I felt a malevolent, stifling presence behind me: Hector the Homunculus was stood in the threshold to the courtyard, glowering resentfully at the new-born. Since he did nought else, and I was in transports of joy and wonder at the birth of my child, I decided to let him be.

'A boy or a girl?' Anima asked, breathless.

Nora, remembering herself, lifted the swaddling cloths to check the infant's sex.

'A boy,' she said.

Chapter 26: The Missing God

We called him Omni and he was perfect. He had the simplicity of a child and the wisdom of an old man; the power of a god and the frailty of a human. The frailty is what made him lovable; his farts were so loud they shook the palace and try as he might, he could not climb onto his chair without assistance. Within seven days, he took his first tentative steps. After two weeks, he stood as tall as Hector and could speak as well as most children of eighteen months. Anima breastfed him only for ten days before he was demanding solids. Around the same time, he began to use the chamber pot. He was a robust little deity, brimming with energy and life. Mentor doted on him.

There were strange and disturbing portents, too. His moods seemed to precipitate changes in the weather. When angry or crying, rain followed; when smiling and happy, the sun came out. He filled all who saw him with a sublime sense of inner peace; I felt absurdly happy just being in his presence.

Then one morning, I woke to Anima's screaming. I came running into her chamber.

The crib was empty.

'Where is Omni?' I demanded, breathless.

'Gone,' she said, eyes wild, hair tousled. 'Gone!' she shrieked.

'Who could have taken him?' I demanded, shaking my wife by the shoulders.

'I don't know!'

'Who was permitted entry to your room! Think!'

'Nestra and Penelope. My handmaidens,' she said, in a small voice.

We stormed through the passage to their quarters, barking commands to the guards to seal all the exits of the palace and be on the lookout for the missing nymphs and child.

Their rooms were empty. Nobody had seen them.

'The wolf!' I said, seized by a sudden idea.

'What?'

'The wolf you summoned when I mounted the dais—'

'The one you killed?'

'I didn't kill him! I turned him into a bee, absorbed him into my brain, then spat him out of my mouth! Why is that so hard to understand?'

'Alright. The one you made into a confounded bee,' she said, impatient and wondering where this was going.

'Yes. Are there others like him who would answer your call?'

'There is a wolf called Huon. He lives in the depths of the pine forest.'

'If we give Huon the child's scent, will he be able to find him??'

She nodded, vehemently.

Then she put her fingers to her lips and made a sharp piercing whistle. A few moments later the white wolf pattered into the bedroom. I had to suppress my natural reaction of panic, for the wolf's demeanour seemed benign. Anima pressed the child's swaddling clothes to the wolf's wet, black nose. The animal sniffed, barked and bounded off across the meadow. We followed; we were able to keep pace, for we were gods. More than that, we were parents fearful for our child.

The wolf led us deep into the forest. I hurdled brambles and briar patches, swerved tree trunks and ducked overhanging branches and skidded down hills on my backside, my wife following close behind. Finally, Huon stopped in a small clearing, barking frantically, but he would go no further.

I saw why: a glorious golden lion stood before us, his jaws red with blood. My heart sank; had this beast devoured our God? Three nymphs lay in bloody puddles around him, bodies limp, limbs gnawed, throats ripped, their entrails dangling loose like spools of rope. And there was the child, sat on the grass, drenched in blood but apparently unharmed. The beast nuzzled the infant and licked blood from his face; Omni giggled with unbridled joy.

Anima approached the lion warily. The beast roared at her; the depth of the noise echoed around the glade and terrified us both. Then he looked to Omni, as if for guidance. With a sympathetic nod from the child, the lion seemed to bow its giant, shaggy head and obediently loped off into the undergrowth. Anima darted in and scooped the babe up into her arms, carrying him swiftly away from the lion who had saved him.

I heard a ragged gasp.

It came from the nymph on the edge of the clearing. I ran across and flipped her over, so she lay on her front. I recognised her golden hair and sour face; it was Ephedra. Her throat was gashed but she still lived. Her breaths came in shallow, ragged little gasps.

'Ephedra! Why did you take my child!' I demanded. I could have struck her, though she was on the brink of death.

She struggled to speak in a hoarse rasp.

Anima said, 'Why did you take him? Speak!'

Blinking with fright, Ephedra jerked forward to get up and run. The little god raised an imperious, chubby little hand – her head slammed back down on the grass again, and an invisible crushing weight seemed to hold her down.

'Speak!' Anima demanded.

Ephedra whimpered and cried. She was terrified, for she had never witnessed the work of Omni before, let alone his wrath.

'It was Nestra's idea, so it was. She'd been talking to the little man. She said the boy wus a barstud seein as you wusn't prop'ly married an' all when 'e wus conceeved and a few of us gurls, we prefer to keep the old ways, else there'll be a bad harvest.' She coughed, hacking her lungs up. 'So we took him. We wos gonna drown him in the sacred grove, loike we would uv in the old days. But now I see 'e is no ordinary barstud; I swear he summoned the lion as if it were a trained dog.'

The godchild shook his head in disapproval.

'Who is the little man?' I demanded.

'The littuw one wot grew in a jar, you know, Hubert or Heston, wossis name?'

'Hector,' I said. The little god's face was troubled at this news; he seemed to understand the gist of what was said.

'Yer thassim. Please, don't punish me none. I just did wot me sister told me, sose I did,' she blabbered, clearly terrified.

'Hector must die,' Anima said, grimly. Omni's blue eyes stared right through me; he knew what must be done.

A shiver ran down my spine. I did not know why, but the child terrified me.

We returned to the palace. Anima bathed the boy, and I found Mentor in the kitchen, fussing over his homunculus. I requested a word in private.

'Very well,' Mentor said, setting Hector down on the ground. He walked over and closed the kitchen door behind him.

'What's the matter?'

'Omni was taken.'

Mentor gasped in alarm.

I held up a placatory hand.

'We have found him. He is well. But you should know, the nymphs who still worship Melea, or your twisted version of her, took him. They thought Omni was illegitimate and should be drowned. They got the idea from Hector.'

'Hector?'

'Do not feign surprise; you know the monster's nature. That is what the girl said, and I believe her. So does Anima, and she is not easily fooled.'

Mentor sighed and leaned against the shadowy wall. The lines on his face deepened to ruts and he seemed unspeakably ancient, like the old oak tree behind his hutment.

'I will deal with Hector.'

'The monster must di—'

He held up his gnarled, massive hand and winced, as if in physical pain.

'I know what must be done,' he said, wearily.

'Hector is a wily little fiend. I shall help,' I said, starting for the kitchen.

'No.' The old man held me back. 'No, I made him; the burden falls on me to *unmake* him.'

I nodded but followed at a discreet distance all the same. I watched and listened closely.

Mentor spoke privately with his little man. Then they came out, hand in hand. Hector sneered at me as he passed.

'You shall like the view very much,' the old man said, his brow troubled, and they walked out across the meadow, headed for Mount Taytos. From the palace, I watched Mentor climb the winding stair path, as the little man sat on his shoulders. Then I saw him stand on the precipice about halfway toward the peak, pick the little man up by his heel and throw him off the sheer cliff. A shrill cry carried on the wind; Hector's tiny, flailing form disappeared behind the trees and there was silence. The old man's gait was stooped, as if under an even heavier burden, as he descended.

****

Weeks later, Anima was keen to resume her duties at the snake-temple. She took Omni with her. She noticed something strange; the mere presence of the child seemed to have a calming effect on the convalescents and even on the dotard-priests. Anastas was a drooling old man who had been insensible from a broken skull ever since his black wedding decades prior. Usually, his milky eyes did not even register Anima when she passed and emptied his bedpan. But even he cracked a smile at the child. Anima decided Omni should spend more time in the temple, and he accompanied her there every day.

And then, one day, when the child was in his mother's arms, he reached out towards Anastas with his chubby little fingers, a desperate, serious look on his fat little face. Anima, curious, lowered the child so he might touch Anastas. The old man chuckled and raised his arm to shake the infant's hand. Quite unthinkingly, he said, 'hello there, little master.'

Anima was stunned. She hadn't heard so much as a word out of Anastas in all the years she'd been tending to him. When she pointed this out to him, the old man blinked and said, 'Yes, I suppose I have been silent a while. But there hasn't been anything worth saying, until now.' Soon he was up and walking again, albeit with the aid of a cane.

Omni touched those patients who couldn't or wouldn't accept Anima's talking magic; mostly long-term cases, elderly priests and nymphs with rotting bodies. His touch did not work in every case, but in those who responded to the child with interest and a willingness to be helped, some degree of improvement was always noted.

One day, a nymph, Rosalia, came in with a gashed hand. She had cut herself in the kitchen, chopping onions. The little god, who was tottering about now, waddled across the marble floor of the temple ward. Rosalia greeted him wearily and the god said, 'hello child.' The child clasped her injured hand in his two chubby little hands. He closed his eyes and furrowed his brow.

And suddenly the wound began to mend; only instead of weeks, the congelation and scabbing occurred before their very eyes, in a matter of mere moments. Rosalia burst into tears; she could scarcely believe it. A once severe wound was reduced to a few faint pink scars, free of blood, before the hour was out.

Omni came to an old nymph, Crita, who had taken to her sickbed with swollen, gangrenous feet. The crone smiled at the babe. Omni took her blackened old hand and regarded her with a look of profound sympathy. Seeing her own suffering reflected back at her in the eyes of an innocent, Crita burst into tears. There was a faint popping sound, and her feet deflated with a long sigh, like a burst pig's bladder. She was cured and could walk again.

Omni's childish oneness seemed to stitch together some primordial open wound inside of people, to put their broken pieces back together; he represented a divine unity, that they knew not, but was nonetheless latent within their hearts.

But Omni's powers had their limits. Certain cases were beyond help. Some seemed unwilling to receive his touch, and these died soon after. He found a dead sparrow in the colonnade. It

301

had flown into a pillar and lay insensible in a pool of blood and feathers. Omni reached down and picked up the bird and tried to breathe the breath of life into its beak. He tried and tried for hours. It was heart-breaking to watch, but the bird remained dead. He was inconsolable for days afterwards.

Chapter 27: The Waking Death

May arrived. The storms of winter had abated. My ship was ready. I felt ready; long since ready, if truth be told, for I had grown bored of my life of idle divinity on Tyria.

'I must depart,' I told Anima, one day, as we strolled through the woods. The grass was greening once again in the high pastures, after the snowmelt. They were dotted with snowdrops and vivid bluebells; pink blossoms and the first shoots of green appeared on the branches of the trees.

'Must you go?' she asked, plaintively.

'Alas, my mother ails. My people need me. And I am ready. Why delay the inevitable any longer??'

'Strife and care await you in the world of mortals.'

'I've had my share of strife and care on these blessed shores! I fear such things are inescapable!'

Anima went morbidly silent for a while and glowered. Then she said, 'I hesitate to tell you this, but the goddess Sofia came to me in a dream and told me that you would die if you returned to Aeonia.'

Dread filled my heart upon hearing these dire words, which had a curious flavour of prophecy about them. I wondered if Anima was trying to trick me into staying here forever, but she seemed to be in deadly earnest. Then I recalled the old man's parable of the man dragged by bandits.

'If that is my fate, then so be it! But I assure you of one thing: I will not submit meekly to the yoke of Death!'

My words seemed to upset Anima even more, for tears welled in her eyes.

'It needn't be this way. Why not reside here indefinitely, in the abode of the gods? We are not immortal, but we might see five hundred summers together if we avoid the tumult of the mortals, their wars and treacheries. Would those not be blissful summers?' she asked, sadly.

'They would,' I said, a tear in my eye. 'But though I be half a god, I am also half a man, and I long for my homeland,' I sighed. 'If truth be told, my life of semi-immortality here on the Forgotten Isle feels like a waking death. Though my days are comfortable, I long for the bustle of humanity, that I might feel myself *truly* alive again.'

She nodded, mournfully, for she knew in her heart the day must come.

'As The Poet once said: "Immortality is akin to death and the gods envy men their brief flame of life. Why else would they strike us down so cruelly for the least display of pride?"'

'I must take Omni.'

She stopped dead on the mud-path, her face icy and poisonous as in the days of old.

'You shall not,' she said, with quiet implacability.

'He is my heir! And if I am to be king, I shall need an heir.'

'He is my heir too, for who else is to take my place on the throne of Tyria when I am gone? Who else is to fill my long, empty days of divine ease, with my husband gone away on some distant folly?'

'I am sorry, but my decision is final.'

'Merely passing the whirlpool is a perilous risk, let alone taking him into a civil war. You would endanger your child, for the sake of your own pride?' she asked, astonished.

'The child has healing power; my mother may need him. But not only her. The whole world is sick and needs a healer – and a new God. Would you deny them their boon for your own sake?'

'I would deny them for Omni's sake!' she shouted, eyes blazing with wrath, like the mother bear guarding her cub.

'Ask Mentor; it is prophesied. The child must accompany his father to the lands of men, where he shall become their new God.'

'Mentors pours poison in your ear. He makes prophesies that they might fulfil themselves – and his own shadowy interests. He is setting you up for a mighty fall. And if you should fail, what price does *he* pay, hiding here in his hut, far from the hue and cry?'

'He is coming with me. He shall share in my rigours.'

Anima fell silent and gloomy; she had not known of this.

'You could come too. Your company would be most welcome,' I said, trying to soften the blow.

But her wall of silence was impregnable. When we came to a fork in the road, I took the right path, and she took the left.

When I woke the following morn, the child was gone from his crib.

'Where is Omni?' I asked my wife, as she sat before her mirror, combing her hair.

'Somewhere on this island. Somewhere you and that wicked wizard cannot embroil him in your vainglorious folly,' she said, without turning to face me.

'Damn it, wife! He is my son and heir; he will be returned to me at once or God help me, I shall choke his hiding place out of you!' I said, raising Mentor's staff.

'You wouldst smite me?' She scoffed, taking up her wand. 'Then prepare to be smitten in return, blowhard!'

We locked eyes. Then she relaxed and assumed a scornful manner.

'Give up your play-acting. You know you cannot harm me without harming yourself! And to kill me would be suicide for I am flesh of your rib! The man who overcame wisdom could not be so stupid!'

I stormed off, cursing, and met Mentor in the passage.

'I heard raised voices. What is the trouble?' he asked, anxiously.

I told him the infant was gone; Anima was hiding him from us so we could not take him with us on our voyage. 'This is a small island. You have lived here longer than anyone. Surely you know the hiding places better than her?'

'I shall scour the island, rest assured on that count.'

****

The old man returned a few days later, shaking his head, ruefully.

'I thought I knew every cranny of this blasted isle, but it seems not, for I have searched all the likely places and have found neither hide nor hair of our Lord God.'

'What then?'

'We could have a word with the new handmaiden. Or lace Anima's wine with truth-potion and put her to the question,' the old man said, his strides lengthening. I struggled to keep pace with him, for he moved with the haste of a restless demon. This child was his life's work; he could not afford to be thwarted now, even by his own beloved daughter.

'Anima has a fine nose for treachery. It would be no easy matter to catch her unawares.'

The wizard's feet stopped their impetuous shuffling. He stood stock still, swaying slightly, eyes closed.

Knowing Mentor's penchant for sudden revelations, I let him be and waited, patiently.

'I have it!' he said, eyes lighting up. I did not doubt that roving mind had alighted on the solution, for nothing could remain hidden for long from such a restless, questing will. 'She's bluffing,' he said, simply.

'What?' I was disappointed; from The Wizard of the Gods, I had expected grander insight, something more…complex.

'Make to depart; be serious about it and do not flinch when it comes to the quick!'

'And what, you expect her to hang around my legs and beg me not to go?'

'And why not? You are man and wife and she loves you, in her way.'

'I don't doubt she doesn't want me to go, but she hates the idea of losing her child still more!'

'Exactly. She wants to be with you both! Make it plain you are not staying, and she will join you aboard ship!'

I laughed, disbelieving.

'If that is so, she has a strange way of preparing for a voyage.'

'My son, you do not understand women at all.'

'Do you?' I said, with raised eyebrows.

'Not really,' he admitted, reluctantly. 'But I know my daughter well enough to know that when she is most silent and surly, she is closest to giving way. She is a strange and capricious girl. Look at how she responded when you mounted the dais! Did you honestly expect to be mounted in turn?' he said, grinning.

'Don't remind me…' I said, ashamed.

'Look, on the off chance I am wrong, she will retrieve
Omni from his hiding place when you have set sail, for mothers do
not like to see their babes in discomfort for long. Drop anchor
beyond the horizon. I shall send an owl to you as a signal that you
should return by stealth with a small landing party at night, on the
far side of the island. Come over the mountains and approach the
palace from the Sun Wing, where nymphs scarcely tread. You shall
steal upon her unawares and together we will snatch the child!' he
said, a demonic gleam in his grey eyes.

'You are the very devil for cunning, old man,' I said, taken
aback. 'I am glad you are no longer my adversary.'

Mentor chuckled.

'Fret not, young one, all this shall prove unnecessary, for
my daughter will yield the instant you set foot on board that ship. I
say this only to convince you to go.'

There was that questing mind again, full of trickery and
practical deceit. Anything, in the service of its goal. Anything, to
bring the dominating idea to fruition in the garden of the world.
Compared to this old man, Nero was a common thug.

'Very well. We set sail tomorrow, at dawn. I shall make the
announcement; it cannot fail to reach my wife.'

And so, the next morning the island's entire populace was
gathered on the beach and the makeshift wooden jetty my men had
erected. The sun had not yet risen, but the first rosy fingers of
dawn caressed the grey-blue horizon, and there was ample light to
see by. The sands were of pale gold and there was a cool breeze; it
was a fine day for sailing.

Anima was there, with her new handmaiden, though she
held herself aloof from the crowds of tearful nymphs and
sentimental old priests. I was surprised by their grief; I had not
reckoned myself as popular as my wife. I said as much to Phidias.

'Oh no sire, if anything, you are *more* beloved than your wife!'

'How so?' I asked, puzzled.

'You abolished the torrid old rituals! Us priests need no longer cower in fear! The nymphs need not incur fresh guilt for battering and mutilating their husbands and drowning their misbegotten children! Once, the nights were filled with their tears, but no longer! Our sons may grow to full manhood without fear of castration! Truly, you are a liberator and enlightener!'

I embraced the tearful old coot.

'And besides, though she be lovely to look upon, she is cold as a statue. You have more *living warmth* about you.'

'Thank you for your kind words, Phidias. I know you sailed to Aeonia, years ago. You may accompany us, if you wish? We are short of oarsmen.'

The priest blanched.

'Oh no, I am far too old for adventures. But I wish you good luck!'

I followed Mentor's advice and did not spare Anima even so much as a last lingering look.

I was the last to board. Mentor called out to me, impatiently, from the deck. I trotted across the jetty and up the gangplank. I began to fear Anima was truly implacable. I dreaded having to steal my own son from his mother – but, after all, she had stolen him from me.

'Wait!' cried a woman's voice.

I paused, turned.

It was Anima. Her green eyes were desperate and bloodshot. The tip of her nose was red with grief.

'What do you want?'

'A word in private with my husband before parting! Or is that too much to ask?'

'I am late; my crew are waiting. Be quick!' I said, crossing my arms haughtily.

'I'm sorry I hid Omni from you, but I only did so because I want you to stay. I want us to be a family *here*.'

'Robbing me of my son is a strange way of making a family,' I said, sternly.

'But you need us, if you are to be king; I am your queen and he is your heir!'

'I will just have to marry an Aeonian noblewoman and have a second son by her; *he* shall be my heir, since you deprive me of my firstborn,' I said, bitterly.

'No!' she cried, stricken.

'I am not proud of my intention, but there it is: you make a bigamist of me!' I shouted, for all to hear.

The crowd gasped in shock; a priest fainted. I knew Anima would hate to be dishonoured before her people, for the humiliation of a leader is the seed from which revolts spring.

Anima's face crumpled into a bleary mess of tears; her heart was breaking before my very eyes. I felt a strong urge to apologise and comfort her, but fought it back, keeping Mentor's counsel firmly in mind.

'There is another way. Wait until he is of age. Then Omni can decide for himself where he wants to live. He could not be of use to you as an heir until such time, anyway,' she pleaded.

I resisted the temptation of this alluring compromise. To tarry on the Blessed Isle any longer would be fatal to my enterprise. Already, I felt my desire to return to Aeonia dwindling with each passing day. Mustering my will, I said, 'My mother and my people need me *now*, not ten or twenty years hence. My decision is unchanged; my will, unyielding,' I said, turning to go.

'Then we shall come with you,' she said, in a small voice.

I froze, halfway up the gangplank.

'You and the child?' I said, turning my head but a fraction.

She nodded, tears dropping from her eyes.

'Where is he?'

'Delay your voyage. I will have him aboard ship by noon.'

The story continues in Ego's Iliad.

Printed in France by Amazon
Brétigny-sur-Orge, FR

19811189R00178